I0665909

Cursed Reflections of the Mirror

M. L. Vanasse

Chief Publishing

Chief Publishing
First published in the United States in 2025
This paperback edition was first published in October 2025
Copyright M. L. Vanasse 2025
Map by M. L. Vanasse

www.MLVanasse.com

ISBN 979-8-9897356-2-4 paperback

All rights reserved. No part of this publication may be reproduced or transmitted in any form or by any means, electronic or mechanical, including photocopying, recording, or any other storage or retrieval system, without prior express permission in writing from the publishers.

This book is a work of fiction. Any similarities are a product of the author's imagination. Any resemblance to actual people, places, or events is coincidental.
This book is not intended to diagnose, treat, or anything else regarding mental health.
If you have any concerns please see your doctor.

Warning
Trigger warning mental health issues with lines blurred.

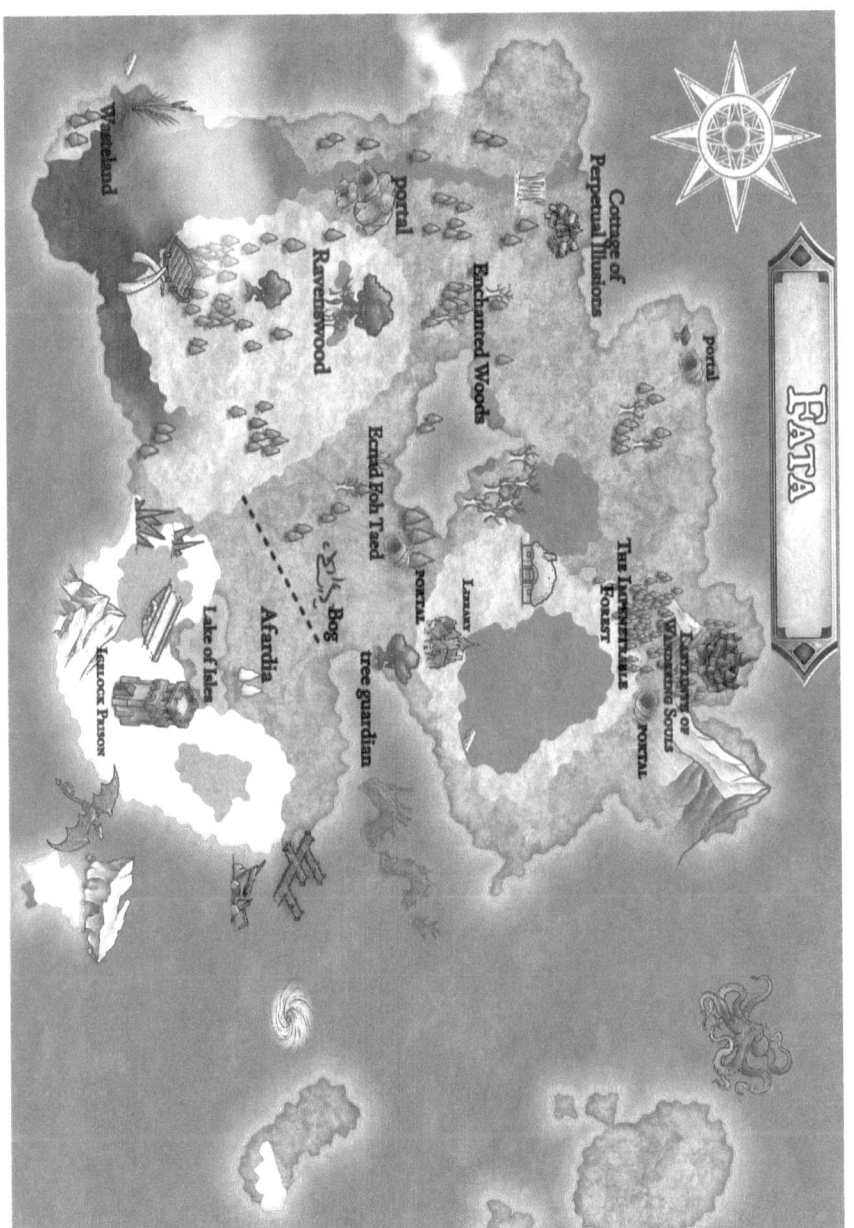

Dedication

To Remy, my rock. Thank you for always being there.
.

Chapter 1: The Awakening

Quinn MacMillans stirred from her sleep. Her eyes fluttered open to an echo, the sound of a voice she recognized. "Your payment is now due," Ophelia declared, sharp and commanding. The sense of urgency conveyed tore Quinn back to the present. She wasn't a Fae to mess with, and a magical pact had been made in exchange for her help.

Quinn sat up, rubbing her eyes to remove any evidence of sleep. "What payment? What are you talking about?" she asked, confusion clouding her thoughts. She looked around her familiar room, but Ophelia's voice pulled her attention back.

Ophelia's face appeared before her, hazy and filled with concern. "You must rescue Puck from the Mirror Prison," she urged. Her knitted eyebrows pinched even farther.

A jolt of surprise shot through Quinn as she absorbed her words. Puck, the Fae who challenged her the most, was trapped in the prison. She didn't care for him at all. The message lingered like an unspoken promise, urgent and demanding of her attention.

Quinn threw her rustic sunflower-themed blankets aside and swung her legs over the edge of the bed. Sitting upright, she rested her feet on the flowered carpet. "Why is Puck in prison?" Quinn flexed her palms. "What'd he do?"

"He will be locked up forever," Ophelia replied, her words catching in her throat. "For a crime most unforgivable. The murder of another Fae."

But how?

Paying the price for such a grave act wouldn't be light. The weight of the situation settled upon her. Confusion flooded

Quinn's mind. She yawned, not fully awake. *Puck, that scoundrel, imprisoned? It couldn't be true. Good, he finally got what he deserved.*

"So, let me get this straight," Quinn said, voice dripping with disdain, her frustration clear. "You want me to rescue Puck? That prick who never missed a chance to torment me or my brother?"

Ophelia's expression remained placid, her eyes scarcely holding back her immense sorrow. "Quinn, I know your feelings toward Puck run deep, but I cannot stand by while he rots in the mirror realm." The pain was evident in her voice.

Quinn's brows furrowed. "Enlighten me, then."

A faint sigh escaped Ophelia's lips. "I wish I could, but my hands are tied. My past in the court prevents me from sharing certain details."

Quinn leaned forward, her annoyance growing. The sunflower nightlight cast a soft glow on Ophelia's transparent face. "So, you're saying you won't help me?"

"I am magically prohibited from *telling*," she emphasized the last word, shaking her head gently.

Quinn's eyes narrowed, her arms crossed, preventing Ophelia from seeing the fists that formed. "How does that help me?" She sighed. "You won't help, and I know nothing about the prison."

"I did not say that. I cannot provide you with direct assistance, but I can guide you and point you in the direction of possible answers. You also know more than you think."

Quinn's jaw clenched, torn between her distaste for Puck and the unresolved emotions Ophelia's presence stirred within her. *I know more than I think. How the hell does that make any sense?* She glanced away. Her thoughts, a fierce whirlwind, threatened to take over.

"I can see the pain in your eyes." Ophelia's voice softened.

Quinn huffed and whipped her head back. "I know you love him, but he's evil. He knew the rules and broke them."

Ophelia's face turned fierce, likely akin to her gaze on the battlefield; her emotions were rarely exposed. "Do not pretend to be empathetic," Ophelia snapped. Her tone effectively shut down that conversation. "I know you are unsympathetic to him."

She had pushed too far. Ophelia's vulnerability was obvious despite her hardened exterior. "Fine. I'll help you rescue Puck, not for him, but for you."

A fleeting smile touched her lips but didn't reach her eyes. "The Mirror Prison is hazardous, a realm where reality twists and danger awaits at every turn. Entering and exiting is no simple feat. It requires mastering the art of reflection and facing your deepest fears. I cannot assist you." Her voice hardened. "You *will* rescue Puck *for* me."

Quinn balled her hands into fists. She accepted her fate, her apprehension transforming into determination. Her mind grappled with the complexities of what may lie ahead. "I'll do whatever it takes. Just tell me where to start."

"Prepare yourself, Quinn. The mirror is a crucible, and you're about to enter its core. This is not something to rush into unprepared." Ophelia's gaze held concern.

Taking a deep breath, Quinn nodded. "I don't know what to do."

Ophelia's lips curled into a small smile, pleased at Quinn's response. "The Mirror World is a treacherous place full of challenges, but I believe you are the only one who may succeed." Something flashed across her face before Quinn could pinpoint it, and then she said, "Meet me at our place when the sun goes down in your realm." With that, Ophelia's hazy face was gone with a shimmer and the scent of blueberries.

As Quinn rose from her bed, her heart heavy with the weight of the task ahead, this journey would test her in unimaginable ways. But she was ready to embark on this mission.

How am I going to sneak this by Baxter? He was her twin and confidant who had his own complicated history with the Fae.

Quinn's disbelief morphed into shock as the truth sank in. *If Puck had gotten himself into something monumental, then he could get himself out of it.* Past events swirled, images of Puck hurling a weapon at Connor and provoking her.

Connor, her mind echoed. A sharp ache stabbed her, constricting her breath. Despite being her brother's best friend, she loved him like a brother. His impeccable hair, his radiant smile, how he effortlessly kindled laughter within her, even while annoying her. A tear formed in her eye, but she quickly blinked it away.

How could he be gone? Now, it falls on me to rescue Puck, with his snarky demeanor, how he held an air of distaste for everything, and how he despised humans. I should've done something to save Connor. Why does Puck get the chance at salvation when Connor didn't?

She wiped away fresh tears that pooled in her eyes. Quinn squared her shoulders and decided to concentrate on the immediate task at hand. Rescuing Puck could be the key to leaving all this behind, the entanglement of Fata and the Fae once and for all.

She had once enjoyed exploring the wonders of Fata, the land of the Fae, but its perils and heartaches had proven overwhelming. Her mother's demise there cast a shadow that made each return more painful.

How could I keep revisiting a realm that deepened my wounds rather than healing them?

Unfortunately, she was a powerful seer with little training. Without guidance, she could become lost within herself, or worse, trapped in someone else's past for eternity. Quinn shoved some toiletries into a backpack.

She recognized the urgency of honing her abilities, requiring the most powerful known seer in Fata, and Quinn's mentor, Seraphina. This demanded her continued presence in a realm from which, she was becoming ever more desperate to distance herself. Seraphina couldn't cross into her realm, or she didn't wish to; it was much the same. Seraphina's nearly violet eyes, rimmed with white, had borne into her time and time again, leaving Quinn uneasy. Shaking off the lingering discomfort she set out clothes for the trip.

My life may never be the same.

Her phone rang. It was Baxter's ringtone. She sighed; emotions crashed over her like a tidal wave when she thought of him. He had already endured so much.

I can't drag him into more chaos. But how could I hide this from him? He knows me inside and out. My feelings are as evident as words on a page. He would read it all over my face if he saw me in person.

His text was short and simple: *hey sis, what r u up 2?*

Quinn made a difficult decision. A text was often vague and ambiguous. Typing out a quick message, her fingers shook: *I thought things were getting better, but they aren't. Please respect my decision and give me the space I need.*

If he knew she was planning to go to the prison, he would try to stop her, or worse, he would want to go along. He'd been through enough. It was her turn to protect him.

His reply was immediate: *Is there anything I can do?*

She typed: *No.*

He texted: *Ok, love you, sis.*

Hopefully, he didn't catch on and try to save the day once more. Knowing him, if one more thing went wrong, he would likely crack. She'd protect him, no matter the cost. A knot tightened in her stomach at the thought of lying to him. When it came down to it, she'd face the consequences and make amends. Her text would wound him deeply, but it was the only way to protect him.

Filled with questions, this was a task she couldn't ignore; she'd made a deal. But it didn't mean she had to involve her brother. Puck was no friend to her, but she'd do everything in her power to help as long as Baxter remained safe. She couldn't lose him, too.

He also had abilities, but he had been through the wringer.

They had lost their mother last year in Fata, and the tragedy cast a dark shadow over their family. The place was far too dangerous for any of them. They couldn't tell their father, Doug, what had happened. He believed she died of a heart attack induced by the stress Baxter caused. The truth was far from ordinary; her body had vanished without a trace. Quinn recalled how their father's grief twisted into fury aimed at him. His neck veins had looked like they'd pop, and the lines etched the corners of his eyes as dark circles grew beneath them. He'd blamed Baxter for the death of his beloved wife and refused to see his son. He had all but given up hope, leaving only bitterness in its stead.

Baxter had watched their mother, Chloe, die right before his eyes, shattering him. Their father had committed him to a mental institution and, consumed by anger, refused to have anything else to do with him, severing ties with his only son. Baxter had endured more than enough tragedy for one lifetime, and Quinn feared one more blow would push him over the edge. But he wasn't crazy. The world couldn't understand what he saw, what she could see now, too.

The extraordinary place, where vast, untamed forests lie, a mystical force, a parallel universe, known as Fata. Where everything was skewed and distorted, and time didn't make sense. Quinn and Baxter could see this realm and even enter it, whereas a Reg, those without the Sight, couldn't.

In the beginning, they kind of stumbled upon the Fae land, not realizing fate had brought them there. Now, Quinn has learned more about her powers and developed them. She ventured deeper into Fata to develop her gift.

Amidst the flowing hills and endless forests lies an unknown secret, its entire existence deftly defying all possible comprehension. The landscapes themselves twisted and turned in unpredictable ways. Among its surreal terrain, time wasn't linear; it looped and distorted, leaving visitors disoriented.

Quinn channeled all her energy into sending Ophelia a mental message. She wasn't sure if Ophelia could receive that type of message herself; hopefully, she was still with Seraphina.

"After I do this, we are even. See you at our usual spot." *Not that I really have a choice. I made a pact. I wonder if I have to agree in order to fulfill it.*

She still couldn't believe it was within her capabilities to send a telepathic message to someone. She struggled to grasp the possibility. Uncertain of her abilities, she hoped the message had been received. Quinn visualized telling Ophelia her answer as hard as she could. With a newly formed headache, she laid back on the bed, exhaustion setting in from the energy expended.

Wow, I'm losing it. Seraphina said if I didn't exercise my magic, I'd lose energy faster when I tried to use it again. Funny how she compared it to a muscle.

Quinn shook her head and moaned. She pushed herself out of bed, driven by the desire to spare an additional burden on Baxter. He didn't need more stress. He'd been trying to move forward, rebuilding his life after the accident. She'd handle Puck's mess herself. Quinn smiled, thinking of how Connor reacted when she agreed to do anything in the first place.

Oh, how he would tease me if he were here. She inhaled sharply; it hurt when she thought of him. *Connor warned me to be especially careful agreeing to things. That I should pay attention to the wording with the Fae. Matt would've agreed with him on that.* Matt was always there for her. The shy guy who, since grade school, harbored a crush on her. Everybody knew it. Quinn chose to remain oblivious.

Matt had been a welcomed distraction. She couldn't tell him what had happened, but he sensed that something more was going on. He moved differently around her. Quinn recalled when Matt sat at the coffee shop table, how he'd looked at her. Her hand was wrapped around the cup of steaming hot coffee that she wasn't drinking, trying to warm her hands. They never felt warm anymore. He stared at her, unblinking for the longest moment. The silence between them was deafening. Her guilt twisted in her gut.

"How is your coffee?" he asked.

They both knew she hadn't even sipped it. She was distracted. He paused again, as if he was saying he didn't want to talk about coffee. He'd wait until she was ready to discuss what was bothering her. Not knowing what to say, she shrugged. Her hands fell onto her lap. He flinched, hardly noticeable, except Quinn knew him so well she knew he was disappointed. They went back to him pretending to stare out the window and she not answering questions. She could tell by the look in his eyes and how he paused, giving her multiple chances to come clean and how he eyed her in long moments, as if he knew she was lying.

She had avoided him since then, unsure if she could handle not telling him. She never told him the truth, and he accepted that. Quinn shook her head, removing any thoughts of him and the disappointment permanently etched into his skin.

Chapter 2: It Begins

*A*fter extensive hours of planning, Quinn rubbed her eyes at the setting sun. She couldn't possibly think of everything, but she certainly tried. Quinn threw on her jacket, hopped on her bike, and pedaled to the meeting spot. She couldn't take her dad's car, not knowing how long she would be gone. It took her longer than expected to reach the forest, even though Quinn had ridden her bike at full speed to avoid being late. She still needed to hike the trails to travel through the portal, and her legs ached. Afternoon sunshine faded, and the trees cast eerie shadows across the path. The forest was unnaturally still, the silence broken only by the sound of gravel beneath her tires.

When she reached the path of her usual hiking spot, her bike skidded to a stop. Her breath came in short spurts. Quinn stashed her bike in the thick overgrowth near the trail's entrance to avoid theft and hoped the brush would protect it from the elements.

The portal might close at any moment, and Quinn still had a long hike ahead of her. Fearing she'd fall, she couldn't run on the rough terrain. Without time to spare, she sucked in a deep breath and took her first step toward her destiny. The leaves rustled with her increased pace and her pounding pulse.

Please be open.

Seraphina warned her that portals weren't permanent. They'd go out like electricity in a storm. They remained open the longest where the veil was thinnest and easier to maintain. Luckily, this portal fell into one of those spots. If the portal vanished, she'd have to search for another way in, an impossible task.

The hike was uneventful, which was almost worrisome. Her footsteps were the only sound. She couldn't place it; something felt off, yet the trail appeared normal. No rustling in the undergrowth, no darting birds between the trees, and no animals of any kind. Not even the chatter of insects.

The silence should've reassured her; instead, it left a ghostly feeling, like the forest held its breath. The farther she went, the more it unnerved her.

She quickened her step, and when Quinn finally reached the stone cave, a wave of relief washed over her. The purple velvet mushrooms were still there, arranged in a circle outside the entrance. They stood out, a stark contrast to the earthy hues of the rest of the forest. Movement caught her eye, a shimmer of light. She blinked. Her nerves were wound so tight she thought she'd implode.

She hesitated, attempting to steady her racing pulse. Her breath came in shallow bursts; she sucked in a sharp breath and forced it out, slow and deliberate. It was now or never. With a final deep breath, she stepped into the cave.

The instant she crossed the portal into Fata, the world changed. The air thrummed with a vibrating energy deep within her marrow. No echoes of footsteps or drips of water, only silence, as the cave consumed all sound. Goosebumps prickled her skin as a chill swept through her.

When Quinn stepped out of the cave, she glanced around and absorbed her new surroundings. The eerie glow of the two moons cast an iridescent sheen across the field. It created elongated shadows, an ominous effect. Though there was no Ophelia in sight, Quinn somehow knew she was there. She didn't fully understand her gift, but she learned to trust her instincts. Like a whisper, deep within her bones.

Her gaze swept over the landscape, the vast expanse of trees, and settled on a decaying log that had fallen long ago, half absorbed by the earth. It drew her attention, and yet it shouldn't have. It was a fallen tree; those things happen in forests, but to her, it seemed out of place. She approached it, and there, sitting with her back against the log, was Ophelia. She was nearly indistinguishable, her head down, with dark hair hiding her face. Quinn wasn't certain whether it was her glamour, a sort of camouflage ability the Fae had, or her unnatural stillness mixed with her combat history that she hid so well. Either way, Quinn crept toward Ophelia in silence, wanting to practice her skills.

As soon as she took her first step, she heard, "May the shadows remain behind you, Shadow Seer."

"How did you know?" Quinn asked, jaw hanging. She took a single step.

"I was expecting you, remember?" Ophelia answered flatly, remaining as still as a fallen tree.

Realizing her mouth was still parted, Quinn's lips curved upward. "Yes, but how did you know I found you?" she asked, her curiosity piqued.

"I heard the portal as you entered." Despite her swords, Ophelia didn't seem to move, as if she were a ventriloquist. Quinn tilted her head sideways to see Ophelia. Finding nothing worth noting, she dropped it for now.

"I didn't know portals made noise." Quinn crossed her arms and impatiently waited for a response.

After what felt like an eternity, which was most likely closer to a minute, Ophelia responded.

"Human ears cannot hear the vibrations," she said matter-of-factly. She remained leaning against the tree, not sparing Quinn a glance. Her arm concealed something. Zmija, Ophelia's familiar, was a snake in its dormant form, an armband.

Quinn circled to Ophelia's opposite side to obtain a visual, as she knew Ophelia wouldn't freely offer the information she sought.

"Okay, but how did you know I was here now?" Quinn uncrossed her arms as she was nearly upon her.

"We planned this time, Shadow Seer." Ophelia hadn't moved a muscle. This wasn't unusual for her, but something was off.

11

"You know what I mean," Quinn said as she approached her.

"Performing magic releases the scent of muskle berries," she answered with a coolness Quinn wasn't used to. "It requires a high-level practitioner to conceal the odor."

Ophelia answered a direct question. Quinn arched an eyebrow. *That's unlike her. Something's definitely wrong.*

Quinn continued her approach with caution. "Is that the blueberry-like scent I always smell?" Quinn stepped back, trying to recall all the times she had scented that hint of blueberry in the air. *What could it have been? Why hasn't anyone told me this before?*

Ophelia moved, ever so slight, Quinn may not have noticed it, prior to her training. Standing to the left of Ophelia, she pivoted to face her head-on. Ophelia had her arm across her stomach with her fist clenched. A dark color, almost black, stained her abdomen. Blood.

Quinn rushed to her side, knelt, and asked, "Are you hurt?" *Of course, she's hurt. She's bleeding.*

Ophelia still hadn't moved. "I will be fine in a few moments," Ophelia said, lifting her arm.

"Let me see," Quinn said, reaching for Ophelia's arm. She pushed it gently aside. "Seraphina taught me some of the healing arts. She always said, 'The greatest threat to mankind, is man.' Healing is important."

Ophelia was on her feet in the blink of an eye and now stood five feet from Quinn.

"Whoa! Was that magic?" Quinn froze in astonishment. "How'd you move so fast?"

"I said I will be fine in a moment. We, Fae, heal faster than you humans. I also took a potion Seraphina gave me and absorbed the essence from this tree."

Quinn's eyes darted to the tree. "What happened to you?" She approached Ophelia as she would a frightened animal. Quinn glanced back at the rotted log. *Was that tree just alive? I don't wanna know.*

Quinn didn't think Ophelia would answer her. During her training with Seraphina, she learned to wait for an answer, no matter how long or awkward. It was a matter of respect amongst the Fae. If you wanted answers, you had to pay the price in time.

Ophelia moved as if she were uninjured, though Quinn knew better. It was a defense mechanism. If you were wounded on the battlefield, you were left behind. Quinn wouldn't leave her behind.

"Let's sit, and you can fill me in," Quinn suggested, her hands up, showing she meant no harm. "That's if it's safe here." She glanced over her shoulder.

"It is safe," Ophelia answered and complied with Quinn's request.

After an excruciating amount of time had passed, sitting in complete silence, Ophelia turned to face Quinn.

"While seeking answers, I tripped an alarm; an arrow struck me," Ophelia said, gesturing toward the wound. "I dodged the others, but I was too slow for this one." She winced. "I think this mess with Puck has weakened me." She gazed into Quinn's eyes and paused. "I need him," she whispered.

Quinn had never heard or seen Ophelia express any sign of vulnerability. It was surreal; she didn't know how to process that information. Ophelia was unmatched by any other, a leader, and a Fae warrior. She was intimidating and fierce. Seeing her now, Quinn felt somehow closer to her. As if she were more human, displaying this emotion.

Ophelia changed the subject and, again became stoic; her facial expression had turned to stone. "The prison does not merely confine prisoners," she said in a cool tone that revealed a history of harsh experience. "It forces them to confront the worst parts of themselves, hidden fears, and shameful secrets. The mirrors, spelled with evil, twist images to create false narratives so convincing they can drive even the strongest Fae to lose themselves."

Ophelia grew quiet, distant, as if recalling the horror firsthand. "It is torturous, planting seeds of doubt that grow into madness from the false narratives." Quinn focused on standing still to be respectful, but she couldn't help but fiddle with her hair. The intensity of Ophelia's words made her uncomfortable. Ophelia continued, "Until they unravel bit by bit, leaving nothing but the remains of a shell of who they once were. None had ever escaped. None were unchanged."

Ophelia paused and inhaled a sharp breath. Quinn thought she heard a quiver.

"You must hurry. Puck will not last long in there." Ophelia stood with no apparent signs of injuries, other than her arm covering her stomach. It rested there as if she were self-conscious rather than hurt. "He has a trickster past," Ophelia said, her voice filled with desperation. "It will haunt him. No matter how far he has come or how much he has changed, I fear the prison will revert centuries of his progress." She took a deep, steadying breath. "He has reshaped who he is…" She didn't finish the thought that weighed heavily on her. She didn't have to. Quinn knew what was at stake and how much it affected Ophelia.

Once she was caught up, the severity of Puck's situation became painfully clear. She was in over her head. Her breath caught in her throat, as if verbalizing her fears made them inevitable. It was more than a mission; it was a race against the odds. Her chest tightened while her emotions swirled like a cyclone. This pressure threatened to paralyze her. Quinn clenched her fist; there was no time for doubt. She nodded to Ophelia. Whatever history existed between them, it couldn't matter, not now. She had to complete this mission, not only for Puck's sake, but for Ophelia's.

Chapter 3: Sometime in the Past

Quinn

If only I had listened. Seraphina frowned at Quinn and warned, "You must learn to walk before you can run, young one. Do not attempt traveling again without completing the task I have set forth."

Those last words echoed in her head, haunting her. Quinn's curiosity got the better of her. She was eager to experiment with her powers and attempted to peek into Seraphina's past. Fractures of memories flooded her. Seraphina and Eve flashed across her mind, but she couldn't piece it together. It was as if they lived the same life. She kept seeing each one doing the same thing. They even slept in the same bed. Eve was the first Fae Baxter had encountered.

It's as if they are the same being. Those who said dreams can't hurt you have never dreamed of Fata.

She found herself stuck in the past for more than a year. Time spiraled, and each time Quinn tried to return to the present, the past swallowed her like a riptide, dragging her further into its depths. Days blurred into weeks, and Quinn worried she might never see Baxter again. While she was living in the past through the eyes of others and jumping from vision to vision, she could still maintain her own thoughts. Even though it was difficult to sort between the person's mind and her own.

I have to learn something from this vision, or I'll never escape it.

15

She gave in and watched as different Fae grew and changed. Quinn let go and succumbed to this vision of the past. She saw different relationships evolve. Finally, the purpose of this vision was clear. Eve whispered secrets into someone's ear, a queen. All Quinn could hear was, "The greatest threat to mankind, is man."

Seraphina always says that.

Then, Eve turned a corner and changed…into Seraphina. *They're the same Fae. She's a shapeshifter.* A coolness washed over her, and she awoke beside a tree.

***

Baxter. Quinn bolted upright, the forest spun. Her body struggled to adjust to the sudden movement after witnessing the past. Baxter would notice her absence. There was no way of telling how long she'd been gone; time moved differently in Fata.

If only I had that artifact Mr. Perry used against us, the Tempus Sisto.

It had the ability to slow time but not stop it. The yin-yang shaped orb appeared to be filled with two types of sand, one black and one white, in water encompassed by gold. Back when Mr. Perry was a teacher at her school, until he went rogue and became a villain. No one knew where he'd ended up or what he did after they confronted him and defeated his fighting champion. For now, he was in the wind.

I can't worry about that right now.

She was near the cave that served as a portal. Quinn stepped through the veil, and the stars and moon shone in the sky, one moon.

Home. But how long was I gone? She checked her phone twice. *My phone must've broken.*

Phones didn't work in Fata. No time had passed. Not a fraction of a second. It felt like an eternity to her. It was unnerving, especially since the last time Baxter had slipped into Fata for a short while, weeks had flown by. Quinn texted Baxter

16

to meet her at Mystical Gems, Celeste's shop and home. Quinn crafted her words with care as she waited for Baxter to arrive.

I can't tell anyone, or I might end up in Oakdale Institute.

Celeste had been the only other person who fully comprehended Quinn's situation. But alas, she was nowhere to be seen. Quinn could only assume Celeste was still in Fata, lost in its twisted time as she once had been. Celeste was quirky. She came from a history of gifted people, able to see the unseen.

Hopefully, she isn't trapped in Fata. I'm not even sure she can go in and out by choice.

Celeste was knowledgeable about parallel universes, yet she possessed a minuscule ability. She knew enough to be dangerous to herself. She relied on charms and potions to glimpse a fraction of what Baxter and Quinn could see with ease. Quinn grabbed her bike and headed to the shop.

If nobody sees me, and I can see Baxter then I can be back to Fata in no time. If I can rescue Puck before Baxter notices I'm missing, he'd be safe. Sweat formed on her brow as she raced to the shop. *Only another mile to go.*

"Hey, Quinn," Matt waved and called to her.

Quinn ducked and turned away. She couldn't hide in the open. She looked back at Matt. "Oh, hi Matt. I didn't see you there," she lied.

Tiny lines formed at his eyes, but he didn't question her.

"I was wondering if you had…"

Quinn pedaled even faster. "I can't talk now, I'm running late," she called over her shoulder.

She encountered two other people along her way. Quinn's absence had gone unnoticed since she returned at the same time. It still barely made sense to her.

She sagged with relief. *Nobody seemed to notice.* No one except Baxter would notice.

She thought that if she divulged some truth, he wouldn't be suspicious.

What if I were stuck in that vision forever? I have to tell him something.

Seraphina had suggested she return to her realm to gather some sense of home and ground herself to the present. Baxter would panic.

She prepared herbal tea while she waited for him to arrive. The tea revealed the truth, Seraphina taught her. She sat in Celeste's kitchen since she wouldn't be using it for a while. This would be a safe place to hang out.

Dried herbs hung from the rafters. The dingy yellow floral wallpaper peeled from the walls, while crystals in the windows scattered bands of rainbow colors across the room. The air was charged. She hadn't noticed this before.

Did my training allow me to sense this now? She was regenerated inside this place. *It must be all the crystals.*

Even the gargoyles around the house gave the impression of security. She thought the gargoyles were fascinating; they even had miniature weapons. Some brandished swords, and others gripped nunchucks and sai. She was certain they had changed positions.

On the steps entering the back porch, the gargoyle with the sword was on the left, and the one with the nunchucks was on the right. She swore it was that way, but the next time she went, the nunchucks were on the left, and the sword wasn't on the back steps at all. In fact, it was nowhere.

A knock on the door pulled Quinn back to the present. She opened the back door of the shop, where the living quarters were. She smiled awkwardly.

"Hey, Ax." She half saluted him and quickly put her arm back by her side.

"Q, what's up?" he asked, arching an eyebrow.

He knows. Quinn's pulse quickened. She took a steadying breath and walked to the table.

"I just wanted to spend some time with you," she lied. Quinn pulled out a rickety chair.

"You texted yesterday that you needed space," Baxter said. The disbelief in his voice was palpable.

Yesterday? It's been about a year. How did time not change here? "I did?" she asked.

"You seem different," he said. "Wiser. And more muscular than yesterday."

Quinn glanced at her hands. She reached for the tea she had brewed and ignored her brother. She needed to think fast. Pouring him a cup, she asked, "Sugar?"

He raised his brows. "Is everything okay?" Baxter asked, taking the mug.

"I'm fine," she said, attempting to cover her misstep. "You know how girls can be."

"Quinn," Baxter started.

"I'm okay, really. I wanted to talk about you, actually." Maybe if she put the spotlight on him, he'd forget about her.

"You look like you've lost weight," he said, perplexed.

Quinn pretended to take a sip of her pre-poured tea. If she drank the same tea as him, she'd end up spilling every secret she'd held back.

"I've been cutting carbs lately," she lied.

Baxter's eyes narrowed, but he didn't respond. He looked around the room, his eyes landing on the strange markings ingrained in the wood. "Did we find out what those mean?" he asked.

I wonder if that's why I feel rejuvenated here. Maybe it isn't the crystals.

Quinn shrugged.

"Is her bird still here?" Baxter asked, gazing around once more.

"I forgot all about that bird," Quinn confessed. "Haven't seen it. I don't know how it would've survived if she wasn't feeding it."

Baxter got that expression on his face. "Should we look for it?" he asked.

"Why not?" Quinn asked.

Baxter stood, and Quinn handed him his mug. He eyed her.

"What?" she questioned. "It'll get cold." He accepted, taking a sip.

They glanced into the rooms one by one, finding no birdcage, only piles of junk.

"Maybe she took it with her," Quinn suggested. *How am I gonna tell him anything without him getting suspicious or trying to follow me back?*

Quinn recalled using the glasses Celeste had given her, which caused her to travel further back in time. She shouldn't have used them. Seraphina had warned her and scolded her after. It had been dangerous, but she was improving in her craft and was faster while using objects. This was the first time she had gotten herself in trouble.

She remembered the scandal when Theo and Celeste had run away together. Quinn had added a 'Gone for vacation' sign outside Celeste's shop to lessen the people missing from town and the questions it may have raised when the store remained closed. However, nothing could be done for Oakdale Institute after losing two patients. Baxter was found, but Theo, Coles's father, had drawn the eyes of the FBI and an investigation into how two patients had escaped.

They interviewed many staff members suspected of providing assistance. The investigators questioned Baxter several times about how he'd escaped. When he refused to provide substantial facts, they eventually left him alone.

Cole, however, wasn't as lucky. He was sent to live with his grandmother when his father disappeared from the institute.

They interviewed him often about his father's whereabouts, expecting him to return to his only son. They were relentless with their questions about his dad's escape.

Cole was already an outcast at school. Feeling bad for him, Baxter had gone out of his way to alleviate some of the pressure. He wasn't sure if it worked. He visited Cole and tried to take his mind off things, which helped distract Baxter from his own worries, a welcomed distraction.

Once the smoke clears, things will likely go back to normal.

Baxter cleared his throat, drawing her back to reality. Baxter's twin senses must've been tingling, alerting him of her wandering thoughts. He straightened, giving her his full attention.

Quinn changed the subject as they headed back into the kitchen. She had no idea how long she'd been daydreaming. "So, when you were released from Oakdale, and you told them you didn't see anything unusual anymore, was that true?" she asked, eyebrows raised. She leaned forward, anticipating the answer.

Baxter's brow furrowed, his eyes searching. "What do you want me to say?" Baxter sighed. "Quinn, I already told you. It's a blur. I don't really remember anything." He pressed his hand to his forehead as if it caused him pain to relive the past.

He's lying. I know it, but do I question him? "Hmm," she mumbled.

But how? Did he know about the Uncertain Tea? He didn't really answer.

Relief washed over her. *It's for the best. Baxter doesn't need to know the specifics, the darkness that briefly enveloped our lives. Plus, if he's attempting to hide it, he won't ask me about it.*

***

Over time, Quinn grew accustomed to the strange occurrences in Fata, finding a sliver of normalcy in the peculiar landscapes and creatures. She had a brief glimpse of her father with a woman, she assumed was her Aunt Dorothy. She couldn't recall the last time she saw her.

Aunt Dot had been diagnosed with schizophrenia and sent upstate after she harmed her dad's cat, Fluffy. He loved that cat and never owned one since. Quinn learned that the cat was her father's familiar and intended to do him harm. She'd have to remember once all this was over to see if Aunt Dot had gifts and was locked up for them.

Meanwhile, Baxter spent more time with Jimmy, one of his closest friends, and avoided their father's simmering grief. Neither dared to bring up Baxter's release from Oakdale, fearing it would reignite old wounds. Her second day back home was enough. She was so stressed she was running late, despite no time had passed at all. She slipped back into the realm once again without telling Baxter.

Chapter 4: No Longer Home

Baxter

Quinn had been acting differently, as if she were hiding something. Not only was she slimmer, she seemed almost wiser. Unable to pinpoint it, yet he sensed something was off.

After his father's anger had finally subsided and Baxter had denied seeing anything unusual, they had released him from Oakdale. With nowhere else to go, he found himself outside Connor's window. The house gave him a sense of peace, even if Connor was no longer amongst the living. Seeking comfort, Baxter had crept inside, knowing it'd be unlocked. He fell asleep in Connor's bed, only to be startled awake by Connor's mother.

She screamed at the sight of him, thinking for a split second that her son had returned. Once the shock passed, she softened, her hand covered her mouth as tears threatened to spill. He recalled the pain in her eyes. It paralyzed him in that moment, like a blow

He'd apologized, offering to leave, but after the dust settled, Connor's mother insisted he stay. She told him it was good for both of them. It gave her comfort to know Connor's room wasn't empty and that her son's best friend occupied it, knowing it's what Connor would've wanted. She then called for Connor's father, who, after a long silence, nodded in agreement. His grief was more guarded, but Baxter could still see the depth of their sorrow.

Although Connor's family had offered Baxter a place in Connor's room, the pain was too much for him to bear. They had questions no one could answer, and the weight of their loss lingered in the house like a shadow. He had to find somewhere else to go before the grief consumed him; he was safe here for the moment.

Connor's parents clung to the hope that their son had run away, convincing themselves that he might walk in the house one day. Baxter, however, knew the truth, and it felt like a knife in his heart to let them believe otherwise. He couldn't shatter their misguided beliefs. He couldn't tell them that Connor had fallen to his death in a pit of thorns. That truth was far too cruel.

What could I possibly say to comfort them? That their son died, and I watched it happen?

But if Baxter told the truth and revealed what really happened, he would never see the light of day again. His current freedom hinged on the lie he'd fed the psychologist. That the shadows and the Fae were gone. That he no longer saw another realm. He pretended to swallow the medications and convinced everyone he had improved, despite the crippling, recurring nightmares.

***

The cuckoo clock on the wall pierced the silence in Baxter's dimly lit kitchen. Baxter jumped, afraid that he'd been caught. Hovering in the doorway, he forced his breath to slow. He snuck into his room to get a few belongings. He just needed a few things. He couldn't simply ask his father if he could stop by. That wouldn't go well.

The ticking brought back a flood of memories; his mother humming while baking. His father was reading the paper, pretending not to hear his mother's jokes as he smirked and quietly chuckled. He enjoyed their playful banter that once made his house a home.

Now, it was silent, apart from the ticking of the clock. His parents had been together since high school, and his father wasn't handling his wife's death well. Not that there's a good way to handle death. But this, this was something else. Doug was particularly depressed. He was alone, swimming in a sea of sorrow. Baxter stiffened when he heard the old wooden chair scratch on the tile.

"I wondered when you'd come crawling back," his father said with disdain.

He clenched his jaw. Doug sat at the table in the dimly lit room. "After all this time, you think you can just show up like you did nothing wrong."

Doug didn't even look up at Baxter. The tightly controlled anger barely leashed in his tone. Doug crossed his arms over his chest, flexing his muscles. His knuckles were white. His father's jaw clenched.

Baxter braced a hand against the worn wooden-paneled wall. His stomach twisted into painful knots. Unable to think of a response, he asked, "Where's Max?"

"That dog ran off when you did," Doug said with growing anger.

Max. Baxter ignored the pang in his chest; he couldn't think about that now.

His father had an untouched plate of food in front of him. He still didn't look Baxter in the eyes.

"I needed to grab a few things, like my license and stuff," he said, his voice quivering. His hands trembled, and he put them behind his back.

A gust of wind whistled as the air pushed past the old windowpanes, startling him.

Doug inhaled long and slow through his nose, as if attempting to rein in his anger. His hands flexed and uncurled. He didn't respond.

Baxter swallowed and cleared his throat. "Arc you..." His voice caught in his throat. "Are you even going to look at me?" Baxter cried, feeling both ashamed and lost. His shoulders slumped forward, as if carrying the weight of the world.

Doug didn't move.

"I'm…" Baxter hesitated. "I'm still your son." His voice cracked.

Doug smashed his fist on the table so hard the dishes rattled. "No son of mine would behave the way you have!"

Baxter recoiled. "I didn't *do* anything," Baxter practically shouted. He shoved his hands deep into his pockets. His breath hitched.

Baxter had never seen his father this angry. His father had always been laid-back, quick to crack a joke, never one to raise his voice. You couldn't take him seriously. Quinn warned him he was mad, but he didn't expect this darkness. He didn't recognize this man.

"She was my mother, too, you know." His voice trembled in sadness. "I miss her, too." A single tear ran down his cheek. He didn't wipe it away. Baxter sniffled.

Doug turned his head slowly to look at him, his eyes empty, shells of what they once were. "You don't have the right to speak to me about *her*." His voice was deadly quiet, which was worse than his shout.

Doug shot to his feet, sending the chair skidding backwards. It flipped over and crashed onto the floor. He looked defeated. For a long moment, Baxter thought his father might say something comforting, that the ice was finally thawing. But instead. he turned away, his head down, shoulders slumped.

"Get your things and go," Doug muttered over his shoulder when he was halfway down the hall.

Baxter didn't say anything; he couldn't. He stood there in stunned silence. After a moment, he composed himself. Baxter tiptoed to his room, grabbed a backpack full of essentials, and quietly crept back down the hallway.

At the front door, he yanked his car keys off the hook. He paused in the entryway and sighed, glancing over his shoulder as if expecting his father to return. He took a deep breath and stepped out of the house he once called home.

His heart ached. This was something no child should ever feel: alone. His father refused to see him as his son any longer. Now, he'd lost both his parents.

***

The bright sun shone as Jimmy knocked on Connor's window, waking Baxter. Referring to the window as anything other than Connor's felt wrong. Despite knowing Connor was never coming back, he found himself hoping his friend would come sauntering in through the door.

Even he didn't know about Connor's demise. Only his sister, Theo, Celeste, and he knew what really happened to Connor. No one could bear to tell them the truth. It was too painful to reveal Connor's death to anyone. Plus, after losing his mother, Chloe, he couldn't face any more loss.

Baxter opened the window, and Jimmy popped his head inside. His goofy grin reached his eyes.

"Hey, B, wanna hike?" He cocked his head to the side as he awaited his answer.

How could anyone say no to him when he was in this mood?

Jimmy, as if he sensed Baxter needed someone, always happened to be around. His go-to distraction was hiking. Baxter couldn't handle the forest; it's how they accidentally stumbled upon the fairy circle that was the portal into Fata. That was where the beginning of the end happened. Baxter couldn't face the woods, not yet. Anytime he thought of Fata, his chest tightened, and he could barely catch his breath.

How could I explain that to him? That our hikes are what eventually led to the deaths of my mother and best friend?

"I'm all set. I got the worst case of poison ivy last time. It was horrible." Although Baxter felt guilty for lying, he couldn't tell him the truth.

"Well, we've gotta do something. You always loved hiking." Jimmy paused. He cocked his head to the other side.

"You can't stay in this room twenty-four seven. It's not healthy. You need some fresh air."

"I like it here," Baxter said, looking around at Connor's belongings. "I feel closer to him, like he's going to come through that door at any time, run his hand through his hair, and say some lame joke."

Jimmy chuckled. "I do miss his jokes."

His smile was filled with pain, which hurt to see. *If he only knew the truth, would he still talk to me?*

Baxter sighed. "I'm not sure I'm up to doing anything." It wasn't a complete lie. He backed up and sat on Connor's bed.

Jimmy climbed through the window. "Let's at least get you something to eat. We could go to Sonny's," he offered.

Sonny's was a classic 1950s-style dining car, the only real attraction, a staple of the small town. Baxter and his friends always went. Lately, he hadn't been able to go, not wanting to run into anyone. Baxter didn't want to answer the inevitable questions like: What really happened to Connor? Why would he run away? How could he not know? Or even worse, their pitiful stares. He couldn't stand having people feel sorry for him.

It's all my fault, Connor's dead, and yet they feel bad for me. They don't even know he's dead. They just think he ran away, not even that he's missing.

It was too late now to tell them all the truth. Together, he and Quinn had decided that Baxter would tell everyone. Quinn didn't want to have to explain everything on her own. They'd forgotten a key component; Baxter was supposed to be in Oakdale Institute when he returned from Fata.

If Baxter told the truth, he would've never been released. Baxter was initially locked up for seeing things; at the time, he didn't know he was a Shadow Walker, meaning he could cross through shadows between realms at will, something he still struggled with. But the thought of telling anyone that Connor died was too much, so he'd kept the secret.

Baxter's shoulders drooped, and his head faced the floor. Jimmy noted his body language and made a poor, but honorable attempt to cheer him up.

He approached Baxter and placed a gentle hand on his shoulder. "Hey, turn that frown upside down."

Connor was the funny one; now, Jimmy's trying to be.

He managed a weak smile and said, "Sonny's sounds nice."

Jimmy's expression lit up; he was practically beaming. It forced Baxter to smile genuinely for the first time in a long time.

His ability put a massive target on his back, and the Unseelie were out to get him. A corrupted group of Fae twisted by consumption. The Unseelie were formed from nature, yet withered, dead or dying like blight. He shoved his hands into his pockets after they slipped out the window and walked to the car. He'd always done this when he was worried.

Maybe he should've told him the truth about Mr. Perry. How his science teacher had gone mad after losing his wife, Sofie, to Fata, which nobody knew. It drove him mad, and he sought revenge, but that revenge had corrupted Mr. Perry. Evil consumed him and sought to end Baxter.

Unfortunately, Baxter had unwillingly enlisted Connor; more like he begged to go. Baxter had a unique necklace that blocked the Fae from feeding off his essence. When Connor wore it, somehow, it magically allowed him to see the unseen.

Normally, only people with a mutation on chromosomes six or thirteen could see the Fae. Connor had neither and complained that he was missing all the fun. Connor eventually convinced Baxter to let him go to Fata, where he met his demise with one of Mr. Perry's booby traps.

Baxter pressed his forehead against the cool window as all these regrets swirled in his mind. He believed Mr. Perry to be his friend. Not that he had ever been his friend to begin with. That hurt deep down. He loved Mr. Perry. That was until he discovered his true nature. That pain had quickly evaporated any affection when Mr. Perry killed Connor. Talking about it wouldn't bring his friend back.

"Hey, man, did you hear me?" Jimmy asked, placing his hand on Baxter's shoulder.

Baxter blinked and swallowed. They were outside Sonny's, and he'd been daydreaming.

I don't even remember leaving Connor's place. "What?" Baxter asked.

Jimmy gave him a look but didn't comment on his inattention. "I said we don't have to go in if you don't want to." He moved to face Baxter head-on. Baxter saw Jimmy's eyes searched for any sign he wasn't screwing this up, proof he was doing the right thing.

Baxter nodded, and Jimmy opened the door.

A bell rang, alerting the staff to a new customer. The last time Baxter had visited, the patrons had grown quiet and glared at him, their stares branding his skin. Their silence was deafening as his steps had echoed on the tile. The following visit, everyone dared to ask him what had happened, a question he desperately attempted to avoid. At least now, things had a semblance of normalcy.

His usual booth was occupied, and while there was an empty table in the middle, it might put a spotlight on him.

Perhaps nobody has noticed I'm here yet.

A dark head of hair in the back corner caught his eye; the all-black attire and pale skin could be none other than Cole.

His pace was deliberate as he approached the table in the back and waited for Cole to look up before he spoke to him. Jimmy was right behind him, until he stopped at his desired table. Baxter cleared his throat and eyed him, unsure if Cole was oblivious or ignoring them. He heard Cole whisper, "Acey."

Acey? His sister, who went missing. He must miss her. "Hey, Cole." His voice was unusually shaky. He ran his fingers through his hair, not knowing what else to do with them.

Cole's forehead wrinkled as if he had been asked about quantum physics. He looked up from his book at a snail's pace and nodded once, then gazed back at his book.

Baxter looked back at Jimmy and shrugged. "Um," Baxter said as he shifted his weight. "Do you mind if we sit with you?"

An awkward pause hung heavy in the air. Jimmy hesitated, withdrawing from the table he'd picked, where he'd been so keen to settle.

Cole shrugged. "It's a free country," Cole said, not bothering to lift his eyes from his book, *The Whispering Shadows of Forgotten Echoes*, even more withdrawn than his usual. "I don't own those seats."

What's wrong with him? Is it his dad? And why is he always reading the same book?

Jimmy approached the table in a huff. "Dude, we're just trying to be polite," he said, frustration dripping from his tone.

Cole, ever so slowly, lifted his head to make eye contact with Baxter. He waved for them to sit. Baxter, knowing this may be all they would get out of Cole, slid into the booth and scooted over for Jimmy.

He shook his head subtly. Baxter patted the seat beside him, urging him to join. Baxter widened his gaze, pleading. He reluctantly took the seat with a sigh.

A waitress wearing a pink and teal uniform approached the table, hand on her hip, annoyance apparent. "Now that you have friends here, are you going to order something or not?" she asked politely despite her demeanor.

Cole looked up at her, his body language unreadable. "I'll have another tea," he said in a monotone voice.

The waitress eyed him with a warning glance.

He straightened. "I'll have the Sonny's special," Jimmy chimed in. His stomach growled loud enough for Baxter to hear, which made him smile.

Baxter looked to Cole. "Me too," he said. "Aren't you hungry? My treat."

Cole paused, clearing his throat. "I'll have the chocolate chip pancakes with an order of bacon," he said with a slight one-sided smile.

Did he not have enough money?

Even the slightest reaction from Cole warmed Baxter inside. Knowing Cole may be uncomfortable with Jimmy, but he was sure to warm up to him. People like Jimmy were hard to come by, and the most loyal friends.

"Do you have any plans for this summer, Cole?" Baxter asked.

Cole shook his head. When the waitress set down the food, he eyed the chocolate chips clumped in the center and licked his lips.

The bell rang, a new customer had entered, and Cole's eyes widened. Baxter hadn't seen Cole react to anything with that much emotion and turned to see what would cause him to display such a reaction. Rust-red hair caught his eye.

It belonged to his former nemesis, Rufus. Baxter had outgrown concerns as trivial as the school bully; he had lost his best friend, his mother, and discovered the ability to travel to parallel universes. Rufus, now insignificant, paled in comparison, no longer registering on Baxter's radar.

Rufus didn't get the memo that Baxter no longer cared what he did. He approached the table with his friends and smirked at Cole. "Finally making friends, I see." Rufus sneered and gestured toward Jimmy and Baxter. "If these chumps can be called that."

The table fell silent, Baxter hoping Rufus would leave if they ignored him. Ignoring him never worked; Rufus demanded attention and always got it, no matter what.

"Hey, Dobber, how's it feel to be out of the nuthouse?" he spewed, cruelty in his voice.

His two friends, Eric Carpenter and Ashton Andrews, smirked beside him but didn't say anything. Eric, with his smooth black hair and round eyes, stood out in more ways than one. His golden skin and five feet nine inches couldn't be more of a disparity compared to Ashton's six-foot stature and pale, scarred face. Beside Ashton, whose mousy brown hair and gray eyes were a stark contrast.

When Baxter didn't reply, Rufus laughed. His smug smile got under Baxter's skin.

Eric appeared gaunt, more than before. He lost weight. *I wonder if something happened to him from that Unseelie feeding off of him last year.*

"Biology isn't the same without your pal, Mr. Perry." Rufus chuckled to himself as he looked to his friends for support. They shifted uncomfortably, one of them even forced a laugh. "It's odd, isn't it?" he paused. "People seem to disappear around Baxter." Rufus turned his gaze to Cole. "Watch out, you might be next."

"Not all of us had to take summer school," Baxter countered.

"That's mint!" Jimmy shouted and laughed. His short brown hair didn't move, despite all the gel.

Rufus flexed his biceps and balled his fists. He pulled back a fist, squaring up to Baxter. The silverware clanked together as Jimmy's fist connected with the table.

"Back off, Rufus," Jimmy shouted, unable to ignore him any longer.

The whole diner looked at them. Cole's cheeks pinkened, vivid in comparison to his pale complexion.

"Whoa, Mr. Tough Guy over here," Rufus said to his friends, pointing his thumb over his shoulder. He elbowed Eric and chuckled once more. Ashton laughed and nodded.

He looks like a clown laughing like that with his red hair. Baxter smiled at the thought, which didn't go unnoticed.

"What's so funny, Dobber?" Rufus asked, his tone anything but friendly.

Baxter ignored him.

Rufus, undeterred, continued, "I'm surprised you haven't taken over for Mr. Perry, adding that strange powder to the town's water supply," Rufus said in a mocking tone. "Probably poison. That's why he disappeared, I bet." Rufus snickered. His pals laughed again.

Baxter's eyebrow raised. *Mr. Perry? The water?* Baxter recalled Mr. Perry said something about spiking the water to allow his minions to do his bidding without outright killing the townsfolk. If he unleashed the Unseelie, there would be mass killings and a lot of explaining to do. However, if he gave everyone Ravenswood, a supernatural tree used to prevent Fae possession, they'd be protected from the Unseelie.

But they would also see things that were unexplainable. I wonder if that's what corrupted the Fae and created the Unseelie in the first place. Seraphina mentioned there was something that caused the mutation from Seelie to Unseelie. If I could stop it, I wouldn't only save the corrupted Fae, I would also take away Mr. Perry's army.

Baxter stood, as best he could, on the inside of a booth and nudged Jimmy out. Jimmy scooted over but didn't exit the booth.

"I just remembered, there's something I have to do," Baxter said in a hurried manner.

"Dude, don't let this clown push you around," Jimmy said, his hand balling into a fist.

Funny, he must've thought Rufus also looked like a clown laughing.

Baxter shook his head. "He's not. I really have something I've gotta do," he insisted and gave Jimmy an encouraging smile.

Cole stood as well. "I'll go with you." He looked energized and eager. This was the first time Baxter saw him excited about anything.

I can't get Cole involved in this again. How can I let him down gently? This is the first time he has spoken up without prompting. I don't wanna crush his hopes.

Unable to devise a good reason why he couldn't go, Baxter finally nodded.

Maybe I can think of something boring to do, and when Cole leaves, I can formulate my plan.

"I'm paying. Check, please," Jimmy insisted as he waved to the waitress.

Her mood had improved somewhat; even seemed more approachable. Now that her tip was imminent, her attitude thawed, almost borderline friendly.

I wonder how long Cole sat here with just the tea.

Cole raised his hand as if he were in class and said, "I'll take three to-go boxes, please." He had no intention of leaving any leftovers behind.

He must be hungry. I've got to remember to help him somehow.

Chapter 5: The Reservoir

The air outside felt cool, a nice contrast to the greasy atmosphere in the restaurant. Cole had walked to the diner, since he lived nearby. They all piled into Jimmy's black Mazda, a gift from his father for his sixteenth birthday. Baxter couldn't help but notice how rigid Cole sat, so straight it was as if he had a steel rod in his spine.

"Where to?" Jimmy asked, his hands loose on the steering wheel.

Baxter shifted in his seat, his hand behind his head. "Well, don't you have something to do?" he answered with a question.

Jimmy faced Baxter and smirked. "Nope. I'm all yours."

Baxter sighed. He hated the idea of dragging Jimmy into this, but how dangerous could the reservoir be? It was unlikely Mr. Perry would still be in this plane, or an Unseelie would be lurking over the water.

"To the Rez then," Baxter said. Cole looked uncomfortable. "Are you okay?" His eyebrow arched.

Creases formed on his brow, and his face flushed. "Yeah. Why?" Cole asked, his eyes staring straight ahead. He remained as rigid as a board.

What's with him?

"Just checking," Baxter replied, attempting to alleviate the tension he had caused.

After a moment, Cole asked, "What's the Rez?" He grimaced as if the question tasted awful.

Jimmy suppressed a laugh, and the corners of his mouth turned upwards. "It's the reservoir," he said as he started the car.

The rest of the drive was filled with silence, thick as smoke. Baxter stared out the window, wondering how he could locate or counter Mr. Perry's destruction. He learned of the death of Mr. Perry's wife, Sofie, from Quinn's vision and how it broke him. She was chasing dreams of Fata. He'd turned evil over time, attempting to resurrect her, and spiked the town's water supply with Ravenswood.

That was likely the reason Theo had gone mad after the loss of his wife and daughter. Shortly after that, Mr. Perry transcended to the self-proclaimed dark king of Fata and ordered the Ravenswood trees to be destroyed. Baxter didn't feel bad for him, even as the pain of losing his own mother and friend ran deep in his veins.

Ophelia, a high-ranking Fae warrior, and her band of Freedom Fighters protected the last known Ravenswood tree. She was once a hero in her day, now forgotten, as peace had no need for warriors. And it's a serious crime to kill another Fae, outside of war.

Mr. Perry had cast out anyone who would stand against him, so Ophelia went into hiding.

Soon after Baxter was released from the institute, he learned that Theo had returned to the land that had taken everything from him. He decided it was better than remaining in Oakdale. This, unfortunately, left his son Cole an orphan. Feeling sorry for him, Baxter and his friends befriended him. Cole could see the Fae but didn't believe it. That made him extremely susceptible to injury or death. There were many dangers when dealing with the Fae, including just existing. But not being able to see them or believe in them was far less dangerous than the alternative.

Sure, they fed like vampires off your essence, but hardly ever left you for dead, just riddled with diseases, like incurable cancer. But to see them and not believe in them was far worse, and the unfortunate reality for Cole. The Fae were capable of convincing people to sell their eternal souls. Some humans accidentally stumbled into Fata, which presented larger issues, like almost getting killed by giant trolls.

Baxter's unfocused eyes were yanked from his daydreams as Jimmy pulled into the long driveway.

"Are you okay?" Jimmy asked.

Baxter nodded once.

The car jolted over a patch of uneven asphalt halfway down the driveway, where it gave way to gravel. The tires rumbled over the stone, loud in the heavy silence. Jimmy parked as close to the water as possible. When the car came to a stop, he killed the engine, and they got out. Cole looked out of place. His movements were jerky, as if he didn't belong in his body.

Has he always been awkward?

Jimmy gave Baxter a side-eye, raised an eyebrow with a smirk, and then glanced at Cole. Baxter ignored it. He strode toward the water's edge; the gravel crunched beneath his shoes; the others followed him. As he scanned the tree line, nothing appeared out of place. The pond stretched out before them was calm, its surface undisturbed and free of any strange colors. As they walked the perimeter, which was at least a three-mile walk, he paused to examine the damp grass. He scooped up a handful of stones, but nothing was amiss.

He pointed across the lake. "I guess we're hiking," Baxter said, voice strained with hints of pain. Memories clawed their way to the surface. The last time he hiked with his friends, it turned out disastrous. Connor never made it out alive. A shiver ran down his spine at the thought of his friend's final moments.

"Hopefully, less dramatic than last time," Jimmy scoffed. "Naomi's not here, so that's a good start."

Baxter gave an absentminded nod. His ex-girlfriend was the last thing on his mind. His past haunted him. He led the way without another word. The stone path gave way to damp earth, the wet ground squishing beneath their feet as they walked. It was eerily quiet. After a time, another shiver overtook him. He wasn't thinking about Connor, and it wasn't cold out. He stopped and observed his surroundings. The others stopped, too. Something felt off. Warning bells sounded in his head.

"What is it?" Cole whispered, oblivious to whatever danger stood before them. He was too close; his shoulder brushed Baxter's.

He stepped forward a step to regain some of his personal space. "Nothing," Baxter responded, not yet having an explanation. He worried something was amiss, yet he couldn't locate a reason why. After he was satisfied nothing was out of place, he continued walking.

They hadn't gone far when Jimmy's voice broke the uncomfortable silence. "What's that?" he asked and pointed to the lake.

He gazed in the direction Jimmy pointed. Something floated on the surface, a small, blue object.

They approached the water, and the object became clearer, a blue plastic container, its wet, glossy surface shimmered in the light.

"It looks like one of those chlorine dispensers people put in their swimming pools," Cole said. He leaned over Baxter's shoulder to get a closer look, once again invading his personal space.

His breath was warm against Baxter's ear. Baxter flinched and stepped forward to regain his space.

Jimmy turned to Baxter. "Was there always one here?"

He shrugged, unsure, but he was determined to check it out. "Not that I remember," he said.

The container floated out of reach. It was too cold to swim. Baxter scanned the area for something to help him and spotted a nearby branch. He picked it up, testing its durability. Once satisfied, he tried to fish the object out, but the branch was too short and only pushed it farther away.

"Not like that," Cole said. "Here, let me." He gestured for the branch.

Baxter hesitated for a moment before he handed it over reluctantly. Cole grabbed it too eagerly, a goofy grin upon his lips. Cole splashed the water, spraying them with tiny droplets.

"Come on, Cole," Jimmy cried, backing away as he wiped drops from his face. He blinked rapidly.

The object floated farther away, and Baxter's shoulder slumped, frustration apparent in the set of his jaw. A few minutes later, the object neared the other side of the pond.

"Great, now we'll never reach it," Jimmy whined as he threw his hands in the air.

Baxter smiled. "No, that's perfect." He doubled back, running toward the other side.

Cole kept creating waves so the object would reach the other side.

Baxter slid to a stop in the wet grass and fell to one knee. "I'm alright," he shouted.

The object was nearly to the shore. He reached for it; his fingers grazed the object, but every time he touched it, the item floated away. He gritted his teeth and yanked off his shoes and socks. One sock had a hole, his little toe poking out. They were Connor's black socks, marked with an orange 'V' to match the tunic he had borrowed, and he was unable to get rid of them.

He rolled his jeans and stepped into the frigid pond, and gasped. Standing still, adjusting to the cold, not wanting the object to float away in his ripples. As he shivered again, he didn't think this was from the cold, though he couldn't be certain.

He waded in farther, the water now to his knees, soaking the bottom of his rolled-up pants. His fingers wrapped around the object, but it felt odd to his touch, like it didn't belong. Regardless, he turned back to his friends on the shore, object in tow.

A commotion startled Baxter. He spun around and scanned the horizon. Then he saw it. Close to where he had left his friends, a large figure approached them from the tree line, moving in an unnatural, jerking pattern.

A walking tree emerged from the brush. Its bark-like skin flaked from its form while it unfolded, now standing two feet taller, no longer blending in. It only took a moment to realize, like a punch to the gut, this thing wasn't a tree.

The Unseelie. How hadn't I realized it sooner? Those shivers were a warning.

The container slipped from his grasp, forgotten. He sprinted as fast as he could toward the others. Jimmy was already halfway to Baxter, eyes wide with fear. The Unseelie drew closer to Cole, who remained in the same spot, alone. Its gait was slow and uneven as its massive body loomed over Cole. A spike ejected from its gnarled forearm as the Unseelie aimed it straight at his heart. Still, Cole didn't move a muscle.

"Cole, look out," Baxter yelled, but he didn't react at all. He was certain Cole saw a deformed tree with hollow, lifeless eyes. Cole acted as if he were enchanted, paralyzed by the Unseelie.

The creature took another step forward, and its spiked limb remained pointing at Cole. The air was suffocating as Baxter's heart hammered against his ribs.

Had poison gotten to Cole's brain? Why isn't he moving?

He ran faster, his breath coming in short bursts. His mind raced with panicked thoughts, thinking of any way to help Cole. As he closed the distance, he only wanted to pull Cole out of the creature's path before it was too late. Baxter passed Jimmy.

Why isn't he moving? I wonder if they can see it as I can.

Movement caught Baxter's attention, and Jimmy was sprinting beside him. He'd turned around.

How the hell is that tree moving?" Jimmy yelled as he ran toward Cole. Jimmy was faster than Baxter.

41

I guess at least Jimmy can see it. But how? The container must contain Ravenswood.

Jimmy reached Cole before Baxter, skidding to a halt a few feet before the towering tree. For a moment, Baxter thought he might turn and bolt, but he didn't. Jimmy took a quick step forward, and without warning, he roundhouse kicked the tree directly in the torso with force. The impact was loud; a cracking sound echoed through the air. The tree barely registered it, stumbling back a step or two, unfazed and irritated. It moved mechanically, pointing its spike directly at Jimmy.

Jimmy froze. Cole still hadn't responded.

Maybe he's frozen with fear. "No," Baxter shouted, panic was apparent in his voice. His bare feet splashed against the ground, making squishy noises as he hurried to close the distance.

The Unseelie turned its head toward him, locking eyes, and halting as if it realized it had been spotted. Before Baxter reached them, the tree moved with an unnatural burst of speed back toward the forest. It was shockingly nimble.

By the time he got there, his chest was heaving. Now that his friends were safe, he could rest. He bent over with his hands on his knees and huffed. His breaths came in sharp, rhythmic gasps.

"What the hell was that?" Jimmy asked, his voice betraying him despite the fierce display of bravery he'd shown earlier. His eyes were so wide they might pop out. He took a step back.

Baxter barely registered what he'd said. He watched the tree line where the Unseelie had vanished. His breathing was still ragged.

Jimmy elbowed him. "Need to hit that treadmill more, B."

Baxter straightened as he glared at him. *How could he joke at a time like this?* Baxter knew how close he'd been to losing another friend, but Jimmy apparently didn't. He grinned, oblivious to how close he'd been to death.

Cole cleared his throat. "That kick was awesome," he said, face bright with amazement. "Where did you learn that?" he asked. The genuine amazement in Cole's remark pierced the tension.

Jimmy tilted his head and grinned. "Karate," he said with a shrug, "for eight years." Jimmy's chest puffed up a little at the compliment.

Baxter approached Cole slowly, not wanting to startle him. He pressed a firm hand on Cole's shoulder and said, "Cole. Are you okay?"

Cole squinted and only smiled with a nod.

Baxter's chest still heaved with exhaustion. Jimmy appeared fine.

"Eight years?" Cole repeated, his eyebrows raised. He motioned a flat hand in a karate chop motion. Baxter had never seen Cole this animated. Jimmy laughed. Meanwhile, Baxter stayed quiet, his jaw tight with tension.

What was that thing doing here? Why did it run when it saw me? His friends couldn't possibly understand the weight of what had happened and how close it was to ending in tragedy.

Reluctantly, he looked away. He wanted to chase after the Unseelie, yet he knew at least Jimmy would follow. "Guys, we shouldn't stay here," Baxter said. He eyed Jimmy, letting him know the seriousness of the situation.

Jimmy's smile faded as he nodded. "Yeah," he agreed. "Let's go."

Turning his attention to Cole, who was still gawking at Jimmy like he was a movie star. "Cole, are you sure you're okay?" Baxter asked.

Cole blinked, the question pulling him back to reality. "Yeah," he said quietly. Shame flickered across his face, and he looked away, his hands twitching at his sides.

The walk back to the car felt far too long. His legs burned with exhaustion. Baxter retrieved the blue container and his shoes on the way back. Normally, he'd take something like this to Mr. Perry. But those days were long gone. The ache of loss pierced his chest, and he swallowed hard. He flipped the container over; it was slick with water and slime.

"I'm bringing it with me," he said, unsure if it was this or the Unseelie that gave him the menacing feeling. He wasn't going to stick around to find out.

"What if you get in trouble for taking that?" Cole asked.

"How will they know?" Jimmy shot back.

"They won't," Baxter said. He didn't bother with his shoes. His feet were already torn up. He'd put them on in the car.

Chapter 6: An Unexpected Alliance

Quinn

T he unsettling serenity of the forest sent chills up Quinn's spine. Not a rustle or a distant bird chirping, only a stillness that set alarm bells off. Standing beneath a large tree, a species unknown to her, she touched the trunk. The bark was velvet-soft beneath her fingertips, and the base twisted and spiraled, ending with a plum-colored tuff of cotton-like leaves. Despite her training and countless trips to Fata, this realm never ceased to amaze her. It remained an endless wonder, full of surprises. The light filtered through the tree canopy, casting a dark purple hue over the area, giving it an ominous tone. The tension was palpable, even the magic felt sinister.

As Quinn and Ophelia hatched out the grim details of the dangers of the Mirror World under the stars, the sky moved closer. Quinn found it difficult to take a deep breath with all the added pressure weighing on her. Despite the enchanted, shining light provided by the stars, which were luminescent, Quinn's distaste for Puck was thinly veiled. Her top lip curled, no longer able to hold it all back.

She sighed. "I don't know what you see in him. He has those classic good looks, but his attitude makes him unbearable." She shook her head in annoyance.

Ignoring her comment, Ophelia looked serious. "Quinn, I cannot help who I love," she said firmly.

Quinn made a face, questioning and irritating all in one.

Ophelia ignored it and continued, "Nor can I say how to help you. I am bound by a blood oath not to discuss any details I have learned as a member of the court." She averted her gaze, avoiding her stare. The weight of her words settled over Quinn, a silent awkwardness forming.

Quinn's mouth dropped. "Can't you help a little?" she asked, voice raised higher than intended.

Ophelia offered no answer.

"What am I supposed to do?" Quinn cried, eyes wide. She crossed her arms with a frustrated huff.

Ophelia, ever so poised, didn't flinch at Quinn's outburst. Her expression remained stony neutral. "I can simply *steer* you in the direction of possible answers." She emphasized the word *steer* and winked. Her reply was deliberate, as if she'd rehearsed it.

Did she just wink at me? Quinn blinked, unsure if she witnessed this exchange.

Quinn, on the other hand, uncrossed her arms and threw her palms up by her shoulders, creating a 'W' shape. Her voice rose in exasperation. "H-how?" she stammered. "I need help." Her tone was sarcastic and ungrateful as she bristled with irritation.

Ophelia didn't react to Quinn's tone. With an eternal calm, she said, "Remember your agreement. No trouble was given when you asked the impossible of me. I dropped everything and aided you."

She rolled her eyes. "And my mother died, anyway." The harshness of her tone shocked even her. Her eyes widened, and her mouth formed an 'O' shape. Quinn sat in a defeated huff.

Ever calm, Ophelia replied, "I could not have prevented that, nor was that a fault of mine." She remained unmoving.

Had she expected this? Did Seraphina predict this conversation and tell Ophelia? How else could she be so calm?

"I know," Quinn said to the ground. "I just miss her." Quinn blinked away a tear. "I still try to call her when I need something." She didn't lift her head, ashamed of how she spoke to her friend. Tears threatened to take over, but Quinn wiped them away.

Silence grew between them. Ophelia was either amazing at psychology or oblivious the weight of silence when used correctly on humans.

The Fae have different concepts of time, so she probably doesn't realize how long this is. Unable to handle another second, Quinn stood.

"Okay, steer me," she sighed heavily. "Where do I go first?"

"I knew you had it in you." She smiled ear to ear, finally showing some reaction. "To start your quest, you must first know what you are looking for."

"What? Come on with the riddles already." Quinn waved her arms in exhaustion. "It's always something with you."

Ophelia was again silent, an unmoving statue.

Quinn crossed her arms with a deep, defeated sigh and said, "Yes, I know what I'm looking for."

When Ophelia didn't answer, Quinn went on after another huff. "Puck!" she shouted. "I'm in search of Puck." Her arms flailed in exasperation.

Ophelia maintained her composure. "You humans are always rushing off to finish. You are not looking for Puck; he is not lost. We know where he is, the prison." She paused. "We do not know where the Mirror Shard is."

"Mirror shard?" Quinn asked. Her eyebrow shot up at this new piece of information.

A wry smile transformed Ophelia's statuesque form. "The key to entering the prison."

Quinn let out a sarcastic laugh and said, "How clever. The key to the prison is a piece of a mirror." *Is it an actual fragment of the prison, like a missing puzzle piece?.*

Ophelia continued with unwavering composure. "You must begin your quest. Time is of the essence." Her tone was rushed.

Quinn turned from Ophelia. *I remember how it hurt to lose Mom and Connor. I suppose it's similar to her losing her concubine. I don't know why she doesn't just call Puck her boyfriend.*

With a sharp inhale, she faced Ophelia. Well, where she was. Ophelia was nearly out of sight.

How'd she move so fast? And so quietly.

Quinn's eyes widened. "Hey, wait up. Where are you going?" Quinn chased after her. Ophelia didn't slow her pace. "I don't know where to start."

Once Quinn caught up, she attempted to catch her breath. "What do I do?"

"The answers you seek are here for the taking," Ophelia said cryptically. "I am off to seek Seraphina. She may show you a glimpse into the Mirror World and all the dangers that will present themselves."

Quinn realized that entering and exiting the prison might not have been as easy as she initially thought. Together, they strode at a brisk pace in silence.

"After this, you will seek the library," Ophelia said curtly. Her pace was unaffected by her speaking.

"Library?" Quinn questioned, her voice raising a few octaves. She stumbled over a root, barely catching herself. Quinn stopped dead in her tracks.

Ophelia didn't acknowledge the question or Quinn's sudden stop. She was widening the gap between them.

Quinn quivered as she tried to catch up again. "Where's this library?" Quinn asked.

Ophelia didn't skip a beat. "It lies just past the border of Afardia. On the way to the prison."

Quinn forced a smile. "Well, at least something is easier for once." Quinn attempted to lighten the ominous mood.

Ophelia's face darkened, her tone sharp as a blade.

"Far from easy. You must cross the border where the Blight lies. It is cursed. It will strangle the life from you," she said, taking a breath. "The air in the poison bog will scratch your lungs. It absorbs everything. Dog-like beasts stalk the perimeter and will eat anything. This will be anything but simple."

The weight of her words hung between them. Quinn was too afraid to speak, worried her voice would betray her. They continued with only the sound of Quinn's footsteps echoing. She hadn't mastered the ability to move as quietly as Ophelia, no matter how hard she tried.

Ophelia stopped before what appeared to be a large stone house, a relic of sorts. The worn slab held countless years of secrets. It looked like a giant rock from behind.

Was it made this way as camouflage, or was the house made from a large boulder?

Bones and feathers hung from a string, with berries woven within. A soft, hollow sound emanated, and the feathers danced. The melody whispered to her.

Once inside, Quinn sat across from Ophelia in the dimly lit chamber. The candlelight danced with mesmerizing movements ,casting shadows upon the room as it flickered. Ophelia's facial features were serene, yet Quinn sensed the underlying tension in the air. Despite her outward appearance, she had to be worried about Puck.

The smooth stone on the outer portion of this house, combined with the crisp air on the inside, created a home-like environment, not that of a cave or dampness under a rock. The aroma of a fresh meal wafted throughout the room, mixing with the scent of herbs that hung from the rafters. Quinn spied a cauldron over an open flame in a fireplace. Something about that fire seemed off.

It took Quinn a few minutes to figure out that, despite the small size of the room, she detected no heat from the flames. It should've heated the entirety of the tiny chamber. Before Quinn had a chance to ask, Seraphina appeared out of thin air with two drinks in hand. The mugs appeared to be handmade, though surprisingly light for their size. Seraphina placed a steaming mug in front of her. Quinn noted etchings on the side, symbols she didn't recognize.

Quinn hesitated, wrapping her fingers around the cup to warm them. She knew better than to drink anything from Fata without the expressed safety and assurance that there was nothing harmful in the beverage. Not that Seraphina would ever intentionally harm her. She may add an elixir that opened her vision further, and Quinn would end up seeing the dead, or hear lies unravel as they were spoken. These may not sound so bad, but the consequences may be dire.

To some, those abilities might appear to be gifts, but Quinn knew the truth: gifts from the Fae often came at a cost. You may have debilitating headaches or be unable to function with all the visions at once. Her training with Seraphina had driven those consequences home the hard way. She quickly learned that nothing was ever innocent or as straightforward as a Fae made it seem. What was inconsequential to a Fae may have dire consequences to a human, let alone a reg.

Once, during their training, Seraphina had handed Quinn a small piece of bread; it looked like a biscuit, called a Rusk. Quinn had inspected it. Since it didn't smell bad, she had brought it to her lips. She had hesitated, remembering to ask, "Will this hurt me?"

Putting the mug down, she smiled and remembered to ask first this time. She'd learn eventually, whether it was the hard way or not; she would learn.

Seraphina's face was unreadable. "Of course not, human. I desire to help, not hurt."

At first, she didn't notice any issues. But some time later, Quinn was seeing double, sometimes even triple. The whole world spun, and her lunch threatened to rise. She blinked rapidly in an attempt to focus her vision, which of course didn't work. Seraphina had said it was a mixture that allowed her to see the past, present, and future simultaneously.

Quinn panicked, turning to find the hut. "What's happening?" she asked desperately, colliding with something solid. Quinn walked with bruises on her cheek; she'd walked right into a tree that appeared to be a hologram.

Seraphina was beside her, hand on her shoulder, guiding her. "Ah, human, you have not learned to see fully yet. Most humans, even with your gift, cannot." She paused and let her hand fall from her shoulder. "The clear path you saw," Seraphina said, her voice calm and slow, "was the path before the tree had grown. It should appear fuzzy, to tell you it is not of this time. The tree is there, and in the future, it is not. The tree was or will be removed," she explained, no remorse in her voice. "Soon, you will learn to absorb all the dimensions of space and time at once. You will gather the information from the atoms in the air." Seraphina smiled and escorted Quinn back to the hut. "For now, the visions overwhelm you."

"You said this wouldn't hurt me," Quinn protested.

"And it has not hurt you. The concoction did not hurt you. Your lack of ability to absorb the information surrounding you is what hurt you," Seraphina said, gentler now. "Remember to always inquire about all possibilities prior to the consumption of anything a Fae gives you."

"Ugh," Quinn huffed.

Training had really taken a toll on Quinn. She lost ten pounds, and when she returned home, everyone was worried. Despite having been gone all summer, she somehow returned with minimal time loss. This was exceedingly difficult to accomplish in Fata, where usually a short amount of time was a huge amount of time in the human realm. Time was like a serene river, appearing calm, yet hidden currents swept you away. The water rushed forward; other times, it stood still. And it might even flow backwards. You never knew when or where you'd wash up.

Ophelia cleared her throat, no doubt to force Quinn back to reality. She dumped the contents of her mug into a chalice. Quinn had no idea where Ophelia had produced that or if she had carried it on her person.

"Oh, right, um, what were we saying?" She blushed, not daring to question the chalice. *The teal colors with the gold trim, are remarkably beautiful. That can't be real gold.*

Seraphina waved her arm as one would wave a magic wand. "I said that you must drink this elixir to view the prison's location, dangers, and secrets. It will not harm you." Her face was an unreadable mask.

How can they keep their faces so blank?

Quinn nodded, raising the mug to her lips. As it was about to touch her lips, she stopped. She hesitated, and the room held its breath. Everyone was waiting to see what she would do. Sensing something amiss but not quite sure what, she asked, "How long will it last?" *She already said it wouldn't hurt. But why do I think there is still something wrong here?*

"You have learned to question before consumption," Seraphina said with a smile. She nodded with encouragement and gestured for Quinn to drink.

Quinn drank the elixir, with hints of honey and blueberry. *It tastes good for once.* All of Seraphina's previous concoctions were difficult to even swallow.

"Ah, human." Seraphina sighed and clicked her tongue with disappointment. "You still did not ask the correct questions, however." Shaking her head, she moved toward Quinn.

Quinn's eyebrows shot up. "What?" Her hand flew to her throat, surveying herself for any inkling of something dreadful.

"While it will have minimal effects, they will still be present. For you will not only see the prison, you will also see the secrets of all you encounter."

"Ugh." Quinn's shoulders turned inward and sagged. *When will I learn? Although this one was unfortunately necessary.*

"If I needed to drink this anyway, what's the point of questioning it? You said you wouldn't intentionally hurt me." Quinn raised a brow in question.

Seraphina tilted her head. "Ah, well. Then I would have offered you this drink instead." She revealed a second cup in her left hand. "This one only lasts a few moments and will have the same desired effect. It will only work on the first thing you ask, and the effects are not painful. I call it Uncertain Tea."

Quinn sagged even further. "Why couldn't you just give me that one in the first place?" Quinn asked, defeat settling into her shoulders.

Seraphina smiled and walked across the room, standing behind a chair. "Ahh, because you have not completed your training, young one," Seraphina scolded and shook her head.

"You could've just warned me," Quinn whined, frowning at Seraphina. Meanwhile, Ophelia was doing her best to become a statue.

"Then you would not learn this lesson and expect everything to be handed to you. This potion has a cost, and I have paid it without asking for anything in return. Most Fae will not do this," she paused, giving a moment for her words to settle on Quinn. "You would be expected to pay the consequences without knowing how steep they may be." Seraphina sat and said,

"Everything comes with a price. You would do well to remember that young Shadow Seer."

Quinn sighed, louder than usual. "Fine. I'll never take anything without asking the price and all the consequences." She shrugged her shoulders. "Happy now?" A fake smile plastered her face.

Her response was slow. "Once you have completed your lessons, you will be happy, not I." Her voice was ominous despite speaking of happiness.

Quinn had the feeling her words were associated with a vision. She knew better than to ask; no answers would be given. She shook her head and looked at Ophelia, her face an expressionless mask.

"Now, see the prison," Seraphina instructed and flicked her wrist.

A cold sensation overcame her, like an icy water crashing over her body. The air around her turned frigid, seeping into her bones and chilling her to the core. Her breath caught in her throat, and the temperature drop sent a shiver down her spine. It wasn't only the coldness of the vision; it was a deeper, more profound sense of dread that left her feeling vulnerable and exposed. It was a manifestation of the fear and uncertainty she long since held.

She stood frozen, trying to shake off the chill, but it clung to her, a constant reminder of the surrounding darkness. With a deep breath, she focused, pulling herself back from the brink of a fear-driven panic attack. The cold, the dread, and the uncertainty were all real, yet she couldn't let them control her. She steadied her breathing and forced herself to concentrate on the task ahead, her vision.

Quinn was catapulted into what looked like water, but as she hit the surface, she was surrounded by mirrors. Not a single room, but an eternity of them. The surfaces shimmered with liquid light, as if the water and mirrors were one. Everywhere she looked, reflections appeared, some transparent, revealing glimpses of other rooms. It was similar to a funhouse maze, yet more complex and strange. None of the mirrors were flat or rectangular; they were twisted and curved into impossible, three-dimensional shapes.

Quinn could see a bridge, but there was more to it; something she couldn't quite grasp. She didn't know what, but something showed her a path across. An unseen force guided her, revealing the way. The path was narrow, perilously so, with gaps that made every step a test of nerve.

It was littered with crumbling stones, the edges jagged and threatening to send her plummeting into the abyss. A keyhole was embedded in the wall, nearly hidden. A bridge with a clue that hinted at escape but not entry. It wasn't the only way out, yet she sensed there was more. Something crucial she was missing. It lingered just out of reach. She couldn't quite tell what.

Quinn also felt an unsettling presence, as if the prison itself wanted to hold her there. Her vision had drawn her here, yet the sense of being trapped was palpable. The treacherous pathways were a part of the prison's design, a cruel trick to lure her deeper into its clutches and never let her go. The lock offered a promise of entry, but the nagging feeling that it would lead to nowhere good haunted her. This place was alive, and it wasn't just showing her the way. It was daring her to take it, beckoning her.

That can't be good.

In her vision, the air was thick with an unnatural stillness, the kind that made every sound feel amplified, distorted, and out of place. It stretched out, looming before her, suspended in a void where the ground fell away into endless darkness. Smoke-like shadows danced along the edges of her sight, and the bridge itself pulsed with a faint, eerie glow, illuminating the path she was meant to take.

Not knowing if she could trust this vision, that it wasn't a cruel trap. An undeniable certainty told her this was the only path forward. One wrong move and it would mean certain death. A slow, agonizing, and inescapable death.

What unnerved her most were the faint whispers that emanated from the depths of the prison, as if the darkness itself spoke to her. One step forward, three to the left, one more forward, and one to the right. She memorized the pattern, knowing that her survival depended on it. The vision felt like a trap, baiting her, luring her into its snare. The prison wanted her. Even in this moment of clarity, she could sense its malevolent intent to twist reality.

Someone flew across the ravine. No, they were thrown. She, too, was hurled, but she curled at the last minute. Not making it across, she scratched at the ledge as she watched herself fall into the void. Her fear of falling came to life as her stomach rose to her throat.

Quinn violently shivered at the intensity of her vision, leaving her breathless. The withdrawal from a vision was sometimes worse than the experience. The air was heavier, and the weight of the prison's intent pressed on her. She feared she'd fail.

The thought gripped her, and an unrelenting fear gnawed at her. It took her a moment to recover, her heart pounding as the vivid images faded. The vision had been so real, so tangible, that she could still feel the echo of the jagged stones beneath her feet and the eerie glow of the bridge seared into her mind. With a deep, steadying breath, she pushed, but the lingering sense of dread remained, the reminder of the danger that awaited her. She couldn't fail. The stakes were too high, and the cost of failure was too great to even consider. The vision had shown her the way, but she had to do it herself. She clenched her fists, forcing her will to comply. She had no choice but to succeed. Her life, and more, depended on it.

Chapter 7: All About Timing

Ophelia made an odd gesture to Seraphina, almost unperceivable. "It's time," she said softly. Her words carried an unspoken meaning.

Quinn's interest was piqued. "Time for what?" she asked, looking between the two of them.

Seraphina hesitated and looked to Ophelia, then nodded.

Ophelia continued, "A good time as any to give her the necklace."

Seraphina nodded and left the room.

Quinn watched her go. "What necklace?" Quinn turned to ask Ophelia, suspicion in her voice.

A hint of a smile touched her lips. "Always in a rush. In due time, answers will reveal themselves," she said cryptically.

Quinn didn't return the smile. Instead, she frowned. Her frustration deepened. "I thought you, of all people, would want some type of urgency in this matter."

"I am not a people, as you say, but a powerful and renowned Fae. You will do well to remember that," Ophelia warned. Her demeanor had changed to that of her warrior self. Her spine was straight as an arrow, and she returned to her unnaturally still form.

Seraphina returned, no doubt sensing the change in the energy shift. She moved with a silent grace, her eyes flicked between them, absorbing the unspoken words.

Could she hear us? Ophelia once read Baxter's thoughts, but that was a spell in her home. I wonder why it didn't work on me?

Seraphina handed Quinn a folded palm leaf tied with a delicate teal vine, breaking her from her internal reflection. Quinn accepted, though she was still cautious of anything offered from a Fae, especially these two, who had repeatedly tested her without warning.

Quinn ran a finger against the smooth palm leaf. "Is this a test?" she asked and cleared her throat. "I mean, will I be indebted to you or owe you in any way for this gift?" she clarified. A triumphant smile crept across her face. She grew to know the Fae well enough to use caution, and if this was another trap, she was determined to find the hidden strings before they could tighten.

I've learned a lot during my time here. Her smile widened.

Seraphina returned the smile; it reached her eyes. "This necklace does carry a cost," she replied, her tone smooth and measured. "But not in the way you fear. The price is simply… friendship. One day, I may ask a favor of you, not a demand, nor a binding pact, but a favor that I trust you would honor."

Her emphasis on the word friendship led her to believe she had read her thoughts.

She paused, letting her words set in between them. Ophelia remained unmoving, perfecting the statue pose.

"Thank you," Quinn said, accepting the necklace with a weak smile. "I do consider both of you my friends." Quinn glanced back at Ophelia, who wore an unreadable expression.

After a moment of silence, Ophelia finally spoke in a dry voice, "Be careful who your friends are." She barely moved, just her mouth.

The words stretched out, heavy with implication. Quinn glanced up at her, meeting Ophelia's gaze, and for the briefest of moments, she glimpsed something guarded there. She knew the Fae were as unpredictable as they were powerful, yet she couldn't take Ophelia's caution lightly.

Quinn shivered at the sudden change.

Friend, I wonder if she considers me one or a mere means to an end.

Quinn untied the teal vine and unfolded the leaf. Lifting the necklace, she slipped it over her head. She pulled it to her face for a closer inspection. A hard, acorn-like charm hung in the middle. Wooden beads flanked the acorn, each etched with intricate glyphs that shimmered faintly in the light. They were unfamiliar to her, with an energy hinting at magic.

Choosing to set aside Ophelia's caution for now, Quinn decided to save it for when she had more time alone, when the full meaning would be revealed. For now, she tucked the warning away, focusing instead on the intricate necklace that now rested in her hands. Quinn rubbed her fingers along the beads, each with different grooves. The texture was smooth and polished, and she was certain the wood had absorbed years of power and history.

"Is this Ravenswood?" Quinn asked, peeking up from the necklace.

Seraphina's eyes beamed, a smile spreading across her face with what looked like pride. "The beads are indeed made from Ravenswood."

Quinn returned the smile as she ran her fingers over the beads once more, admiring the craftsmanship that had gone into it.

"Before you ask, it is to provide longer protection," Seraphina said, her voice quiet and confident. She watched Quinn closely. "Not as strong as ingesting Ravenswood, but this," she gestured to the necklace, "does not wear off." Seraphina smiled, pride exuding in that all-knowing grin.

Does she know what's to come?

A silence spread like a blanket over them, each lost in their thoughts.

Before Quinn had a chance to dwell on it further, Ophelia cleared her throat. She'd perfected her statuesque stillness so completely that Quinn had almost forgotten she was there.

An annoyed pause as she glared at Quinn and said in a huff, "The beads were hand-carved by Seraphina, and the glyphs were etched by me. Enough questions. It is time." Ophelia's tone was clipped, her irritation barely masked. She stood abruptly, her urgency woven into every deliberate movement. "Now, head south," Ophelia instructed, an unspoken command. "Do not stop until you see a dead oak grove with its twisted and gnarled branches reaching toward the clouds. Then head southeast to the library."

The finality in her words left a bad taste in Quinn's mouth. There was no room for argument. The gravity of the situation weighed heavily on Quinn.

She jerked her head toward Ophelia. "You're not coming with me?" Quinn whined.

Ophelia ignored the question, her stony silence an answer in itself. Seraphina's eyes held Quinn's, her expression serious yet gentle, as if she understood the weight of what was about to happen. The reality of the journey settled in for Quinn, as she had to face it alone.

Seraphina stepped closer, her presence warm and reassuring. "The prison is in another realm," she explained gently. "As your world is closely connected to Fata, the Mirror World lies beyond a thinner veil. You may not even notice once you cross into it." Seraphina paused, her eyes growing distant. Then, she continued, "The colors are all muted like the dull, shadowy reflections on the backside of a mirror," she explained, her voice soft like she revealed a secret.

She reached into the folds of her forest green cloak, producing a small, intricately wrapped package. "Here, take this," she said, holding it out toward Quinn. "But do not open it until you feel all hope is lost," she added cryptically. She gestured for her to take the offered item. Her face was once again a mask.

Quinn hesitated and waited for an additional explanation. None was given.

"What is it?" Quinn asked, her eyebrows raised.

Before she accepted the small burlap satchel in Seraphina's hand, she needed to decipher if it was another test. She didn't want to accept another mysterious item without understanding its purpose. Seraphina merely gestured for her to take it, and Quinn reluctantly complied. As it touched her palm, a warmth radiated from it. The sensation was both reassuring and unsettling, and only deepened her curiosity. She searched Seraphina's face; it remained blank, revealing nothing.

That warmth has to mean something, but what? And what does she mean by 'when all hope is lost?'

Seraphina's smile was tender, easing Quinn's ever-racing mind. "Hope, the most powerful thing I can offer," she explained.

Relief washed over her. The doubts she'd harbored were almost too much to bear.

"Use it as you see fit. There is no test. I know you assume there is." Seraphina turned to leave.

Quinn raised her palm in protest. "Wait."

Seraphina floated from the room without acknowledging her plea.

So, is it a test or not?

Ophelia moved stiffly. "Come, I will walk you to the forest."

Quinn sighed, emulating a child in a tantrum. "You're really not coming with me?"

Ophelia shook her head. "I cannot, child." Something lingered in her unspoken words. Quinn couldn't quite place it.

Is she sad?

Swiftly moving toward the door, to the trees beyond, shutting down any more questions. Quinn followed without a word. Something had caused this change in her demeanor, but the cause remained a mystery.

She must really miss Puck.

Quinn trailed behind as Ophelia came to an abrupt halt. "This is where I take my leave of you," she announced, her tone short and curt, leaving no room for argument.

Her heart clenched with fear, the weight pressing on her. She wasn't sure she could handle this alone.

As if she sensed the fear, Ophelia said, "Head in this direction until your instincts tell you otherwise. You will know what needs to be done." Her words held such conviction that Quinn's doubts temporarily melted away.

How am I supposed to know when to turn? Quinn did her best to suppress a sigh. She didn't want to seem ungrateful.

Ophelia continued, "It is the burden of the Freedom Fighters to guard the Ravenswood tree now that Mr. Perry is in the wind, that it might remain whole despite his wishes."

The comment felt abrupt and out of place, and Quinn wondered if Ophelia had mentioned it to reassure her that she wouldn't be sitting idle while Quinn faced the dangers ahead. Regardless of the reason, it gave Quinn motivation. She steeled her spine, lifted her chin, and nodded.

Without another word, Quinn walked into the forest, the dense canopy closing around her like a living tunnel. She didn't look back. She didn't want to know if Ophelia watched her. Instead, she focused on the path ahead, trusting her instincts would guide her. The trees swallowed her shadow as she disappeared.

Chapter 8: Past and Present

Quinn

Quinn's walk was uneventful; she fell into a vision haunted by images of Theo and his wife, Cara, barely realizing reality had slipped through her fingers like sand. Cara's resentment was palpable, as though she teetered on the edge of an epiphany. Although she had no solid proof, she believed in a divine world that was just out of her reach. Her family was ordinary in every way, but her great-grandmother had a connection to Fata. She recalled the many stories that had been told.

Cara was well aware of the townsfolk whispering that she was a little off, but nobody knew she was right. When she discovered Theo's ability to perceive magic, a truth he refused to believe, she was infuriated. Her lips pressed into a thin line as this revelation sent her over the edge. How different it was for Theo, how easy. His family had long been unable to see any kind of occult. Theo didn't understand it. He thought he was going mad as he tried to explain the unexplainable happenings every day. The fact that he refused to face and so casually dismissed what she yearned to discover was unfair. Cara had watched Theo treat his gift like a curse; it was a vicious irony.

Theo accepted that life was unpredictable; he even attempted to use medications to lessen the illusions that plagued him. Unfortunately, the medications only dulled the vision, leaving him groggy and worse than before.

The aftermath of his wife and daughter's disappearances sent him spiraling down a rabbit hole. He pored over all of Cara's notes and books, obsessed and desperate for answers. Page after page, the pieces of the puzzle came together, but his understanding came too late. They were already gone, forever beyond his grasp.

When Theo discovered the illusions were real, he stopped taking his medication. This raised his doctor's concern, as he began acting differently, isolated and withdrawn. Theo spent all his time reading fantasy books and chasing rumors of portals. Eventually, he managed to traverse the plane to Fata, yet he returned empty-handed. Soon, he found himself a permanent patient at Oakdale Institute.

He learned that the patients at Oakdale were especially at risk, and no one believed them when they tried to tell the doctors what was happening. It was chalked up as another illusion. The Fae had been feeding off the patients. Theo discovered that the Fae had a portal within the institute. *How else would they feed off the patients, undetected and so easily?* He even found a way to use the portal, yet try as he might, he couldn't locate his family. Every failed attempt deepened his internal torment, and his obsession made him seem madder.

The vision shifted to when Theo discovered the Unseelie siphoning the souls of its victims through a spike in their wrists. Quinn had to remind herself that this was Theo's memory as the Unseelie extended its arm and the spike shot from its wrist with a deafening crack.

The ivory spike glinted in the moonlight as Theo held his breath. It glistened with slickness, as the unsuspecting victim, paralyzed by an enchantment, was lured closer by an invisible tether. The creature crouched on the human's shoulder, inching closer to his jugular. When the spike was driven into the victim, a squelching sound caused Quinn to turn away, stomach churning.

The pain spread like wildfire as their essence was withdrawn, but the prey was unable to scream for help. Nobody would be unable to see the Fae without Sight or a charm. When the Fae was sated, the spike retracted, slick with blood, leaving a hidden wound that no doctor could trace. Often, the patient would develop an illness, such as cancer or an autoimmune disease that doctors would be unable to diagnose.

The pixilated image faded away as Cara came into view once again. She acquired a rare, enchanted object from Celeste's store. It was the only thing that allowed her to see the concealed world inhabited by the Fae and other beings beyond ordinary sight.

Gidcon's Tear, the crystallized charm, granted her the uncanny ability to glimpse into the world her husband's family unwittingly shaped. Doubting which object was the functional one, she decided to bring all three of the items she had purchased from the shop. Without the object, she was another outsider, watching the ordinary world without the power to penetrate Fata's depths.

***

Quinn woke to the hoot of an owl. She looked around. She must've fallen face-first into a pile of leaves. Luckily, her head had landed on a mossy bed instead of a rock. Typically, she could sense a vision coming, giving her time to sit.

Cara's feelings were still wild in her mind, and she couldn't help being upset with Theo. A stone circle surrounded her, and her legs were covered in large palm leaves. Someone or something had covered her and placed her here. Oddly, she wasn't scared. Had it intended to harm her, it wouldn't have looked after her.

Chapter 9: Not So Sweet Dreams

Baxter

He let his head hit the pillow, hoping to get a few hours of sleep without having another nightmare. A bead of sweat dripped into his eye, blurring his vision. Baxter ran at a full sprint, well, more like floated through one, in what could only be described as a funhouse maze. The twisted walls distorted reality, with hundreds of different long versions of himself. The warped reflections churned his stomach, and his world came to a crashing halt. There, before him, was his best friend, Connor. Well, multiple Connors. It was difficult to tell if any of them were real. He was lying on the dark stone floor in the fetal position. Connor always had that boy-next-door look, accompanied by perfect skin, and blond, swept-back hair that never seemed out of place.

With dark smudges on his skin and his hair brown with grime, this version of Connor was sickly.

The darkness and silence of this place reminded Baxter of a dungeon. He reached for Connor, but his hand was halted. The cold glass created yet another barrier between them. Ten versions of Connor appeared; all crumpled on the ground.

"Connor," he whispered, but no sound came out. Baxter made a fist and pounded the glass. The floor opened beneath him, sending him tumbling onto a familiar carpet. Connor's room came into focus, telling him it was all another twisted nightmare.

Sweat ran down his brow, and Baxter wiped it away with the back of his hand. The alarm clock showed 3:13 a.m., the witching hour. He often had dreams of Fata around this time for some unknown reason. He leaned against the bed, still on the floor. Eve had told him it was the time when the veil between realms was thinnest. He rubbed his shoulder and winced at the touch.

That will definitely leave a bruise. He let out a deep breath. *I really miss him.* He no longer had dreams of only Fata. Now, he had reoccurring nightmares of finding his friend alive but unable to speak to him. He didn't know what was worse, night terrors involving Fata or Connor.

***

Mirrors again. The warped maze of the funhouse nightmare had returned, and with it, a giant worm-like creature covered in twitching antennas. Its mouth unhinged to expose sharpened teeth. It roared, rattling his bones, before disintegrating into a mountain of smaller worms. Their wriggling forms searched for something. Baxter followed it, hovering about like a ghost. His breath hitched in his throat.

They're after Quinn.

He tried to hit the creature, but to no avail. He kicked at one of the worms, and nothing happened. A thick, gelatinous mucus oozed from it and splattered on the ground. That repulsed him.

He yelled to Quinn, but the words wouldn't come out. She was okay, but whoever was with her didn't look so well. A figure was crumpled on the ground. Quinn pulled the body to the side and froze. Shaking her head, she changed direction. She barely made it anywhere when she stopped, and multiple reflections of her looked at him.

"Baxter?" she asked.

He couldn't say anything, so he pointed. She didn't look. He signaled again, more firmly this time. She'd forgotten her backpack. Quinn turned to retrieve it, and Baxter gasped as if he had just been drowning and could finally breathe. Bolting upright, he let out a sigh. He was in Connor's bed.

It was only a dream. Baxter looked at the clock. It was 3:13 a.m. *Didn't I just wake up after a nightmare? A dream within a dream. Is this lucid dreaming? No, I saw Quinn. I know I did. That look on her face was so real, no dream could mimic that. She looked surprised and guilty. Why would I dream that?*

He recalled Celeste saying, "Some dreams are whispers. Others are warnings. His are a curse."

Baxter reached for his phone and texted Quinn: *Hey, what r u doing?* When he didn't receive an immediate reply, he called her, but it went straight to voicemail. *She wouldn't. Maybe she's sleeping. It's 3 a.m.* Baxter hopped out of bed and dressed in record time. He slipped out Connor's window, not daring to risk waking Connor's parents. The cool air was refreshing. He shook his head, raking a hand through his hair. *No way she'd go back there.*

Chapter 10: Gathering Knowledge

Quinn

A sense of foreboding grew as Quinn thought about what she'd learned of the Mirror World's unpredictable nature. She embarked on a journey she didn't fully understand, seeking answers about the enigmatic prison. Walking through the lush forests and vibrant meadows, a few Fae sat along the side, locked in conversation. The tallest one had long, vibrant green wings, another was brown with earthy tones and with stubby wings, and the last Fae, a female, did not possess visible wings but resembled an aluminum figurine. Quinn strode up to them, hoping to glean any fragment of information that could aid her quest.

She approached the group of Fae gathered beneath a towering oak-like tree, their laughter creating melodious notes.

"Hello," Quinn began, her voice carrying an air of urgency. "I'm searching for knowledge about the Mirror Prison. Do you know anything?"

The Fae exchanged glances, their expressions shifting to unreadable. A tall, silver-haired Fae with unnatural stillness stepped forward, breaking his statue-like posture. "That prison is no laughing matter, human. Its secrets are as elusive as it is dangerous."

The other male Fae said, "Not a place for humans." A sneer etched upon his face.

Unflinching, Quinn pressed further. "Where can I find the information I need to access it?"

Her attention was drawn to an odd wind chime apparatus hanging behind the Fae. It looked to be made of bones, berries, and feathers.

The Fae with the translucent emerald-colored wings flapped them as he curled his fingers in a dancing motion, conjuring an illusion of swirling smoke. "A rumor of a hidden library nestled deep within Fata that bears the ancient secrets of all that is. It may contain the knowledge forgotten by time itself. Perhaps there you will find the answers you seek." His ice-blue eyes bore into her, searching for something she didn't know.

"I've seen that before. What is it?" Quinn asked, pointing to the chime. *Where did I see that?*

Only the female looked over; the earthy Fae kept guard.

As if I am some sort of danger to them.

Once she looked back, she said, "A Verachime, merely a ward."

"What does it ward from?" Quinn asked, genuinely curious.

"Any with intentions of ill will," the Fae with short wings answered. His answer was curt, and it was clear he didn't wish to speak with her.

"It will sound if someone with bad intentions approaches," the tall Fae answered.

"How do you know if it's the ward or the wind making the sound?" Quinn asked.

"It does not make sounds in the wind," the Fae answered flatly, as if he were speaking to a child, and she should've known this already.

"That doesn't make sense," Quinn countered, approaching the wind chime and exposing her back to the Fae.

Some lessons she'd never learn. "How can it not make sound in the wind?"

"The wind is not what causes the sound," the Fae explained with reluctance or annoyance; she couldn't distinguish which. Their mask-like faces kept all their secrets. "Ill will releases the spell bound to the bones, and the berries release an energy that rattles them. The feathers turn toward the perpetrator and dance."

"Would it make a sound if you had ill intentions toward me?" she asked. *Seraphina's, that's where I saw it. Does she wish me harm?*

"It would work if that is what it was set to do," the female answered cryptically.

A non-answer. Typical. She fought hard not to roll her eyes.

With his rustic brown and umber hue of his bark-like skin, the other Fae easily blended into the natural world around him. His hair resembled a cascade of intertwined twigs, giving him an air of harmonious coexistence with the forest. As Quinn thanked them and prepared to leave, he stepped forward. His concerned gaze locked onto hers with an air of wisdom.

"Beware of what you seek," he cautioned. His voice was a soft murmur that carried on the wind, one that didn't set off the wind chime. "For the prison holds secrets that can both liberate and ensnare. Its mysteries are as intricate as the roots beneath the surface, and venturing too far may lead to your undoing."

Quinn regarded him, her curiosity piqued by his cryptic words. "What do you mean? What dangers lie within?"

The Fae's blue eyes pierced through her, seeing into the depths of her soul. "The prison is not a realm to be trifled with. It mimics the physical world and the echoes of one's desires and fears. Those who enter may lose themselves amidst the illusions, trapped by the reflections they seek to navigate."

His warning lingered in the air like a gentle breeze, leaving Quinn with a sense of dread. She couldn't help but wonder if his words were a cautionary tale or a challenge of her resolve. With a nod of appreciation, she turned from the Fae, his cryptic presence etched into her thoughts.

Quinn thanked them repeatedly and headed out in search of the mysterious and legendary library. The directions were vague, but something deep in her bones said she was heading in the right direction. Traveling through the dense forests, she found the trees crowding closer together, the terrain thick with overgrowth and difficult to traverse. She ducked and squeezed between branches. The path was gone; she let her instincts guide her.

Eventually, the woods became sparse. There were shimmering lakes that resembled the constellations and rolling mist-filled valleys that added a layer of ambiance. After a time, she approached a mammoth, overgrown path. She couldn't tell where the path was, yet it beckoned to her.

Quinn passed a dead oak grove with Spanish moss clinging to its gnarled branches. The moss shimmered in the wind. She recalled the directions: the dead oak, go southeast, and the library would be there. Quinn glanced at the map she'd snuck from Baxter's belongings.

So which way is southeast? She was heading west, according to the map. She walked toward a marked path, and it moved as a GPS would. She adjusted her direction and saw a path she would've missed. It was overgrown, hardly visible until you were upon it. Quinn peeked at the map again, and it realigned, guiding her onward. A sigh of relief escaped her lips.

Taking a turn onto another path that led her into an expansive opening, which revealed a large building. *This has to be the entrance to the library.* Plant life, similar to ivy, covered half the building. She took a deep breath and headed to the entrance. The stone structure rose three stories high. Light from within cast shadows on the outside.

The large wooden doors could fit a truck through them, and with centuries of neglect, it looked as though one had tried. Quinn paused a moment before pushing the doors; they didn't budge. She attempted to jar it open with her shoulder, but the doors remained unyielding. Quinn sighed and knocked three times on the weathered door with its peeling golden paint, revealing years of neglect. A rumbling caused her to jump. Painstakingly slow, the door to the left creaked open.

She slipped her head inside. "Hello?" she called into the vast entryway. Her voice echoing was the only response. *Well, I guess they probably aren't used too often if the doors hardly open.*

She crossed the threshold into an enormous chamber lined with dusty shelves, endless tomes reaching the ceiling. The leather-bound tomes were a spectacular sight to behold. She could spend forever here. Alas, time was of the essence, and she must figure out how to locate the books she needed. A hundred years of reading wouldn't cover half of the tomes.

Delicately, she ran her fingers along the spines of the books in the entryway. Her mind raced; she didn't know how far back the library extended. She found herself walking to the room on the left, even larger than the great hall she'd left. This room was rose-colored, or it had been before it fell into disarray.

Her eyes crossed, and her head ached, but a vision of what the room once looked like appeared before her. Shaking her head, the image left her, and she was back to her present time. In the vision, she noticed a hefty tome with bronze edging upon a pedestal in the back of the room. She approached it, but it was empty save for cobwebs. Not knowing why, she wanted to locate that book.

Who could've taken it?

A Fae's face appeared in her mind. A sudden flash, and it was gone. A hidden passage, a small door behind a decorative vase. She approached it, pushing on the wall. Nothing out of the ordinary. Quinn knocked on the wall to see if there was a hollow area.

The wall fell back, revealing a hidden staircase.

I haven't made it through a fraction of this library, yet I know this is the way.

The stairs were dark, so she left the door open to cast some light. Once she reached the bottom of the stairs, she could see again. There was a fire in the fireplace, yet she could see no wood burning. It was also contained by a transparent force field; she could barely see it and had no idea how she knew it needed to be contained. She had the distinct feeling this fire was never-ending and that, if released, it would wreak havoc on the library. The alternative was that someone had recently been here and lit the fire. She had a feeling that wasn't the case.

Opening the first book, shapes formed letters she'd never seen before. This library wouldn't be any help if she couldn't read its texts. *I don't even know what language this is.*

Frustration overcame her. She stomped her foot, and dust cascaded from the walls, making her sneeze. Sighing, she left the room, her head hanging low, and found herself back at the main entrance. She was so overwhelmed that she had to get some fresh air and escape from all the tomes.

How can I save anyone if I can't even read these books?

The air outside was a welcome reprieve, but the events of today still took their toll on her body. Fatigue pulled at the seams of her consciousness as she approached a tree. Sliding to the ground, she leaned against it, promising herself she would only rest her eyes for a single moment.

A sudden noise jarred her awake from the unexpected nap. A blurred figure stood before her. She blinked, and it remained; she rubbed her eyes. It was a creature. *How long was I asleep?*

It spoke to her, barely above a whisper. It said, "Sleeping on the job, I see." Its ears twitched as if in anticipation of her reply. It looked like an overgrown mouse. Fur covered it from head to toe, and whiskers sprouted from its face. "You seek answers, and they lie before you, unseen. How is it that you cannot perceive them?"

Of course, there are more riddles.

"Wait, perceive," she said, not finishing her thought out loud. The creature helped her realize she could use her power of sight to read or interpret the books. All she had to do was merely try to see it, not read each individual word, to obtain the knowledge within.

She looked up at the creature, but it was gone.

That was odd, convenient, but odd. I wonder if it is a sort of librarian or caretaker here.

She hurried back into the library. The secret passage was too easy to find. She returned to the book she had left open.

After combing over a few books, the words were a river that flowed into her mind. She absorbed the information. Quinn still didn't know the language, but she understood the gist of the book. She skimmed titles for anything about mirrors.

Mirror Realm Creatures, Cursed Reflections of the Mirror, Alchemy of Mirror Realm, How to Create a Mud Monster.

As hours passed, each book she reviewed wasn't what she was looking for. Until she discovered a section of tomes that offered glimpses into the prison's history, its rules, the scary inhabitants, and how it came to be. She read of a creature that lived beneath the prison, to deter prisoners from attempting to dig their way out. This world's cryptic nature became more apparent to her. Reality could shift and change without a moment's notice, which presented a significant challenge even the most skilled Fae couldn't conquer.

Well, everything in Fata's more complicated than it needs to be.

Her right hand skimmed an ancient tome bound with faded red leather, written by another seer. The pages were filled with cryptic prophecies and riddles. Quinn saw the vision of the author rather than the words. When she read a particular passage, it sent a shiver down her spine.

> "The mirror's realm, a tangled fate,
> The reflections change and equate.
> Fear the shadows, for they deceive,
> Only the pure of heart shall ever leave.
> You must choose one to go with you,
> Ensure your decision is tried and true,
> One you will leave behind,
> And one you will free but not find.
> Obtain the answer before your breaking,
> The decision may be your unmaking."

As she read those words, something gripped her heart, squeezing it. The Mirror World would be unpredictable; its very nature was to deceive. Quinn realized that her journey wouldn't be easy. Armed with this knowledge, she left the secret room of the library, her confidence wavering as the overwhelming task lay ahead. How could she possibly get this done?

She read a tome about the Tempus Sisto, with the ability to alter time. The yin-yang-shaped orb was filled with black and white sand in water, encompassed by gold.

Certain she had enough information; Quinn exited the secret chamber. In the antechamber, she noticed the same gargoyles as Celeste's shop. *Did I miss it?* She hadn't noticed them before. *There's so much to see.*

Quinn shook her head. No time to worry about medieval statues. She had to get moving, time was of the essence, and everyone was depending on her.

She opened the large door with ease and descended the steps.

A rustle in the overgrown bushes caught her attention. The brush reminded her of wisteria, a presence that made it seem more alive. Vines spiraled and twisted slowly, curling around everything in its path. The movement was subtle, unnoticeable, unless you knew what to look for.

The delicate, lavender blossoms hung in clusters, swaying gently as if it was a breeze that didn't exist. The soft fragrance, intoxicating, alluring, masking the danger that slowly crept. The beauty was a weapon. You would never imagine its destruction.

The vines were relentless, suffocating life from anything within its grasp. At first glance, it appeared harmless, even enchanting, but left only decay as it strangled the life of each victim.

"The lotus flower will help stop your visions temporarily once you inhale its aromas to help you focus on the task ahead." Quinn heard a voice; the speaker was invisible.

Quinn reached out and plucked a lotus blossom. She held the flower close, its soft petals brushing her lips as she inhaled the calming aroma. Instantly, her racing mind slowed, and the visions became manageable. For the first time, she felt as if she could focus since she awakened her visions. As if the haze lifted enough for her to concentrate, the relief was fleeting.

The crunch of dried leaves beside the tree caught Quinn's attention. Something crept along the ground. The leaves and even the earth itself moved. She jumped back as a large tangle of gnarled roots or thorny vines moved toward her. It suffocated the surrounding plants, sucking the life and color from them.

A tree inside? How does it get light?

The brambles, with their claw-like thorns, scratched at her like a wild beast, threatening to ensnare those who dared to venture too close. A scent of decay filled the now heavy air. She grabbed her pocketknife and cut the branch. It split in two and immediately doubled in size. The now-cut vine, a whole new entity, even thicker. Quinn crawled backward like a crab to get away.

It rose, blocking the light above her. It lunged for her once more, and she fell. The vines narrowly missed her. A small bird flew overhead, but it was not as lucky. The vine recoiled and dragged the bird into its depths. A blur of movement flashed before her. Quinn recognized the gargoyle; it had swung its sword and chopped off a tendril of the vine. The brambles were satiated for now. Their suffocating embrace vanished into the ground. *I knew I saw them move.* The gargoyle vanished as well.

Quinn was thoroughly shaken. She knew of the infinite dangers, but attacking plants was a step too far. Fata was crawling with vegetation. Everything was a danger. *How did I ever get this far without being attacked?*

Quinn took a steadying breath and closed her eyes. She couldn't afford to fall apart now. But which way should she go? She'd seen maps of the realm and where the prison was, but how should she get there? *Am I still in the library, or was that a portal out?*

When she opened her eyes, the answer came to her. She'd go behind the library. There was no time for second guesses. This was the way; it had to be.

Chapter 11: Trials of Preparation

*A*fter walking for what felt like several hours, Quinn set up camp. Exhaustion settled deep within her bones, and her legs ached with every movement. She unrolled her sleeping bag and padded it down. It did little to mask the sharp blades of grass. After a quick nap she'd be refreshed.

On her way to her camp, she noted dog-like beasts that were feral and ravenous. She had luckily passed without them noticing her. Their frog-like skin made her shudder. She could no longer wander aimlessly. It was challenging when her confidence morphed into worry, which led to doubt. Quinn believed she was heading in the right direction, but what if she wasn't? With a deep groan, she slid her pack from her shoulders and let it fall onto the ground.

Rest was her only option; she'd sleep here for now. Despite the daylight, Quinn knew better than to trust Fata's time; the sunset wasn't a daily occurrence. She'd sleep and feel more confident after. Quinn glanced around, weary, as she absentmindedly rubbed her legs.

I just need a little rest, and I'll be back at it tomorrow.
The forest was calm, and soon sleep overcame her.

A branch snapping jolted her awake. Her hand shot for the hidden dagger concealed in her boot. She scanned the tree line for anything out of place; her heartbeat rang in her ears. There was no sign of movement; the forest was unnaturally still. She held her breath, assessing the air around, but her thundering heart made it impossible to focus.

Behind her, a presence lingered, something foreign. She called out, "I know you're there." She tried her hardest to keep the emotion from leaking into her tone.

"Very good, little human," Seraphina called back. She emerged from her camouflage with a sly smile on her face, amused. "Now that you have obtained the knowledge, you must undergo additional and rigorous training. Magical preparation is essential if you are to succeed."

Quinn rolled her eyes. There was always one more step. She wisely chose to remain silent. *More training.*

Without a word, Seraphina turned and walked away. Quinn didn't have time to pack up her camp; she knew Seraphina expected her to follow, and there was no time for hesitation. She'd have to make do without her belongings or retrieve them later, whenever that might be.

Seraphina only stopped when Quinn's forehead glistened with sweat, while the Fae remained pristine, not a single drop of moisture marring her. Quinn sighed inwardly, trying to keep quiet. Seraphina wouldn't like the sound, and she wouldn't appreciate her frustration, finding her ungrateful.

The greatest lesson she had learned this summer was the value of silence; it was her best defense. Her mouth had gotten her into enough trouble: extra laps, longer nights, and endless work.

Seraphina waved her arm in a graceful sweep when they reached a clearing, and a training ground appeared. Within a painted circle, three targets materialized. Near the edge, a wide variety of weapons glinted in the light. A dilapidated building rested in the back. Quinn had grown accustomed to Seraphina's power, though she was unsure whether it was already here and hidden by glamour. Or moved here with the wave of her arm.

Magic must've hidden it. It doesn't matter.

At the back of the area, the door to the small shack burst open, and there, with her signature bandana and flowing skirts, was Celeste. She waved and glided down the stairs with ease, running to Quinn.

"My darling," she said, her arms wide for an embrace. The fabric of her skirts shifted, dragging on the ground as she moved, catching the stiff, glass-like blades of grass. The delicate fabric caused it to crack and break, creating a rustling sound that made a melody of destruction. Her movement was an enchantment that echoed through the forest, amplifying the melody of her body.

Quinn smiled as a wave of relief washed over her. She waved back, not realizing how worried she had been for this woman. An invisible weight lifted from her shoulders.

"Hi, Quinn," Celeste said, wrapping her arms around her, a smile reaching her eyes. "I made a vitamin drink for you."

Quinn eyed Seraphina. *She knew I'd be here?* Glancing between the two women, she decided not to comment on it.

As usual, Seraphina revealed nothing. "There is no time for that part of your training," she said dismissively. "Celeste is human, as you are. She can't perform the spellwork the Fae can." She waved toward Celeste.

Quinn hesitated, eyeing the bubbling green concoction in Celeste's hand; the color alone told her enough. This would taste horrible. She grabbed the glass and attempted to stall.

"How's there time to train? I thought this was a matter of urgency?"

Seraphina gestured for her to drink the glass as she said, "It is, young one. If you encounter anyone in the prison realm, you will need to be able to handle yourself, or you will meet your demise."

"Did I not make it? Did you have a vision?" Quinn asked. *Am I not ready?*

"Careful with questions you do not wish to know."

Quinn gulped, her fingers tightening around the glass, and took a tentative sip of the ominous green shake. To her surprise, it had a pleasant blueberry taste. She had been expecting something pungent. Cool liquid flowed into her mouth, refreshing despite its thick consistency. The light, almost airy flavor was a welcome contrast to its heavy appearance.

She blinked in surprise, taking another gulp. This was good.

Celeste smiled knowingly as Quinn took another sip. "I've been working on it. You're going to need all the strength you can get," she said.

The cramping in her legs dulled like she had returned from a day at the spa.

"That recipe Baxter had made these, too. I call them Runezests."

The bar-shaped, bread-like food was etched with markings.

"I don't know what that means, but the recipe said to add them. That's why it has rune in the name," she said.

Quinn inspected it.

"It's like a superpower against Fae. It might even grant temporary magic. I'm still perfecting it. Part of the paper was torn."

"That's incredible," Quinn said.

With that, Celeste turned. Her skirts flowed as she made her way into the shack. As the door creaked shut behind her, Quinn's training began.

This sudden session wasn't random; it was likely triggered by one of Seraphina's visions. She needed to learn this new skill, as her life literally depended on it. Whatever the training would be, it would likely alter the vision.

Whatever was foreseen must've been terrible. Hopefully, this will alter it.

Taking a steadying breath. "Where do I start?" she asked, reluctant but understanding the necessity.

Seraphina's gaze bore into her. After a long pause, she pointed to the glass. "You start with the drink," Seraphina said.

Quinn eyed the half-finished shake in her hand. Of course, it wasn't just vitamins. It never was in Fata.

The blueberry, it must be a muskle berry. That means it's magical.

Quinn smiled, hesitating for half a second before tipping the glass back and finishing the drink. An electrical current coursed through her. Her leaden legs felt light and powerful; the exhaustion evaporated. She straightened, feeling revitalized, her body humming with renewed strength. Whatever was in that drink, it had done more than refresh her. It had transformed her.

I have to remember to thank Celeste for making it taste better. A smile crept along her face. *And Seraphina.*

"I have a question," Quinn announced.

Seraphina lifted her chin.

"I saw a gargoyle. It defended me," she explained.

"A rare incident, indeed," she responded cryptically.

"It defended me," Quinn repeated.

"They are picky about who they defend. They can be useful when they want to be. Come. We have much to do." She walked away, leaving no room for further questions.

***

"You must filter," Seraphina had said, walking around her in a circle. "Not every vision is meant to be seen, focus only on what calls to you."

For hours on end, they performed meditative-type exercises. "Take it in and move past, do not block them. You control the visions with focus. They do not control you."

The air was alive with electricity. Seraphina taught her to navigate her mind, letting the chaos pass over her like water instead of trying to stop them like a dam. Quinn could slow the flood, but it remained difficult. She had to control her state of mind at all times. Not easy for a teenager.

"Those glasses," Seraphina had said as Quinn put them back, "are a crutch. You need to learn to see without them. It will be harder if you rely on them."

Quinn wore the glasses and carried the rock, making her see two things at once. A blurred vision made her feel disoriented and faint. She recalled the black obsidian stone Celeste had given her last year, which clouded her sight and made her vulnerable.

Quinn shuddered at the memory. Her training, distant in her mind, wasn't helping in this moment. The stone enhanced her gift, honed it even, allowing her to focus, but carrying obsidian too long had devastating consequences. Even using it and her glasses nearly ended her.

***

Training had progressed steadily under watchful eyes. Each session pushed her to her limits, forcing her to hone her skills. Every moment was a step closer to something bigger. Now that she had learned about the tool, one essential for navigating the treacherous prison, she could proceed with caution.

The device was unlike anything she'd ever seen. It wasn't merely an object; it was a piece of the prison itself. In a guided vision by Seraphina, its power emanated. It pulsed with an energy that hummed as though it were alive. Without it, crossing into the Mirror Prison would be impossible undetected, making her mission fail before it even began.

She wrestled with her old doubts. *What if I'm not strong enough? What if this was all too much?*

As Quinn's practice intensified, she noticed subtle shifts in her surroundings, her sharpened vision. The daily drinks may have been behind the change, or perhaps it was the air itself in Fata, filled with energy. The air crackled as they practiced detecting spells in the secluded clearing.

Quinn could detect spells, traps, and glamours; even Seraphina couldn't hide them from her now. She couldn't do magic on her own, but she could avoid, counter, or heal. Quinn also learned to mix herbs commonly found in Fata to create a flash bomb.

Gathering the common pink moss, she wrapped it in a large leaf, shoving an abundance of Shimmering Cane Flower into another leaf. Lastly, she added a drop of nectar of the Starlight Fern Flower, a rare ingredient to find since it only bloomed in darkness. Fata didn't have regular night cycles, so it became exceedingly difficult. Quinn gathered a larger fig-like leaf, wrapped them together, and tied them with a vine, completing the concoction.

"Yes," Seraphina said encouragingly. "Now throw it as far as you can and look away."

Quinn hurled the concoction toward the ground. The vine entangled with her finger at the last moment, resulting in the bomb going off at her feet. A painful, bright light exploded. Quinn fell to her knees as a cloud of smoke engulfed her. She was blinded for two sleeps, a length of time she had come to measure. Essentially, it was equivalent to two nights. The excruciating headache that followed was tormenting, pounding against her skull, a reminder of her failure.

I'm never going to get Puck back.

After that disaster, Quinn named this particular concoction the Blinding Light, a name well-earned. She vowed to herself never to drop it again.

The days stretched into what felt like weeks as Quinn honed her skills. Celeste and Seraphina joined her daily in her preparations as they sparred and tested their herbal mixtures. They exchanged knowledge, blending Celeste's non-magical methods with Seraphina's intricate spellwork.

"I feel like I'm in potions class," Quinn remarked one day with a wry smile as she mixed a batch of foul-smelling herbs.

Celeste laughed as she passed her more ingredients. "Careful, if you mix too fast, you may find yourself at the end of another disaster."

Quinn held her breath, frozen in place.

Celeste smiled and said, "At least you're learning."

Quinn stuck out her tongue and hoped she'd never make that mistake again. She learned from every failure, perhaps more from failing. Each one brought her closer to mastery.

Chapter 12: The Lamiank

$\mathcal{A}$ meek voice startled Quinn as it echoed through the clearing, breaking her concentration. "Quinn, you must acquire a tool before you head to the Mirror Prison."

Quinn and turned, her curiosity piqued. A squirrel-sized animal with long, fluffy fur, faced her. It was the color of a Siamese cat, with big fox-sized ears and large, beady eyes that were solid black and half the size of its tiny head.

"What kind of tool?"

Wait, how does this creature know my name? Is that one of Seraphina's familiars, Reza or Ezra?

Its eyes held hope and wonder. "The Mirror Shard can manipulate reflections, a crucial tool to navigate the mirror realm."

Quinn's eyes flared. "Where's the Mirror Shard?" *I can't believe I forgot it.*

Its face twisted into an awkward smile. "A well-guarded secret amongst my kind, hidden deep within the heart of the Enchanted Woods. The ancient Tree Guardian can grant you access." A serious look shadowed its face, and it said, "Mirrors were banned in Fata for a reason. You must seek and use it with extreme caution."

Quinn's heart pounded in her chest; she had a new sense of purpose. She was steady and certain of what she must do. The endless hours of training had consumed her, forgetting her task ahead. She needed to embark on this new journey into the

Enchanted Woods. There, she'd find the Tree Guardian, and she'd ask for the shard.

Taking a moment for herself, she decided it was time to say her goodbyes. Facing each of them individually proved harder than she had expected. Only the Lamianks, Seraphina's familiars, and Celeste stood out in her mind. Celeste's quiet smile, even Ophelia seemed more withdrawn, she only nodded when Quinn said goodbye.

"Good morrow, human," the creature spoke.

Quinn was almost certain it was Ezra. She smiled and waved.

Celeste, with tears in her eyes, said, "This isn't goodbye." She sniffled. "It's see you soon."

Quinn's heart melted. It was harder to leave than she thought.

***

After a brief, uneventful journey and one portal, Quinn emerged at the entrance of the Enchanted Woods. The teal grass, damp with cool moisture, combined with the canopy of trees blocking out much of the light, created an ominous effect. The light shone through and made a silvery gleam shimmer off the water droplets. The wood was silent, aware of her presence.

The large roots breaking through the ground made walking through the terrain difficult. Quinn stumbled, causing her to run to catch her balance. Hands out, she caught herself on an enormous tree, its bark pressing into her calloused hands. It vibrated against her palms.

A pair of cold, narrowed eyes peered at her. She jumped back. "Why have you assaulted me?" Its deep voice rumbled like distant thunder, shattering the silence, threatening to unleash its temper.

"It-it was an accident."

It examined Quinn silently, then said, "What is the reason you seek the Mirror Shard, young one?"

Quinn had never imagined the Tree Guardian was an actual tree. No mistake could be made; this towering tree was the Guardian.

How does it know what I seek?

Quinn's voice rang true, solid, and firm, "To free a Fae trapped wrongfully within the Mirror Prison, I must right this grave injustice."

After learning more about Puck through visions, she understood the reasoning behind his behavior. Compelled to save him, something pulled her toward him. A vision had what he'd done to save many more. Knowing he hadn't killed out of evil, but rather on the behalf of the greater good, eased her mind. It wasn't easy, but he had to kill to protect his love and the realm.

The Tree Guardian's gnarled and contorted branches creaked, as if they might snap with the unnatural movement. A glass-like case emerged containing the shard before Quinn, suspended in mid-air before her. It appeared to be made from a type of stone, like quartz. It was completely clear.

Quinn gasped as she caressed it. Cold and almost painful to touch, it shocked her. Her hand recoiled involuntarily. She reached out again and grabbed it. As he held it, her body heat was absorbed, and the shard's warmth increased with each passing moment.

A surge of energy coursed through her when she touched it, connecting her to the Mirror World's essence. The reasoning for the reflections and a power that could aid or be the undoing of her purpose was clear. *But how do I open it?* With that thought, the tree's branch contorted again. *Is it trying to point me in that direction? Could it read my thoughts?*

The Guardian shuddered, returning to its normal position, as if in answer. Quinn didn't second-guess the directions; she followed the path. Hours later, her hair matted to her forehead, she needed to slow her pace.

Do I even know what I'm doing? I hope this is the way. It always somehow works out. No point in worrying.

The shard pulsed in her grip as her fears bubbled to the surface. Failure was not an option. Too much depended on her to quit now. Her inner struggles and fears resurfaced. The weight of the task overwhelmed her.

What if I can't do it? How can I find the prison and jailbreak Puck when no one's ever done it before? Could I really succeed without an inkling of what I'm supposed to do? I'm just a girl in a wondrous world I don't fully understand.

Quinn had come too far to turn back now. She willed her heartbeat to slow, taking deep, revitalizing breaths. With the Mirror Shard in hand, she was ready as she'd ever be.

Chapter 13: Crossing the Threshold

Her walk was endless and uneventful. When she finally reached the next portal, she was exhausted. Once she crossed through it, everything was backward, as if the portal transported her to the back side of a mirror, distorting reality. The colors were muted and gray, unlike the vibrant hues of Fata. The ground beneath her feet seemed like a gateway, pulling at her perception. An unsettling thought crept through her.

Was this place a portal within a portal? Quinn had since trusted her instincts; she could sense realities, but this was too far-fetched. *How could I tell the difference between a gateway and an entire separate realm? Is this place altering my consciousness and distorting my intuition? Was that the very purpose of this realm, to deceive?*

A soft glow lit the ground beneath her, and on inspection, it was her acorn necklace. *What would Ravenswood do here? Maybe it's the glyphs.* Her instincts told her this place was something far more complex and darker than she imagined, a threshold between dimensions where reflections within the walls no longer matched her movements.

They showed something slightly off, her face lingered too long, or shifted the wrong way. The closer she got to the prison, the clearer the mirrors became, yet they grew more distorted. Initially, they were small due to the surfaces having bumps or cracks. Then, the textures changed; some had a weathered glass appearance, whereas others had frost on them, despite the warm temperature. They reminded her of quartz, how some were smooth and transparent, while others were rough and cloudy.

It felt like hours walking in the terrain leached of color. All the surfaces were lifeless gray or reflective, which made for a boring time. This place was devoid of living creatures, no signs of life anywhere. She quickened her pace. The jagged stone made her uneasy. Her necklace pulsed.

What could that mean?

Time blurred, and Quinn hesitated before the entrance. She'd arrived. The surrounding air was magnetic. She swallowed hard and took a steadying breath; with an exhale, she stepped through the shimmering veil of the Mirror World. A humming sound vibrated in her ears and deep in her bones. Quinn turned with deliberate slowness, taking in the surreal landscape before her. Moisture clung to her skin, making her shiver.

The images showed a different version of this world in each mirror; they were both familiar and foreign. The illusion held multiple scenes in view at once. It was enough to confuse anyone's reality and fracture their sense of direction. If she stumbled onto the wrong path in this realm, she may never return. It was easy to imagine how one could get lost here, in a place where physics didn't obey logic. Her throat tightened as the fear of failure rose, but she forced it down.

A heavy gloom clung to the air; it turned the depressing gray realm into a smoking shroud that cast strange shadows across the landscape, dulling the already dim light. Quinn squinted, straining to see through the haze that blurred everything. The ground beneath was uneven.

A dark shadow passed over her. She originally thought it was a bird passing. She glanced upward, and her eyes adjusted to the light. There was no bird in sight, but several feathered dragons soared past, each no larger than a horse. The iridescent feathers shimmered in reflective light, reminding her of gemstones.

The one directly above her had the markings of a tiger's eye stone. Her breath hitched; astonishment and fear paralyzed her momentarily before a dragon swooped down, its eye matching its hide. Its gaze locked onto her, swerved, and flew away. The powerful wings sent a gust of wind toward her, and the flapping sound was mesmerizing.

A flash of movement brought Quinn back to the situation. It was herself. A hundred different contorted versions of herself stared back at her. Some were impossibly tall, and morphed into grotesque, shrunken, and hunched images. She ducked behind a nearby rock to avoid the dragon. Its shimmering reflection showed the great beast soaring away. She remained hidden for quite some time once her pulse steadied enough to move again. While sitting, she spotted a polished sliver of a mirror, resembling a walking stick.

This'll come in handy. She lifted it, feeling light and solid in her hands.

Her nerves were frayed after seeing a dragon. Some images appeared to move in time with her while others moved in the opposite direction. A few had faces that were almost right, while others were warped into grotesque caricature versions, with twisted smiles and elongated features that made her stomach churn.

One made her heart skip. The face was hers, but the eyes were all wrong. They were too large and hollow. Her lips were pulled unnaturally into a grin full of teeth that was terrifying. Quinn recoiled, her breath catching in her throat as fear overtook her.

Her beat-up black combat boots echoed off the rough surfaces as she moved cautiously forward, the sound oddly muffled by the haze. Each step felt uncertain; the ground beneath her wasn't smooth as glass but strangely bumpy, as though something burrowed right beneath the surface, causing slight ridges to form, throwing off her balance. She had to shift her weight carefully to avoid stumbling. Boots clinked against the surface, a reminder that she was still grounded.

Ahead, a crack in a shattered mirror glinted in the fading light, catching Quinn's attention. The remnants of where a portal had been were a reminder of how delicate the barrier was between worlds. She pressed her hand to the cool surface, an almost tangible link to yet another twisted realm.

The Mirror World pulled her in, like the irresistible allure of a lover, drawing her deeper into a passionate embrace. It was dangerous to allow it to suck her in, but her instincts told her it was where she needed to go. This surreal place shifted reality like sand.

Beyond the mist ahead, Quinn glimpsed a flicker of movement. The fog beckoned her with ghost-like tendrils, as if the mist itself wanted to claim her, to be its prisoner. A shiver ran up her spine.

Puck, she thought, her breath hitched.

At least, she hoped it was him. The mist warped everything, making it hard to be certain. The figure was distant, but familiar. If it was Puck, she had no time to lose. Her muscles tensed as she darted through the maze of mirrors with swift steps. The mirrored walls stretched endlessly in every direction, far into the distance, and others curved back on themselves in impossible loops.

She saw ahead and behind at the same time with a kaleidoscope of images shifting around her all at once, fracturing her vision. It was challenging to navigate. Her reflection multiplied with each turn, some running ahead, others moving behind, and some walking sideways.

It couldn't be Puck; he was in prison, and she hadn't found it yet, in this sea of looking glass.

***

After hours of walking, Quinn took a break. She sat beside a large, shiny rock, leaning back against it. She placed her walking stick on the ground beside her; it had saved her from falling more than she'd like to admit. A noise startled her. She ran from it, not wanting to find out what it was. She turned and slammed into a massive, fur-covered chest.

A low growl sent goosebumps racing across her skin. Her heart tried to beat its way out of her chest. Quinn yelped, stumbling backward until she fell hard onto the ground. Towering over her was a two-legged bull with wide, flaring nostrils. Large ivory horns protruded from its head. A glinting key swung from its nose ring. Neither of them moved.

"Um," she said. "I'm so sorry. I didn't mean to—"

The Minotaur snorted and dug a hoof into the ground. It swung its horns at her, leaving shimmer dust in its wake. She narrowly dove out of the way at the last second, landing on all fours. Caught off guard by the confrontation, she momentarily froze.

The Minotaur charged away. She glanced up in time to see the beast charging back at her. Rolling out of the way just in time. She did a kickflip onto her feet and brandished her walking stick, swinging it at the Minotaur as he skidded past, striking him.

The beast stumbled and tumbled into a somersault. It puffed out an exhale and rubbed its head and charged for her once again. This time he stopped short of contact. Quinn would've been hit, unable to move fast enough. Her gut reaction caused her to flinch and land on her bottom. Without a word, it offered her a hoof up. Quinn cautiously took it.

"I am so sorry, um," Quinn said.

Confusion consumed her. It shoved her. She stepped back, not losing her footing. Its foot pounded the ground and lowered its head to swipe a horn at her. She ducked and kicked it, retreating.

"Had enough?"

Quinn cautiously nodded.

"Is that all you got, bald one?"

"I'm not bald," Quinn said, touching her hair to ensure it was still there.

"Your fur is indeed missing."

Quinn blushed. *This is weird.* "I don't even know your name."

She fought with a Minotaur and then asked its name.

It forcefully expelled air through its snout. "My name is Bertha. You can call me Big B," it said with a slight bow of its head.

Quinn stared, mouth parted. *This is a female Minotaur?* She closed her mouth; it was rude to gape.

The Minotaur snorted. "I'm kidding. Humans love humor." The Minotaur dug its left leg in the dirt with the same intensity a bull would prior to charging.

Quinn crouched, arms extended in a defensive position; she'd be ready for a battle with the beast.

The Minotaur shook its massive head; its flowing mane waved to and fro. "Easy there, human," the Minotaur rumbled. "I kick my leg when excited. I get excited to battle as well. You may call me, Cornelius."

Quinn couldn't help but laugh. *This Minotaur's funny.*

"What's so funny?" Cornelius asked with a stern look upon his face.

Quinn's smile faltered. "You keep giving me the most ridiculous names. I thought your name would be Asterion..."

Quinn's voice trailed off as the creature's displeasure became apparent. Her smile melted completely and was replaced by an apologetic look.

Cornelius flinched as if he'd been struck. "What's so funny about my name, human?" the Minotaur roared, emphasizing its irritation as a leg stomped the ground. "Asterion was a mythical creature, make-believe. Although I think it was named after my cousin, Ashter."

Quinn stepped back. "I'm sorry. I thought you were teasing me again," she said.

"Why would Cornelius be funny? It's not a funny name," the Minotaur asked.

"You said your name was Bertha. I thought…" Quinn clamped her lips together mid-sentence as the Minotaur chuckled.

"I'm kidding, human. Don't be so uptight."

"I was gonna say Cornelius is quite the ridiculous name."

The Minotaur pounded its leg. The scrap of cloth covering his lower half rustled with the movement. "My name *is* Cornelius."

Quinn smiled, but the Minotaur didn't seem to be laughing. Her smile melted. "What's with the key?"

"I cannot give you this key for nothing," the Minotaur said, his voice deeper than before. He swept his arm wide as if encompassing the world.

"What? I didn't ask for the key," Quinn protested, her brows furrowed with apparent confusion.

"You will, they always do," the Minotaur said and pointed to his eye with a hoof.

I can't even see his skin with all that fur.

Quinn started, voice filled with sincere regret, "I'm sorry. I've never met a Minotaur before. The only other creature I've met was a troll, and it…" Quinn was cut short as the ground trembled beneath her feet.

The Minotaur slammed his leg again and huffed a loud snort through his nose.

"Now you compare me to those vile and filthy trolls. I hang out in manure fields, but I'm not filthy. I bathe," Cornelius bellowed from the depths of his lungs.

Quinn wavered and took a step back. "Um, that's not what I meant," she protested.

"I didn't insult you, you furless, hoofless, human."

"I'm sorry." Quinn held up her hands, palms facing the Minotaur. "What can I do to make it right?"

The Minotaur scratched the coarse scruff of his chin with a massive hoof. "Hmm."

The massive horns were intimidating. Large brown eyes bore into her without saying a word.

It's difficult to read his expression. It's probably all the wild fur.

Quinn took a step and leaned forward. "Really, what can I do?" she implored the beast. *I hope I don't regret this. Please don't make me regret this.*

The Minotaur's face softened. "Well, I've had trouble with the ladies. I think if I had my hair braided by my ears, I would look more dignified."

The Minotaur flipped his head and pushed his hooves up toward his shaggy brown mane.

Quinn bit back a laugh. Her lips curled at the edges. "You want me to braid your fur?" she asked. Nervous, this was another poor attempt at humor; she didn't want to offend the creature once more.

"Yes, it'd look cool. Don't you think so?" he asked her.

Quinn nodded. "Of course, it would look cool," she said. "Braids are making a comeback."

"Comeback? They were never out of style. I can't reach up by my ears," he said as he demonstrated.

It created quite a comical scene, a Minotaur, large and mighty, attempting to lift bulging muscular arms up to his head. They could only raise to about ninety degrees.

Quinn faked a cough in an attempt to hide her laugh.

She expertly orchestrated the strands into neat, intertwined bindings. Once Quinn had successfully twisted the hair around the Minotaur's ears, she rested her hands on her hips with a satisfying sigh.

"There, I think that will do." *It's strange to feel comfort here.*

"Will do? How does it look? Am I positively distinguished?"

He shook his head left to right in an attempt to show off the braids. He bent his ear back and then turned them forward, one at a time. The movement was deliberate, assessing the effect of his newly braided mane.

"Absolutely," Quinn said with a smile. *Come to think of it, I haven't smiled in a long time. I can't remember the last time I did. Despite this being quite the side quest, I think it may have been beneficial.*

"Well, then, I suppose you can have the key now," Cornelius said as he attempted to remove the key from his nose ring.

He huffed through his snout and motioned as if he were going to rip it out in frustration. His hooves weren't conducive to removing the key.

Quinn approached him with care. "Here, let me," she said as she reached it. *It's a cruel joke to leave a key here like that. I wonder who did it and why.* Quinn shook her head and her thoughts away. "There, how's that?"

"It actually feels lighter. I can swing my head without it hitting me." He bared his teeth.

Normally, Quinn would've been frightened by this toothy display, but she'd gotten to know Cornelius during this exchange. He attempted to smile. She didn't have the heart to tell him how intimidating it appeared. The braided fur somehow made him even more frightening.

Quinn pocketed the golden key. It weighed more than a key should. *That must've hurt his nose. He's probably happy I took it.* She smiled at the thought.

"Well, I should be going. I have a quest to finish."

"I love quests. Can I come?" His voice filled with childish excitement.

Quinn paused for a moment, weighing the benefits of having a bodyguard versus a loud Minotaur. She looked away from him, unable to concentrate.

Cornelius snorted. "I'm kidding. I must say you humans aren't the jokesters I was told you were."

Quinn smiled again, finding herself warming to the idea of a companion. *It might not have been so bad to have someone on the journey.*

"Goodbye, Cornelius." She waved and walked away.

"See ya, human," he called after her.

His voice bellowed, an eerie echo. He blew air from his snout. She had the distinct impression that it was his happy noises. She smiled to herself as she continued on her journey.

Chapter 14: Quicksand and Riddles

With the key in hand, she could begin her quest. Quinn didn't even attempt to check if it would fit the stone that encased the Mirror Shard. She had a gut feeling it would fit; she'd wait to open the stone until she got to the prison.

Quinn retrieved the map from her pack. Although she had to head south, the dotted line along the page made her pause. It appeared to be a border of some kind, but something told her it was more, perhaps a portal. Her intuition was rarely wrong.

How do I know that's a portal? It must be the potion I drank.

Quinn tucked the map away and continued walking. It was eerily quiet. The tiny hairs on the nape of her neck rose. Her vision was fuzzy on the edges.

Something's happening.

Recognizing this feeling, she sat down, crossing her legs beneath her. She was having a vision. Her mother's voice rang in her ears. Unable to hear what she caught only the echo of her voice.

Could my mother be calling out to me from beyond? Am I hearing a past echo of her? She's gone, I can't see the future.

Quinn shook her head and dismissed it as grief. She didn't lose the sense of her surroundings like she had with past visions.

She palmed the ground, pushing herself up as she heard her mother yell, "Help."

Quinn stood and scanned the tree line. *Could I be losing it? That's definitely my mom.* Against her better judgment, she tentatively called, "Mom?"

A flash of Chloe banging on a reflection of herself appeared for a split second.

"Mom!" Quinn shouted. She looked all around but saw nothing related to her vision. *Was that what happened to Mom?* A single tear ran down her cheek. *Mom.* Quinn wiped it away with a sigh and headed over to the dotted line on the map.

Hearing no response, she shuddered as a wave of overwhelming disappointment washed over her. She'd give anything to hear her mother again. Quinn took a steadying breath and walked once more. Her footsteps echoed in the silence, reminding her once again that she was all alone. She beat herself up for getting her hopes up. *Stupid, stupid, stupid. Mom died.* She curled a strand of hair around her finger.

Encountering no further signs of life, Quinn hung her head in quiet reprieve. She pondered how to get Puck out once she got there. She couldn't walk right in, even if she had the key and turned around and fled.

Were there guards there? How many? There has to be traps. Baxter is the one who's good at navigating the dangers of unknown places. The popular dice game with the dungeon master had prepared him for that.

At the threshold of the border on the map, Quinn stopped, her doubt getting the better of her. There wasn't anything noticeably different, but not everything was as it seemed in Fata.

This is it. I can finally see why this line's here.

She slowly crossed it, and the map updated with her movement. Standing on the other side, she didn't notice a difference at first. When she crossed back over to the previous side, still nothing. Quinn released a deep sigh, hoping to calm her frayed nerves. As she exhaled, the scent of blueberries lingered.

Someone must've performed magic recently. Maybe I triggered a spell or trap, or has this scent lingered since a spell was cast?

She steeled herself, crossed back over, and picked up her pace. Goosebumps formed upon her arm. As she pulled out her jacket, her gaze landed on thousands of carcasses scattered across the border that she hadn't seen earlier. They were creatures she'd never seen before. She broke into a jog, distancing herself from the decaying graveyard. A fog formed with her breath. The jacket wasn't enough to block out this cold, and a shiver shook her whole body.

It's colder here. How didn't I notice? Must be the adrenaline.

Black clouds rolled in, deepening the already darkened sky. The menacing wave sent electrical shock throughout her body. Despite the ominous feelings, Quinn's excitement was rekindled. It coursed through her veins as she realized she was so close to her goal. The hard-packed ground rumbled beneath her, loosening so that her feet sank into the dirt about an inch.

Quicksand?

The land trembled again, and she sank deeper.

No, not quicksand, but what could it be? On second thought, I shouldn't stick around to find out.

Quinn ran with childlike abandon or fear; she wasn't sure which. Her throat was tight, as though her heart was trying to climb out of her mouth. She wheezed, gasping for air. She'd never been much of a runner. She was too determined to stop at this point, not when she was so close to escaping Fata and this quest.

The sky darkened, casting an eerie shadow upon the land. The temperature dropped even further, and Quinn looked up from her reprieve. There, towering over her, stood a mountain, but not quite. Made from the same shimmering material that encased the shard, only this time it resembled the shiny stone, mica. She learned about it in science class; that stone had been her favorite. She'd peeled back the layers until it was more transparent. Something deep within her told her this mountain wouldn't peel back so easily.

The Mirror Prison.

Quinn released a big sigh. She found it.

How long was I running? I zoned out. Her breath still hadn't returned to normal. She bent forward, putting her hands on her knees to lessen the burning in her lungs. Her muscles started to cramp.

I could really use one of Celeste's drinks right about now.

She paced in a circle, feeling her cheeks flush. With a final steadying breath, she squared her shoulders and approached the enormous rock. She knew this had to be the prison with every fiber of her being.

Now, if only I could find the door.

Circling the rock proved to be more difficult than she had originally thought. The ground pulled at her like a magnet. If she stopped for too long to inspect a crevice that may have been a keyhole, her feet sank. The dirt completely engulfed her boots as she tried to keep herself moving.

Quinn could sense its presence, as if the prison itself were a living being. She firmly squeezed the stone that encased the Mirror Shard. Retrieving the key she put it into the stone and opened it. A flash of light momentarily blinded her. Placing the stone that encased the shard into her backpack he held the Mirror Shard in her hand. She closed her fingers around it, causing her hand to bleed, a sacrifice that must be paid in order to activate its properties.

Quinn had no idea how she knew that; perhaps it was the elixir she had consumed. She stepped forward, and a dizziness encompassed her reality, contorting her perception. She wasn't prepared for the transition; it was disorienting. When her vision cleared, another realm appeared. It was both familiar and new at the same time.

The entire realm appeared reversed, but different from before. A reverse image almost, as if it were flipped upside down. Tree roots reached up into the sky. Her heart pounded in her chest as she took in the surreal scenery, her surroundings defying all the laws of nature. She stepped over tree branches instead of roots; it was disorienting.

A small creature with large, luminous eyes darted past her, making a chattering noise as it scurried away. Its eyes glowed in the darkness, reminiscent of fireflies at night. The teal-blue creature resembled a mouse with long, spiky hair, yet it had two sets of transparent wings. It presented her first challenge as it spoke to her in nonsensical riddles.

"Answer me this, young seer, if you dare. If you are correct, you will receive care."

Quinn sighed, struggling to hear the creature's words. *Must it always be riddles?* She rolled her eyes.

Quinn attempted to decipher the meaning behind the last cryptic phrase as it uttered another.

"I am not one but two,

When you see you, you look at you."

"You look at you," Quinn said, more to herself, but the creature made a loud, ear-piercing buzzing sound.

"Does that mean I guessed wrong?" she asked. The creature made a purring sound as its eyes brightened.

"I wasn't really guessing. I was thinking out loud," she said.

She took a deep breath and relaxed her shoulders. "Okay, so with each correct answer, the creature's eyes light up brighter, and wrong answers blow my eardrums," she said aloud in an attempt to interpret this puzzle.

The creature made that cooing sound, and its eyes brightened once more.

"But if you can talk, why not just say if I'm right or wrong?" she asked.

The ear-piercing buzz sounded.

Quinn covered her ears. "Is something preventing you from speaking the truth?"

The creature's entire form shifted, and as it vibrated, its eyes grew bright. It cooed once more.

"Okay, I need to figure out this riddle," Quinn said.

It cooed again.

"I am there, but I am not,

I vanish right before you do."

Quinn thought for a long moment, this time not guessing out loud. "Is it a mirror?"

The creature vibrated so much its form became completely blurry. A noise behind her startled her. Quinn looked over her shoulder, as the wall retracted within itself. It revealed a hidden passage, leading deeper into this realm of mystery. It appeared to be the passage into the Mirror Prison, a funhouse labyrinth at a carnival.

Her eyes struggled to focus on the two-layered realities at once, like staring through a rearview mirror and forward simultaneously. Taking two cautious steps, her third step was more confident. The area was silent, and only her footsteps echoed. Picking up her pace, she walked right into a mirror.

"Ow, that's gonna leave a mark." She rubbed her forehead, winced, and slowed to a snail's pace. Quinn walked with her arms stretched out in front of her to prevent a repeated close encounter with another mirror.

Chapter 15: The Inmates

*A*s she continued her journey in the prison, she encountered twisting pathways that shifted as she passed through them. It was a moving maze. When she took a wrong turn and attempted to retrace her steps, the path had already changed. Each step formed a new puzzle that toyed with her reality.

After what felt like hours, frustration set in. She whimpered, nearly surrendering. One could only walk into so many walls before quitting. The corners were what got to her. She'd have her arms extended, feeling nothing, until a corner struck her face. The tunnels and stairs made the trek challenging, chipping at her already frayed resolve.

This almost impossible adventure was wearing down the last thread of her strength. After a blow to her temple, she decided she was done with it all. As she squinted, she somehow activated her Sight capabilities. The mirrors now emitted a dull light, just enough to prevent her from colliding with the transparent walls. Her breath fogged rows of walls.

Movement caught her attention far off, in three places at once. *I will never go into a funhouse again.*

Quinn's gaze was drawn ahead as she spotted a Fae's sudden freeze. It resembled a tree stump when motionless. Had it not been for its nature-like appearance, she wouldn't have thought twice about it. Somehow, she knew it had been much taller, but as punishment, it had been chopped down to its current size.

She didn't think trees belonged indoors, but then again, not much in Fata made sense. Baxter had told her about the Tree of Life. She'd never wanted to see anything like that, let alone hear about it. How it absorbed sustenance from all living forms.

Has this Fae always looked this way, or was it spelled to resemble a tree?

The Fae turned toward her; dark eyes contained only black where the sclera should've been. Its gaze was menacing. She crouched in an attempt to hide, but it didn't make a difference.

How can I hide in a world of glass? Glass prison would be a better name for it.

She quickened her pace, not wanting the Fae to alert the guards or attack her. Unsure if the Fae's cell was locked or if it was loose in the maze she'd been wandering through. *That would be punishment enough, walking into walls all day.*

This corridor's image depicted Quinn, but elderly. They flashed in and out as she walked with a limp, hunched over. Panic threatened to overcome her. The labyrinth fed off her fear. It grew exceedingly difficult to maneuver as her terror intensified. She stumbled and caught herself; her hand brushed against the cold, hard surface of the glass. The touch was grounding, and she used that moment to pull herself back from the brink of self-destruction.

She couldn't afford to slow down. Quinn's muscles ached as she pushed herself harder and faster, the echo of her boots a steady rhythm, and the only sound piercing through the unnerving silence. The figure ahead wavered like a mirage, slipping into the thick mist. Fear tugged at the edges of her mind, but she shoved it away. Her breath came in sharp, uneven bursts, her lungs straining against the cold.

Don't lose him, she repeated silently, her pulse thundering in her ears.

The figure flickered into view once again, then dissolved into the mist, and Quinn's heart leapt. She had to trust her instincts and cling to the connection, no matter how fragile.

The maze, with every reflecting path, twisted and bent in ways that defied logic. Quinn kept her gaze fixed forward, determined to catch a glimpse of the Fae once more, refusing to fall for the tricks. The maze could turn all it wanted, but she wouldn't let it deceive her.

Exhaustion clawed at her, but giving up meant abandoning Puck forever. She had to find some clue where they kept him. *Focus,* she told herself, studying the reflections. Every step felt heavier, and her limbs screamed in protest, yet she pressed on with sweat trickling down her back.

Just a little farther.

Quinn stopped to rest, bracing her hands on her knees, as she caught her breath. Her heart pounded. With sweat-slick palms, she clenched and unclenched her fists. Finding Puck wouldn't be as easy, and breaking into the prison was a challenge, especially in another world.

Sure, it'd be tough, like finding the prison and getting in.

Naively, she'd assumed that once inside, locating him would be simple. This wasn't her small-town jail, where all the inmates were in neat rows, visible at once.

She glanced around, never having imagined this level of complexity, nor did she ponder that this would be the case. A near-impossible task. This wasn't a mere maze; it was a meticulously designed labyrinth intended to disorient and deter visitors. Each hallway led to a different reality, testing her courage at every step.

The sound of rushing water caused further confusion. She was cold, fogging the glass with her breath. Even as she looked down, the distant sky was visible. Through gaps in the shining rocks, scattered throughout, created a sensation of motion sickness.

The prison was built to blur the line between reality and illusion, displaying a world of muted colors and distorted reflections. It forced self-reflection and often false images, breaking the prisoners one by one as it drove them mad. The falsehoods they witnessed repeatedly for an eternity convinced them of alternate realities.

On the rare occasion someone was released, they were never the same, but a hollow shell of their former selves. Unable to contribute to society, they were often made to be a jester or pet, unfit to even complete the task of a servant. The atmosphere here was heavy with regret and sorrow. The edges of her view blurred as a vision came on.

In the deepest part of the prison held a prisoner so feared that his name was seldom spoken aloud. Despite the mirrored walls, the faint light that reached him wasn't intentional. It was due to the difficulty in preventing mirrors from naturally reflecting it; otherwise, he'd be in complete darkness.

Although the reflections were crafted to both punish the prisoner and enable the guards to observe their condition from afar they also carried unintended consequences. The reflections might leak energy that the prisoner may absorb.

His posture was wrecked, and he reeked of smoke. His fiery red eyes were the only remnant of the strength he once possessed. He was known as Ignatius. Brief glimpses of his crimes indicated a reckless use of Pyrocraft, a firepower that once burned with such intensity it destroyed his entire community.

People had revered him for his power in the past until he had gone too far. In a moment of uncontrolled rage, he unleashed his flames, which spread beyond his control and consumed everything and everyone he loved. Some whispered it was deliberate, not an accident, as he claimed. His greed had led him to an ancient tome that required this destruction.

According to it if he burned everything he loved, he would achieve unprecedented power. The Fae before Quinn now was a hollow shell of the man he once was. The fire in his soul had dwindled to a flickering ember, thanks to his cuffs, a stark reminder of the devastation he'd caused. The shackles around his neck and hands were called Praesidium, a metal forged to prevent the wielding of power.

Despite his cell being warded, he was too powerful to test the limits. Every precaution had been taken to the extreme. He was given a bland, cool diet, out of fear that spicy food might trigger his flames. She scurried from him with haste.

Quinn remained standing during that vision. It took her a moment to keep walking, hoping not to meet that Fae.

After a while, she came upon a Fae with blank white eyes sitting cross-legged. The vacant stare, seemingly unaware of all. His stare ensnared her, rendering her motionless. Her limbs felt heavy. She instinctively touched her temple, brushing the skin. The pearl-white eyes were foreboding; something deadly hid behind them. She'd heard of their premonitions that almost always came true.

"I am called Niveus. What is your name, most peculiar human?" the male asked. He tilted his head to the side.

Quinn paused, unsure whether giving her name could hurt. "My name's Quinn," she said in a meek voice.

"In the world of the Fae, names carried deep significance. They weren't simply labels, but the very essence of a being, bound to their soul. Knowing someone's true name meant possessing a piece of their essence, their power."

Her own name floated to the forefront of her mind, a name she never spoke of: Alisandra, Truthseer, Conqueror of Shadows. It was hidden from her, it felt dangerous. She felt both pride in the name as well as fear that others might discover it.

"Few humans know their true name, and those who did never understood the power it held."

Alisandra, the one who survived. It was a name forged in fire, marked by all the trials she'd been through.

"Your name is a living thing that grows and evolves as you do."

Something warned her not to reveal her true name. She blinked and saw the male clasp his hands together, overly excited to gather information. His visions were as accurate as they were condemning. Nievus's prophecy about the last Fae Queen, forewarned she'd lose her empire to an evil king, and her demise was so clear it was thought to have influenced fate itself.

The Fae spoke of how a changeling from an unknown family would trick the king and lead in his stead. The Fae blamed the seer for turning his vision into reality. His punishment was imprisonment in the Mirror Prison, where his sight was a curse. He was haunted by futures of his wildest imagination. Yet, he didn't see it as an influence. He warned them of the future, yet the fools refused to believe him, saying he caused these visions to be true by magic.

The next blink, she was standing in front of his cell. *That's the fastest a vision has come and gone. I couldn't feel it coming.*

"The Fae do not believe in premonitions. They lock us up," Niveus explained. "An abomination, they say. If you hear the prophecy, it becomes self-fulfilling. By hearing them, it's believing in them, and in some aspects, you act differently, thus fulfilling the prophecy."

Quinn listened in silence. *Does he know what I saw?*

"They say we spread false wisdom, like an evil prophet who misdirects."

"Does every eye color mean something?" Quinn asked.

"Mostly, the rarest eye color is red, for they represent all three sects and can create Pyrocraft."

Quinn nodded, absorbing the knowledge.

"We often link that eye color with a ferocious temperament. You would do well to be wary of those with red eyes. They are in dungeons for committing unspeakable crimes or expending too much energy, attempting the forbidden. The latter is a solution in itself. Their expended energy is reabsorbed amongst the enchanted receptacles nearby and reenters the reserve."

"What's the reserve?" Her eyebrows raised.

A devilish smile crept along his face. "It is a collective pool."

"Like a well of power," Quinn said, leaning in.

"Similar," Niveus replied. "When one's personal reserve is depleted, they end up burning themselves up, in actual flames."

Quinn's tiny hairs on the back of her neck raised.

"Some Fae pull from their surroundings, but if they draw too much or have evil intent, blight is formed."

Quinn was still determining if the Fae was attempting to manipulate her or if he was reformed. But she recalled that encounter outside the library. *That must've been blight.*

"Some seers seek prophets to determine accuracy, yet they used their powers for their own gain and condemned us all."

After a brief silence for Quinn to process, the Fae continued.

"Most fairies have violet eyes. Although there are many other colors, there is no specialty, just living magic. Browns and greens are earth magic. Blues have air magic."

"I didn't know the color of eyes meant so much."

"Only the inverse can undo or combat one another, like charity counters greed. Patience counters anger. Humility counters pride. Contentment counters envy. Self-control counters lust. Diligence counters sloth. Abstinence counters gluttony," he paused and tilted his head. "Air magic counters fire or magnifies it. Each has a time and place where it may be even necessary; however, the overuse can…"

Quinn heard a faint calling, breaking her from the spell. She couldn't quite make it out.

"I should go," she said.

His words were hypnotizing; she could've stayed there forever. The Fae only nodded.

A time later, she passed another prisoner. She blinked and realized he was carrying the mistakes of his ancestors as well as his own. Caelm, a name uttered with scorn, was the last of a mighty Fae lineage. By siding with dark forces, his ancestors betrayed their own kin, seeking power.

Despite living righteously, Caelm was burdened by the sins of his forefathers, leading him to this wretched prison. Haunted by the sins of his family, he was forever tethered to a past that cast a dark stain on his life.

That didn't even feel like a vision, more like a walking premonition.

She left him without much interaction. Then a pale, gaunt figure lurked at the edge of the darkness. He was Maros, a power-hungry Fae who had stolen the life force of three others, using their power for his sinister rituals.

The magic he sought was deemed forbidden. The collective was meant to connect to the earth, to heal, but Maros had transformed it into a weapon designed to kill. With the stolen energy, he attempted necromancy to raise the dead.

When it backfired, it left him scarred beyond repair. The power was now a curse that bound him to the prison. He then annihilated his entire family, absorbing their power. He used too much of the collective and absorbed the essence of three Fae around him. Causing their death from consumption, granted Maros the ability to perform dark magic.

Quinn couldn't face what he'd done with that power. She scurried away from him in haste. Her power was growing at an alarming pace.

Seraphina said something about magical powers. Could this be it?

Once she reached the prison's darkest depths, she found a sorrowful figure sitting in a corner. Her face was etched with extreme sorrow.

"My name is Amethyst."

Quinn could see why she bore that name, as her eyes were the most spectacular shade of violet she'd ever seen. Even her hair had different shades of purple streaks in it.

The Fae spoke of her crimes; she was accused of betrayal of the Fae court. She spoke of her lover, whose jealousy was unmatched. He fabricated a lie so convincing that Amethyst was cast into prison. If she wasn't his, she'd be no one's.

The lover's deceit was a desperate attempt to keep Amethyst close, ensuring she'd never belong to anyone else. In his selfishness, Amethyst was condemned to an eternity of isolation. Her innocence would forever be hidden. Each prisoner's magic and life were warped by their tragic past, whether it was due to their decisions or their inherited destiny.

The Mirror Prison, a place where echoes of past sins resonated endlessly, was their purgatory, offering no solace, only the cold reflection of their losses.

"It may take longer, but your path is already planned out for you. Even if you go around, backward, and in circles, you will end up at the same destination. The journey might be long, but your course is already set. Whether you go straight or take a detour, the final place you reach will be the same."

Quinn leaned forward, eyes narrowed, when she noticed something behind Amethyst's cell. She moved around to examine a peculiar stone. At first glance, it looked like any ordinary rock, except for the faint shimmering aura that danced around the surface.

Intrigued, she pressed her face closer, her nose nearly brushing it, when all of a sudden, the stone moved. She gasped as a slit appeared, and a glowing yellow eye blinked at her with glistening green scales. Her heart leaped.

Oh my God, it isn't a stone. It's an egg! A dragon? A real dragon!

She tumbled back onto the ground, astonished. She never thought, in a million years, she'd see a dragon. Dragons weren't real. Well, she also thought fairies weren't real, either.

"You were destined to encounter that being. However, it may distract you from your purpose."

Quinn glanced back at Amethyst. *I have to keep moving. With all these distractions, I'll never find him.*

"I have to go. I'm sorry." She turned and ran from this Fae as well.

***

She hesitated. The farther she went, the darker it was. The weight of the world pressed in on her. As she plunged deeper into the maze, each twist and turn brought her closer to Puck.

The hair on her neck rose, her senses heightened as she navigated the labyrinth. The temperature plummeted the deeper she went. In the distance, whispers echoed, and she formed illusions to visualize what she heard. A shadow flickered at the corners of her eyes, bouncing off the mirrored walls and scurrying away. She trembled, unsure if it was due to the temperature or the creature. No telling how far away it was, thanks to all the mirrors.

There he was, Puck. He appeared in the distance, his figure distorted, and she only caught glimpses of him. Relief rushed through her, only to be replaced by disappointment a moment later. No matter how hard she tried to reach him, the maze twisted, resulting in a dead end. Every step took her farther from him.

The reflections turned into grotesque shapes, bending the world like a kaleidoscope. It was designed to challenge her and tear at her sanity. Her instincts would be her only weapon as the labyrinth of mirrors tricked her, but they could also be her downfall. Every turn revealed another endless corridor, each more confusing than the last.

The image of him focused for a brief moment, long enough to see his face. Quinn chased after him, yet no matter how hard she tried, she couldn't reach him. His lips were moving, yet she couldn't hear anything.

She took a deep breath and tried to calm herself. This was a test; it was why Seraphina and Ophelia challenged her so much. This place was designed to break her, but she couldn't let it. She had to focus and complete her mission.

Quinn traced the edges of the mirror with her fingertips, searching for a clue, anything, maybe a premonition. There had to be a way through.

The only question was, could she find it before the prison transformed her beyond recognition?

Glimpses of the other inmates sent her body into hyperfocus. She was practically trembling. She was in uncharted territory. No one but guards had been in here, and once you went into the prison, you never came out the same.

I can't worry about that now. I need to find Puck first.

"I knew you would come, human," the seer said. Quinn jumped when she heard her voice. Not expecting a living creature, especially when you could usually see them coming, was eerie. The Fae looked so much like Ophelia that she almost asked her for help; the only difference was that the female's eyes were all white. Ophelia's were a deep purple.

A seer, I wonder if they are related? Wait, how is Seraphina free?

"You will see who you wish for the most, child of interlaced time. But when you see her, she will once again be lost to you. Immense joy shall be followed by vast sorrow. Truth carries a heavy price, and you pay in pain. When it all crashes in rubble, she will not be buried."

Quinn's chest was a vice.

"You end where you began. As all daughters of the Sight are."

"Why are you here?" *That's a dumb question. All the seers were locked up.*

The seer tilted her head as if in answer.

Can she read my thoughts like Ophelia read Baxter's? No, Seraphina practiced blocking with me all summer.

The Fae moved with slow, deliberate grace, analyzing Quinn.

A shiver overtook her self-control. She didn't want to seem weak in front of the Fae.

"Do you know where Puck is?" Quinn asked.

The seer reacted as if she'd been struck across the face. She hissed, backing up.

Quinn jumped, then collected herself. "Puck is the reason I am here to begin with."

"Puck?" she asked. "He goes by many names, but I know of whom you speak. He turned me in so he could save my sister. She also possesses a little psychic power."

Ophelia.

"She can read people's true nature and intentions, aiding her on the battlefield and at court. I got her that bandolier she wears over her shoulder and the belt equipped with knives as a gift. I saw she'd need them. Even gave her a spell with several charms to allow her to enhance her power and read thoughts of those not protected within a small area."

She'd read Baxter's mind at her house.

"Puck set the prophecy into motion by betraying me. It was his undoing and why he is here. I did try to warn him. He wouldn't hear anything but Magnus."

Quinn's head swam with information. She didn't want to mess with fate or prophecies. "I just need to find him."

"It will not lead you to *your* desired outcome. If you continue on this path, you will be forced to choose a most heart-wrenching fate."

"Please," she said.

"You will not like the answer." It sounded like a warning.

"Please." Quinn let every bit of pleading drip into the word, all her desperation. The whine even astonished her; how desperately she wanted this to be over.

"Finding him will only extend your time here, human. I'm sure my sister warned you." She tilted her head again.

That motion created enough doubt to stop Quinn momentarily.

What if they were only training me for this outcome, knowing I wouldn't like it? Seraphina can see the future, and Ophelia only cares for Puck. What if?

She shook her head. It didn't matter, anyway. She made a pact. Even if they knew her mother couldn't be saved, she still agreed. *I'd best get this over with.* She released a deep sigh.

"Where's Puck?" she asked with such force she felt a shimmer of something move as she demanded her answer.

Was that magic? The Runezests? I don't have time to figure it out now.

The seer was unmoved by her tone. After a moment, she merely pointed in a direction and turned her back to Quinn, ending further communication.

"Thank you," Quinn whispered and scurried away.

Chapter 16: A Seer's Warning

Quinn shuddered as she was propelled into another vision. This one was of Ophelia's history, one riddled with heartbreak and turbulence. Not only was she a high-ranking member of the Fae Court, a highly coveted position, she was also the leader of the Freedom Fighters.

One position required cunning and strength to navigate the complexities of politics, whereas the other required her and the resistance group, to challenge the evil that threatened to overtake her lands. Her ability to balance her duties was no small feat.

Her personal life was even more complex. Puck wasn't approved of by her family, nor the court. His history was known for more than his mischief. Puck was reckless and unpredictable, an ill-suited consort for Ophelia, given her high stature.

The very presence of him in her company threatened to jeopardize her titles. Ophelia's family fervently disapproved of any union between them. Lyra, her sister, was a forbidden seer. While rare, the Fae viewed it as an abomination rather than a gift.

Lyra had foreseen her sister's future. In it, Ophelia was desperate and broken. The cause, Puck. He begged her not to speak of this vision, yet Lyra wouldn't listen. He told her it was incomplete and not fully formulated. Though the vision was fragmented and unfinished, the weight of it would destroy Ophelia.

A prophecy was dangerous; it had the power to change destiny. The very act of speaking a prediction would set it into motion, disrupting the natural flow. Lyra refused to listen and voiced her vision to her family. She knew it was reckless, and she'd kept the secret this whole time.

When her eyes changed to show her true nature, it was Ophelia who helped her hide the color using herbs. It was irresponsible, and Ophelia could be seen as performing an act of treachery by the Court. Puck knew the truth would be revealed and turned Lyra into the court. \

He learned that one of Ophelia's enemies within the court was planning to use it against her, and she'd lose her seat. That a Fae named Magnus would take over the entire realm and sentence Ophelia to death. The Fae did not believe in ending lives, but Magnus was no ordinary Fae. Lyra saw him gut the entire Court.

This created a huge rift within their family. It fractured their relationship, and it took Ophelia a long time to forgive Puck. Her love for him and the anguish of her sister's imprisonment left her broken beyond repair. Ophelia was a fighter, and she never let others see how much this damaged her. She felt isolated.

Only her family and Puck knew of the prophecy, but it clung to her like a leech. She couldn't escape. She questioned him often, which tainted their affinity, as she was nervous she couldn't trust him. Despite it all, Ophelia refused to extinguish the embers of their connection.

She held on to the hope that their love would defy destiny and forge its own path. Their love would rewrite any prophecies that came their way. Yet, when left alone with her thoughts, doubts assaulted her. Had her sister's words sealed her fate?

Quinn bowed her head. Ophelia had lived through so much pain, and this was a small piece of it. No wonder her friend was so hard on her.

***

Quinn rubbed her head and blinked away the vision. Reality returned to her, and once she collected herself, she resumed her walk. Her thoughts swirled of Ophelia's past.

After a while, she spotted a hunched figure in the corner of a cell. Its shoulders were turned in, arms wrapped around itself. Quinn stepped forward to get a better look. She gasped.

Puck was directly ahead of her. His normal lean, muscular physique was thin. His spine was hunched, and his shoulders turned in as if the world's weight crushed them. His long, dark hair was unruly, instead of its usual pulled-back ponytail. No longer had that threatening air about him, but Quinn knew better. Despite his stature he could tense and pounce before she blinked.

The path through the maze to reach him glowed in her vision. There was a trap along the way; a green wire that lit up across the aisle. Easy to step over as long as she remembered where it was. A distant walk was required to get near his cell.

She noticed his cell was smaller than the others. It had more glass walls, and they were thicker, harder to see through. Two guards appeared to rotate rounds every few minutes. Her watch didn't work here and time moved differently.

Finally, some guards, not that I wanted to see them.

Her desperation fueled her ambition. She had to navigate to him without being seen and manage the maze. The glow of the glass was increasingly difficult to see; each turn led her farther astray. She was unsure if she could even get to him.

The path was so clear a minute ago.

"Puck," she whispered. No response. Hopefully, no one else heard her. "Puck."

He didn't flinch.

Could he hear me?

On her path to his cell, she lost sight of him. The atmosphere grew thick as the humidity rose. It was increasingly difficult to walk. She passed another prisoner. This one didn't appear to have his own guard duty. He had fiery red hair and an arrogance about him that drew her closer. She needed to go around all the glass walls anyway, so why not look at this Fae?

An eerie air about the Fae occurred as approached. He lifted his head as if he could sense her and turned with a panther-like grace. Bracelets adorned each wrist. Praesidium, the Fae was unable to take them off, bound by magic. The Fae had a shimmer coming off his skin like the pavement on a hot day. Quinn remembered the warning regarding the red-eyed Fae. They were the most volatile and dangerous with a ferocious temperament.

The Fae slammed into the glass with such speed it startled Quinn enough to make her stumble back. She landed on her bottom with a sharp intake of breath, stifling a scream.

"Hello, human," he said with sinister disdain.

He tilted his head in the most unnatural way. A crinkling noise was made from his crusted skin moving. His fiery red eyes had an orange ring around them.

Quinn took a steadying breath and regained her ground, standing on her feet. Acting calm, a tightness in her throat said otherwise. Looking around revealed no clue that anyone had heard their transgression. Nervously, she used both hands to smooth her hair.

"So many humans here. I wonder if it's an epidemic."

That piqued Quinn's interest. *How many humans could be here?*

As if sensing her interest, the Fae curled his fingers, beckoning her to approach the glass. Despite it being a cell, Quinn still feared the creature. She tentatively approached, and the Fae smiled approvingly.

He placed his palm on the glass and gestured for her to match his hand against the transparent wall. He nodded eagerly. Drawn to the creature, not knowing if this was part of his predatory nature, or if her future depended upon it. She placed her hand on the cell wall.

As Quinn hesitantly touched the glass, a searing heat surged to an unbearable temperature, and her hand recoiled of its own accord. She jumped back, this time remaining on her feet, and cradled her hand against her chest. The interaction left her breathless, a stark reminder of the perilous magic this Fae could perform even with the bracelets on.

I can only imagine what could've been unleashed without them. He could easily melt the glass and my bones. I gotta be more careful.

After a moment, she inspected her hand. It was marred, surely, it would scar. And the raised area formed a symbol.

That can't be possible. It's just a burn. I should've known better. All my training warned me. Despite her teachings, she couldn't stop herself; the Fae had somehow compelled her.

***

A reflection of a familiar face appeared before her. A Fae she'd known in Fata, but all twisted and distorted, and then it vanished.

What was that about?

Quinn recognized the next prisoner from the battle in the arena. She swore she saw that wild hair in the crowd; it stuck out like willow branches, with pink flowers.

As she passed more inmates, some of them offered her guidance and wisdom, hinting at the inner workings of the prison's secrets. Although cryptic, it was helpful. While others hindered her progression with false directions and advice. She sensed their deceit. Their intentions were as chaotic as the realm, and she attempted to avoid anything these prisoners had offered.

Each prisoner added a piece of the puzzle to help solve this maze. Amongst the prison's challenges, a soft, familiar voice called to her. It was almost a whisper, echoing in the corridors. Her stomach flipped. She couldn't let herself be hopeful.

"Quinn, my baby, remember who you *are*."

The emphasis on the 'are' made her pause for a moment. The ghost of her mother's voice was missing her undertones of joy. It awoke feelings from her past and stirred unprocessed sorrow. A shiver overtook her. Shaking her head, she dismissed the voice as a figment of her ever-present grief-stricken imagination.

As Quinn delved deeper into the prison, the Mirror Shard's glow grew stronger. Quinn found she could almost manipulate the reflections and see farther ahead by bending light and shadow to her will. Every distorted glass was a gateway, each one offering a possible path to Puck. She'd lost him and was still unsure how to get back.

Although she could see farther than before with the Shard, the only issue was that she had to hold it up to her eye. The world shifted and changed as she passed each mirror. The chaos of the illusion gave way to the clarity of her reality. After a while, the shard was warm, then hot, and she wrapped it in a cloth and put it away. The bright light it gave off was a beacon for the guards to find her anyway.

Her courage wavered. Confusion set in as to whether this was the truth or a hallucination. She was so close to Puck and now so far. Another test of her abilities might be her breaking point. The continuous deciphering of the riddles and small traps was too much.

She could barely keep track of her path through the mirror's twisted maze. Unable to shake the feeling that her mother's voice held some significance, one that may unravel her, preventing her from the outcome she sought.

Chapter 17: Allies and Adversaries

Quinn's spine remained straight despite facing dangerous adversaries, each with unique powers and motives. Some Fae were purely evil, vicious creatures. They all wore Praesidium cuffs on their limbs, etched with symbols that shimmered in the dull light, binding their power. Some Fae bore only one cuff, others wore multiple. The cuffs called to her own power.

The Fae that she encountered were a mix of benevolence and cruelty. A few of the Fae wore cuffs on their limbs, necks, and waists. One of the seemingly kind Fae told her that the larger the cuffs, the more powerful the Fae.

The tension in Quinn's head increased; a premonition was coming. She sat on the floor in case she lost consciousness again. A whisper called in the darkness. "You can only choose one to leave."

In a haze-filled corner of the prison, her mother, Chloe, appeared, banging the glass with her fists. Tears stained her cheeks, and she fell to her knees in frustration. Chloe stood and paced the perimeter of her cell before striking the wall again, this time with her knee. It went through the wall as it morphed around her leg, almost as if it were made of a gooey substance.

It isn't glass.

Chloe crouched and stuck her hand through, and judging by her reaction, it was extremely cold. She shrugged and stuck her head through.

125

Quinn hovered over the room like a ghost. "Mom?"

Chloe peered into the adjacent room of mirrors. She shivered, and all went black.

Quinn woke up still trapped in the suffocating depths of the prison. *What was that? Was that really a vision or another trick of this maze?*

***

Quinn was forced to form alliances as her path intricately entwined with the fates of its inhabitants. She shivered as the cold, damp air clung to her skin; the stench of sweat and decay caused her nose to crinkle. She encountered a wide variety of inmates, some appeared reformed, others malicious; their true intentions were shrouded in ambiguity.

In this place, she wasn't certain of anything. Some prisoners seemed out of place, wrongfully twisted in a fate they didn't deserve. While others were exactly where they belonged, the darkness within them permeated through the mirror, the prison's own cruelty. A warning to all those who entered.

Haunted eyes peered at her from the shadows of a cell. The Fae's hollow gaze startled her. He stepped toward her, entering a beam of light that reflected throughout the prison. His thin frame creaked with the movement; he trembled as he approached the transparent barrier that separated them. The tip of his ear was missing a chunk.

"Please." His voice was raw and cracked from lack of use or desperation; she couldn't distinguish which. "I am innocent," he claimed. His voice made Quinn's heart ache.

Quinn hesitated, her chest tightened, unsure what to do or if what he said was true. His plea gnawed at her conscience, stirring emotions, mixed with fear, conflicting with her insides, making it hard to breathe.

As if sensing her indecision, he spoke again. "A jealous Fae locked me in this prison a hundred years ago." A sense of urgency painted his tone. "Please, you have to believe me," he pleaded, sending a shiver down Quinn's spine. His breath fogged the glass. The sharp scent of iron and stone alerted her to the spells that prevented magic.

Why would he need spells if he were harmless? Was this another manipulation waiting to unfold?

His eyes gleamed with something like truth, but she had been fooled by Fae before. Quinn wavered as she contemplated his plea. Could she trust him? Compassion wrestled with caution, each pulling her in opposite directions.

She swallowed hard, the taste of uncertainty bitter on her tongue. She weighed her options, torn between compassion and caution; ultimately, she chose to aid him when she came back. First, she needed to get Puck.

"I'll come back for you," she whispered, her voice strained. Her words felt flimsy and weak, as though they might shatter in the cold air. "I promise."

The Fae slammed both hands upon the transparent wall. "No, please. Help me now." Despair was evident in his words. The cuff on his left hand was cracked.

Quinn forced herself to turn away. "I can't. I'm on a mission. I'll come back for you."

Glancing back, she saw the Fae's hands slide against the barrier, leaving streaks from his palms. His face twisted with wildness and panic.

"No! Please," his voice broke, all calm slipping away.

That look over her shoulder was a mistake. His desperation tore at her heart.

"Help me now," he shouted as he slammed his fists against the glass with a vicious force, the sound reverberating through the narrow corridor. The vibrations crawled beneath Quinn's skin, not only making her flinch but deeply affecting her soul.

How can I just leave him here? A tear formed in her eye; she blinked it away before it could overtake her. She took a step away from him. He made her doubt everything. *Would walking away condemn him if he were innocent?* She forced herself to stay focused. She couldn't save everyone, not now. Quinn took another step, determined this time.

"Do not leave me here," he snarled, his voice tinged with anger. He pounded the wall once more.

His outburst frightened her. Quinn jumped, turning toward him, and his eyes flashed with a danger she hadn't seen before. She feared he'd break the wall.

"I can't," she forced herself to say as she walked away. Her feet were made of lead. "I'm on a mission. I'll come back for you." Her heart pounded painfully against her ribs.

The Fae's hands squealed, sliding down the glass. She assumed he had fallen to his knees in defeated. A choked sob escaped him, echoing after her, a knife to her heart.

"Please... don't leave me," he cried. His voice trembled with despair.

Quinn, riddled with guilt, didn't turn back. She couldn't. Not yet.

***

The echoes of past encounters still resonated within Quinn. The weight was almost too much to bear, pulling at her heartstrings. His pleading words echoed in her mind, haunting her like a waking nightmare. How many more innocents would she encounter and be forced to leave behind, trapped and forgotten? It left a suffocating feeling within her chest.

As she wandered deeper into the maze of cells, she caught glimpses of shadowy figures shrouded in fogged glass. Most were quiet. Some watched her with a distance in their eyes; others were still, in eerie silence.

Were they dead, ignoring her, or simply broken by the prison's relentless ability to force you to examine the depths of your soul?

She couldn't tell, and the uncertainty gnawed at her. She navigated the smooth mirror floors as silently as possible. Each step betrayed her, sending reverberating footsteps that echoed through the stillness. The noise ricocheted off the cold walls and amplified her presence, unwilling to let her enter unnoticed. The glassy surface beneath her feet showed her reflected form in an unnatural, fragmented manner. It showed shadows of herself she wasn't ready to face.

Her heart pounded in her chest. It grew louder with each step; she could hear it in her ears and felt it at her temples. The beating caused tension to coil tighter within. Her senses were heightened here, each sound magnified, vibrating through her bones, and the silence was almost deafening when she ceased to move.

Quinn's hands twitched with every step forward, her muscles tightly preparing for something unknown, primitive, and predatory. She thought the prison was sentient and assessing her, breathing her in, its silence causing this reaction, suffocating her.

Her eyes darted to every dark corner, anticipating. The unmoving cells increased her anxiety. The distorted reflections of those trapped behind the glass appeared out of nowhere and everywhere at once.

The slightest sound would cause her to flinch in terror. Stopping to collect herself, she noticed a prisoner staring at her; their stillness was unnerving. The hollow gaze followed her with deadly precision. Half hidden in shadow, she kept moving, not wanting to find out their intentions or their fate.

The silence wasn't the only thing that disturbed Quinn, but the feeling that something larger was watching her, hunting her. This was no mere prisoner lurking in the shadows; it was something ancient, far more sinister, a dark energy. It pulsed within the walls, a presence slithering with every step she took.

She shivered as a cold sweat engulfed her. She needed to get out of here before she found out what was stalking her. Creeping paranoia burrowed into her skin, a prickling sensation that crawled deep inside. If she wasn't fast, she might end up losing herself here. Quinn forced herself to keep moving.

Every shadow contorted unnaturally; every trace of movement caught in the corner of her eye had reached out for her. It was her reflection, one of many within the mirrors. She swallowed hard, her throat tightening.

The ancient presence was everywhere and nowhere, and her fear crept closer, overwhelming her. An invisible force tracked her, breathing down her neck. The very air hinted of malice and promises of doom.

One misstep and she'd be lost here, swallowed up, consumed by the prison. An intrusive thought crossed her mind.

If that's how the presence survived, off the essence of creatures held within these walls, then that's why the prison was built here.

Her instincts told her she was correct. It wasn't a coincidence that the presence anchored itself here, growing stronger with each tormented victim.

Was the prison built to siphon energy from the prisoners and devour them, or did the presence find the prison an easy feeding ground?

This force was violent, slow, and deliberate. Taking its time, wearing down the will of anyone who lingered too long, savoring their fear. The thought of becoming like them, an empty version of herself alone and forgotten, made her sick to her stomach.

She picked up her pace. The tapping against the mirrored floor was louder, forcing her already frayed nerves to the brink of combustion.

This must be what happened to the prisoners. Years, centuries in here, no wonder they stared off into the distance, with a ghost-like gaze.

Her heart raced, she slowed her breathing to a shallow inhale as she strained to hear over the clicking of her shoes and the pounding of her pulse. Despite her intuition, there was nothing. No voices, no movement, no surprise attacks, only the endless, suffocating quiet and miles of reflections.

The empty cells felt more like a catacomb, heavy with the weight of forgotten Fae. The damp air carried a lingering scent of mildew, mixed with something rusty and metallic. It reminded her of the distinctive stench of blood left to rot.

The first encounter with that smell was in Fata, and she was thankful Baxter was home, completely unaware of all this. She imagined him playing video games with Connor. She sucked in a deep breath. For a brief moment, she forgot Connor was gone. Her throat began to close. The reek of festering and pain threatened to smother her.

Her skin prickled with an awareness, attuned even to the air. The walls were closing in, reminding her of how vulnerable she was, and of the potential danger that lurked in the shadows.

She peeked into the cells as she passed. Many were quiet, too quiet. The inhabitants were too weak to respond or chose to ignore her. The silence was worse than the heartbreaking pleas. As a calm before a storm, it was oppressive.

Quinn pressed on; she forced her mind to calmness. The unsettling feeling that ran down her back was almost painful. It was as if a long fingernail scratched down her spine. Each step dragged her farther into the maze of reflective glass.

The whispers of her mother's presence or a human that resembled her had echoed through the dimly lit halls. It unnerved her, but she had a job to do. Each time the sound reached her ears, it served as a haunting reminder of the painful past. Her shattered family, side by side with the shattered reflections. Or the mirror she wished to shatter; the parallel wasn't lost to her.

"Quinn," her mother's distorted whisper called to her.

As Quinn had discovered that she could only free one prisoner; Puck or her mother. It only fractured her further. She didn't think she could break into small pieces, but she did. She pulled herself together, creating a mosaic, something new, born from her devastating past.

As the weight of her decision bore down on her, she steeled her heart and made the only decision she could; Puck. She made a binding pact, and she didn't wish to discover the consequences if broken. Despite her decision, it still tore at her insides. The memory gnawed at her about the promise to Ophelia.

As she gazed upon Puck's reflection, an agonizing internal struggle pulled at her. Puck, the loathsome Fae she despised, was now within view. Now, his eyes possessed a vulnerability she'd never seen.

Her emotions wavered as she knew her choice. Walking toward him, she kept hitting dead ends like a cruel joke. She'd bump into fake walls of glass. The harder she tried to reach him, the farther she got. Trying a different approach, she turned her back on him and walked away.

Quinn started to get close. She recalled reading in an ancient text that you couldn't merely walk in and go where you desired; instead, you had to surrender and let it take you to the destination.

She could still hear her mother's voice. Brokenhearted, Quinn turned from her mother's echoing whisper and searched for Puck. She didn't have to walk far. His chamber loomed before her. This wasn't an illusion; her necklace lit up, lighting the path.

Her hand shook as she touched the glass. It trembled beneath her touch. A surge of magic sparked, and the color of the wall changed. She drew close to him. Puck turned, his form blurred, and then solidified. He limped out to where Quinn was as if he walked through smoke. The shard must've unlocked him.

The moment I chose it became easy.

The decision weighed heavily on her shoulders. Bittersweet relief and grief washed over her at the same time. She met Puck's gaze, guilt-ridden, no words needed. He knew the sacrifice and nodded. A silent understanding had passed between them.

Puck knew she had chosen, and in doing so, she had decided on a course of events that would forever alter her life. She nodded back, and he staggered. Quinn's instincts moved to catch him. He leaned most of his weight onto her. She supported him without faltering.

"I've got you." Together, they proceeded to move carefully down the hall.

Chapter 18: Confronting the Past

Silence stretched between them. The close proximity allowed Quinn to explore Puck's history, both willingly and not. She uncovered his motivations and deepest regrets, piecing together that he had been saving Ophelia from being murdered when he killed the Fae.

It wasn't a cold-blooded act, but one born of desperation. He didn't commit the unforgivable crime out of malice or cruelty, but out of love by defending Ophelia's life; he had saved her from a fate worse than death, to be forever cursed and bound as an Unseelie. He didn't belong in the prison world. She felt for him. He was only protecting his lover. She would've done the same for her brother.

Her heart softened as her perception of Puck shifted as she learned about his complexities and vulnerabilities. She still thought of him as an arrogant prick, but his motives weren't evil. His actions were harsh but weren't sinister, and he didn't deserve to be locked away.

She also learned that "Puck" wasn't even his real name, but a persona, a mask, to hide behind. Beneath it, he was far more vulnerable than she'd imagined. Despite her attempts, she couldn't uncover his real name.

"Names are different in our realm," was all he would say on the matter.

Past events and choices came back to haunt them both, adding emotional depth to their strange connection. Learning of the ridicule he'd endured as a child, and how he was meant to be switched into the human world as a baby, that his parents didn't want him. He was an orphan.

The stillness of the halls left Quinn unsettled. Occasionally, she'd see artwork disintegrating on the walls. The quiet was the prelude to something huge. Not a tapestry rustled, nor a single creature scurried. The air pressed in around her like a fog enveloping her. The glow of reflected moonlight painted silver patches on the moss-covered ground, illuminating everything between them.

Puck's mischievous stance was replaced by a rigid posture with his back to her, his arms at his sides. That effortless smirk, with all its arrogance, was gone. Instead, raw emotion, something he'd never displayed, at least not to Quinn.

"They got rid of me," he said, his hands curled into fists. "I could not understand." He paused. "Why?" His breath hitched.

Quinn could sense his pain. She placed a tentative hand on his arm.

"What happened?" she asked, her voice soft.

Puck let out a bitter laugh. "I was supposed to be switched with a human." The disdain in his voice was heavy.

No wonder he hates humans.

"To be traded like garbage," he said. Then he whispered, "They did not want me." He turned toward her, pain and something darker in his eyes. "The exchange never happened. Some seer changed that. So, they abandoned me." His eyes filled with unshed tears.

She'd never seen this side of him. She'd been certain he didn't have a soft bone in his body, but now, seeing him so full of pain, she understood the tough facade. Quinn's stomach knotted. It was easier to hate him. But now, he was open, so vulnerable.

"I was orphaned," he continued. "Not because my parents were killed. Because they left me."

Quinn didn't know what to say. He looked into her eyes.

"I wasn't good enough." Puck's voice cracked as he spoke. He inhaled sharply and shook his head. "And you know what the worst part is? Everyone knew." He turned away.

Quinn tried to move to face him, but he wouldn't let her.

"I was unwanted by everyone. What other choice did I have but to become what I became?" he turned and asked her. A single tear escaped.

Quinn's throat tightened. She could imagine little Puck, sad and alone, developing that defiant arrogance as a protective mechanism. Being too young and learning how cruel the world could be.

She rubbed his arm in a comforting manner. He twitched but didn't pull away. "They were wrong to leave you," she said.

He looked back at her.

"You deserved better. Parents are supposed to take care of you," Quinn continued. The silence stretched. She thought he wouldn't say anymore. Quinn removed her hand.

"Funny. I pretend it does not matter," he said. He paused and glanced up. "But it does."

"You matter," Quinn said.

Puck wore a faint smile and said, "Thank you."

She smiled back, no words needed.

Her feelings had shifted; she felt bad about his past and found his vulnerabilities made him more relatable. The growing hostility spurred by their interactions in the past began to give way to a new, yet reluctant understanding. She started to recognize the complexities and multi-layers that defined him.

While discovering Puck's past, tensions escalated as Quinn delved deeper; her probing questions caused hints of his arrogant demeanor to return. His time in prison, completely giving up, had changed him.

He softened and ended up answering her inquiries. He had nothing left to lose and everything to gain, his freedom.

Having dug into his past, armed with questions and her new power, Quinn learned of the struggles to Puck endured to persevere. He'd been the outcast, ridiculed by his peers, and faced the hardships alone; his family wasn't known to him. He had been abandoned, an orphan, and unwanted by his parents. He was to be switched with a human child, which added an additional layer of misery to his story. He later discovered he was the son of a slave and royalty, so he fit in nowhere.

Quinn never would've guessed that this journey would shatter her perception of this Fae who had once been her foe.

She pulled from her newly gained knowledge from the ancient texts to unearth the exit, for one couldn't exit the prison the way in which one entered.

She had a waking dream that Puck's parents hadn't abandoned him but were killed. She wasn't sure if he could handle that truth in this moment. For once, she was unsure if it was even true; the realm was making her doubt everything. It was best not to mention this now.

Her heart ached as all the pieces fell into place. Puck wasn't only the arrogant jerk who had constantly challenged her; he had a vulnerable side. He was in love and willing to make the ultimate sacrifice. A pang of sympathy ran through her, making her shiver.

Quinn's conflicted emotions swirled within her. Despite what she uncovered, she still regarded Puck as the selfish Fae who infuriated her, yet realizing his complexities and vulnerabilities tugged at her heart. This world had a way of confronting the innermost elements of a person, laying bare their deepest regrets, desires, and true selves.

It wasn't lost upon her, the parallel between herself and Puck. They both had faced isolation and hardship due to forces beyond their control, which led them to lie about their actions. It was as if the mirrors held a reflection of her soul, forcing her to see things as they truly were and confront her insecurities.

As Quinn and Puck's paths continued, a bond formed between them. A connection forged by shared pain and regrets.

Although Quinn's perception shifted, that didn't mean she liked or even forgave him for how he'd behaved. It meant he wasn't the evil villain, locked up for a product of his circumstances. As she journeyed through the prison, each layer unveiled a new level of humanity. She was forced to have visions of the prisoners, seeing how some were innocent.

This added a new depth of emotion and complexity to her mission; she knew she couldn't veer off course, or she'd fail. She was unsure if the prison or its inhabitants could morph her sense of reality. All she knew was that nothing could have prepared her for this, not even with her gift of Sight.

Chapter 19 : Trials of the Heart

Quinn's emotional stability wavered with each reflective corridor. The passages folded into in endless loops, yet she couldn't figure out how to stop. Puck wasn't any help at the moment, he barely said a word. The images pulled at her heartstrings or taunted her. She saw visions of her turning away from her mom while saving Puck. Her mom falling to her knees crying.

Her mother reached for her with tears in her eyes, then the image faded. Each one increased her doubt. Puck trailed her and in a reflection she saw him stop and whisper to a Fae whose face twisted into a mocking smile. Quinn turned to catch him in the act.

Puck raised an eyebrow at her but didn't say anything.

Am I the hero or hypocrite here? Puck needs my help, but do I really want to help him, or am I only doing this for Ophelia and Seraphina? If they found out, would they still consider me a friend, or would I become a foe?

Each difficult decision she'd made caused small pieces of her to crack, like broken bones, and forced her to question her values, losing some of her empathy.

How can I leave these Fae here, knowing some are innocent?

The growing connection between Quinn and Puck complicated her commitment to the mission. She'd learned there was another human in the prison and couldn't help but wonder if it was Connor. The body was never recovered, and the possibility that he fell through a trapdoor remained. One never knew in Fata.

Dismissing the thought, as the odds of a loved one being in this prison were minimal. She didn't want to get her hopes up.

There's no way Connor could've survived that fall.

This prison was treacherous, proving to be a journey through each of her emotions and breaking down her inner self. The dilemmas presented to her in this realm tugged at her values and morals, forcing her to make difficult decisions that may weigh heavily on her.

Who could I save? Could I leave a loved one behind?

As the challenges progressed, they increased in difficulty. Quinn was faced with obstacles designed to push her boundaries, blurring the lines between right and wrong. She wanted to help everyone, and yet she couldn't. She began to question her sanity.

The reflections showed more than glimpses of herself, moments from her past where she had failed others. Things didn't go as planned, adding to her momentous guilt and self-doubt. Among all the added pressure, she couldn't breathe. Alternate versions of how the turn of events should've or could've gone bore down on her.

Am I making the right decision? Is that what happened? It messed with her mind.

The cool and dampness here was like a basement. Quinn hated basements. Her first panic attack was in a basement. She accidentally locked herself in as a child, afraid of the dark.

Visions of Baxter haunted Quinn as they flashed in the corridor. A scene depicted her leaving him when he needed her the most. Baxter was on his knees, pleading with her to help him and not go to Fata.

His voice rang out among the other horrors. The vision showed her turning her back on him, then the image shifted. He was lying on the ground, and his chest wasn't moving.

Oh, Baxter, what have I done?

Quinn's throat tightened as she choked back a sob. *This isn't real. I'd never leave him, but I did. He didn't ask me for help, though.* She shook her head and ran from the sight. She couldn't handle letting her brother down or worse, causing his death.

Celeste tried to teach her to see what was real, yet she ignored her warnings. She guessed what happened with the glasses and stone incident. Her pride had gotten in her way. She possessed more raw power than Celeste could ever dream of, but she lacked the discipline and knowledge to wield that power safely.

I should've tried harder, practiced longer.

She thought she knew it all, but her arrogance had risked the safety of her friends. A fleeting vision of her pride cost Connor's life. If she had only listened, perhaps Connor might've been alive today.

A single tear ran down her cheek. Some scenes suggested that saving Connor would have endangered or caused her to lose Baxter. If given the choice, Quinn would choose her twin every single time.

That realization twisted her insides so tight she thought she'd burst. That made her the same as Puck, a selfish person. She loved Connor and never wanted anything bad to happen, but she'd sacrifice him to save Baxter. This forced her to grapple with who she was as a person. Who was she to prioritize lives?

Could I make a decision?

It felt like an arrow had pierced her heart. Heat rippled through her as she understood Puck better. He'd do anything to save Ophelia.

How could I blame him for having such convictions? At least he was firm in his beliefs. She'd never been this honest with herself. *If given the opportunity to redo it all, I'd probably hesitate and lose them both. Puck's been so quiet in allowing me to process.*

"I need a moment," Puck said before collapsing to the tiled floor. Sweat covered his brow.

"Are you okay?" Quinn asked, kneeling beside him.

"I will be," he said with stain in his voice.

She made sure he was comfortable, allowing him to lean against the wall and her body. His skin felt clammy.

Quinn dug through her pack and retrieved the snack Seraphina had folded in a leaf for her. The only comfort in this hopeless place. She gave some to Puck.

He eyed it but said nothing. It was working; his complexion was returning to normal, but not as fast as she wanted. He wasn't as much of a shell of his former self. They rested only for a few moments; it wasn't safe to linger.

"We have to keep moving if we are to escape," Puck said.

She offered him a hand, which he declined with a half-smile.

As they walked, Puck didn't have so much of his weight on her shoulder. He even started to gaze up. The cruel illusions tricked her. Though she thought she was moving forward, in reality, they retraced their steps. She'd dropped torn pieces of the leaf as a sort of breadcrumb trail. Still, she returned to the trail of leaves twice.

Is this my trail of leaves or an illusion? She crumpled the remaining leaf in her hand and discarded it.

Visions of the exit were before her. When she followed, she was back where she started, angry and with frustrated tears pricking her eyes. Puck even had trouble navigating; he seemed so weak.

One image of her transformed her into a woman she barely recognized. This version of herself had complete control over her powers, effortlessly commanding Fata and bending its laws to her wishes.

An intoxicating thought, the idea tempted her, implying that acknowledging her abilities could stop future tragedies. Yet, Quinn recognized the vacant look in her eyes; this path could risk her compassion or even her humanity.

The vision showed that if she went down that path, there would be no coming back. She'd be consumed by power, as Mr. Perry was. She sympathized with him, yet no matter how sincere and innocent his intentions were, he was unable to save the day or a loved one. She couldn't lose herself in the process, or it would have devastating effects. Perhaps an even worse outcome for those she left behind.

Quinn caught glimpses of Connor or her mother in fleeting visions, but she couldn't trust them to be real. All the illusions confused her. They lingered long enough to tear out her heart. She had to complete this task, or Fata's illusions would be the end of her.

Each interaction was a precarious, delicate dance when one's life depended on the rhythm, and the other didn't know the moves. The unspoken tension tore at the last thread of her humanity.

As they continued their journey, they overcame challenges together, strengthening their bond, which neither had expected to form. Puck helped her see she had to leave this place for her own well-being.

"If not, we will both be captured, and you will be of no use to anyone. You can return at a later time and rescue the people you desire. Right now, we have about five minutes before the guards notice I am no longer in my cell."

She found she'd rather like his company despite the setting. He was particularly comforting when she had an emotional breakdown. She teetered between hyperventilating and passing out.

Her heart pounded viciously as it attempted to escape her chest. Puck guided her gently, his hands steady on her shoulders as he coaxed her to place her head between her knees. Her breath came in shallow gasps.

With a firm but gentle hand on her shoulder, he murmured, "Take a long, slow, deep breath, let it fill you completely. Now hold it." His voice grounded her like an anchor in all her chaos. He dropped his hands from her shoulders.

Quinn nodded as she complied; the whites of her eyes grew smaller.

"Good," he said in a steady tone. His voice comforted her. After a few moments, he continued, "Now let it out, nice and slow. Force every bit out, and with it, all your tension."

He placed a reassuring hand on her back, moving it in a circular motion. "Just like that," he said. His touch was filled with a gentleness she didn't think he was capable of. "Now, do it again."

She followed his instructions and nodded as each exhale released the death grip on her lungs. Her wild eyes gradually softened, and her breath returned to normal; a serene calmness washed over her.

Is this his power, to influence or heighten emotion?

"Excellent," he said. The audible compassion in his voice helped relax her further.

After a time, once Quinn's breathing steadied and her thoughts cleared, Puck unleashed an epic confession. "I overheard the guards talking," he said, his voice barely above a whisper. "They mentioned another human here." He hesitated. This information could push her over the edge; she already teetered on the brink of a panic attack.

Upon discovering this information, Quinn struggled to breathe. A jolt of possibility and devastation flowed through her veins. The possibility of someone else trapped within the prison sparked the belief that Connor could be alive.

Her visions were true. A body was never recovered; he merely disappeared. However, that fall would be extremely difficult to survive. Her heart skipped as a glimmer of hope grew. She forced herself to dismiss the notion before it took hold. Her stomach grew warm despite her attempts to ignore the idea.

"I have to find them, whoever it is."

"I know," he said. "Can we find the exit first?"

Quinn knew the odds of Connor and her mother both being imprisoned here were highly improbable, yet the twist of fate was so outlandish it almost seemed plausible.

She had witnessed stranger things, but she couldn't allow herself to believe it, not when the stakes were so high. She had to remain focused no matter how tempting it was. There was no way Connor could've survived that fall into the abyss.

Her inner struggle mirrored the trials she faced. Her commitment to disposing of Puck clashed with tangled feelings. Despite warming to him, she was still left with the ghost of Connor's absence. It lingered and may forever haunt her. She recalled how callous Puck was to her friend.

They pressed forward despite the way her heart hurt, and each breath was an agonizing squeeze. Puck's limp had improved. The path ahead would determine if she honed her skills enough or not.

Am I ready?

It would require an unwavering command of her emotions and her commitment to her values. The courage to confront the complexities without wavering would be a challenge, but she was ready to face it. Either way, this would be over soon.

Quinn changed her mind. "I have to try and find the other human while we're here. I may never get another chance. I can't leave without at least looking for the other human. I'd have to live with myself if we escape. This might be my only chance. Once it's discovered that you've escaped, they may lock down the prison, and we'll never get back in."

Taking a steadying breath, she turned around in search of the human.

Puck nodded. "I knew you would say that."

145

Chapter 20: The Other Human

Quinn clung to the faint promise that the trapped human might be her mother. All she knew was she had to rescue whomever it was. She couldn't leave an innocent person in this chaos.

Along the way, one prisoner had intentionally sent her in the wrong direction. Puck was feeling better, but not enough to navigate the maze. Her instincts had kicked in after a few minutes, and she realized the prisoner had lied to her, and she doubled back.

Quinn had quickly adjusted her path, and her persistence was rewarded. After hours of searching, finding dead ends and twisting paths, she found the cell that contained the human. She approached the glass, seeing the round ears, lack of intense colors, and no exaggerated shapes on the skin like bark.

Although the clothing was tattered, she recognized him instantly. Her shock hit her like an earthquake; it shook her to the core. Connor was alive. Her breath caught in her narrowing throat.

Tears formed in her eyes. Her dear, sweet, goofy, Connor. Elation replaced the shock. Her happiness overwhelmed her, so intense that her knees wobbled.

She flung her hand to the cold, reflective surface to steady herself. Puck was there in a split second, his piercing gaze slid from her to Connor, a smirk on his face.

Could this be an illusion?

She shook her head; she'd know him anywhere. While it was definitely Connor, something about him was somehow different. A strangeness clung to him like a shadow.

Did he develop some kind of power, an unnatural resilience from being exposed to something here?

Maybe a twisted "gift" left by Mr. Perry, who'd vanished without a trace after the battle in the arena. Whatever Connor had endured, it marked him and altered his fate. After a moment, she called to him.

"Connor." Her voice was tentative and low, barely above a whisper. He didn't move. "Connor?" she asked, more to herself. She made a fist and hit the glass with her hand. "Connor," she repeated, louder this time.

He finally moved, albeit sluggishly, as if swatting at a mosquito that was annoying him. With a wave of his hand, he let it drop back into place, lifelessly.

"Unless you are trying to alert the guards to our location, I suggest you lower your voice," Puck hissed. He held her up by the elbow. Quinn only nodded.

"I thought you were dead," Quinn explained. Her mouth quivered as if she'd seen a ghost; well, in this case, she had. "Answer me," she demanded.

The person rolled over, possessing very little energy. It was definitely Connor, yet he was a shell of his former self.

"Another hallucination," he said, and motioned his finger in a circle. Then he turned back over as he said, "Yay."

"Connor, it's really me," she said in a desperate voice. She took a steadying breath. "There isn't time for this. I've come to get you out."

He flipped back with a groan, without enthusiasm, still not convinced. "Stop lying, or I'll get the de-*fib*-rillator," he said. He eyed her, disbelief written all over his face.

"What happened to you?" she asked. Not waiting for a reply, she pressed, "How did you get here?"

"Quinn never got my jokes, fib… Never mind." His eyes widened at the sight of her, and he blinked. Then he noticed

Puck, and his face twisted into a scowl. "Get away from her," he shouted, pointing at Puck.

Puck feigned insult. "Well, isn't this a touching reunion," he said.

"Shh, you'll alert the guards," Quinn warned and placed her index finger to her lips.

Connor rubbed his eyes and sat up. "What's he doing here?" he asked with evident disdain as he continued to point at Puck.

Puck bowed. "I would not miss this for the world," he said, and his mocking smile reminded her of the first time they met.

How infuriating he was back then. Gone was the kind, gentle Puck she had come to know.

"There's no time," Quinn said, slicing through their hostile, glaring contest. "We've gotta get out of here."

With a dramatic sweep of his hand, Puck gestured for them to exit the area. "Then, by all means, let us go. We can catch up on all these pleasantries later."

Connor stepped back. He crossed his arms. "I'm not going anywhere with you," Connor snarled.

Quinn sighed in frustration. It hadn't occurred to her that this may happen. Connor might not leave with her. She shook her head and dismissed the possibility.

"How did you end up here?" she asked, fumbling through her backpack for something.

Connor shrugged. His exhaustion was apparent, but something else was there as well, irritation.

"I don't know. I fell and woke up here."

Puck scoffed.

Connor's eyes shot daggers at him.

Quinn shifted her gaze between the two of them. Connor was holding something back.

"That's it?" she asked, eyebrows raised.

"It's a long story. One, I'm not sure I'd say in front of him," he said, jabbing at Puck with a sneer.

Puck had threatened Connor by throwing a dagger past his face. She wasn't sure what Puck's intentions had been when he threw that dagger. Connor's mood was understandable, but Quinn didn't have time for this.

Quinn suppressed her sigh. It wouldn't help. So, she tabled the conversation for now. Quinn fished out the cloth-wrapped shard and attempted to locate a spot to unlock his cell. She felt for an invisible keyhole.

Puck's cell had been easy. Why was Connor's so much harder?

"I can't find the damn lock," she said.

"I checked this entire cell. I never felt a lock," Connor replied. His shoulders slumped.

Puck, with his height, reached up and grabbed onto an invisible ledge. He maneuvered himself up into a pull-up position with ease. Quinn hardly believed his fluidity despite his weakened appearance. He crouched on a transparent platform, his knees up by his chin. Puck leaned forward, extending his arm to Quinn, fingers splayed.

"Give me the key," he said.

Connor said as he stepped forward, "Don't do it, Quinn." He reached the edge of his cell and placed both palms on the glass.

Quinn froze. She had to trust Puck to get out of here. She'd never be able to reach that high.

She handed Puck the shard. A sizzling sound caught her attention; the shard must be burning him. He lifted the shard to the lock he found with haste and passed it back to her. It felt cold in her hand.

"What was that?" she asked, eyes wide.

"Nothing," Puck said and looked away. He opened a mirrored door, which became visible once it was open. Puck reached down with his arm for Connor to grab. Connor stepped back.

"Connor, please," she cried. "There's no time. We've gotta get out of here."

Connor wrinkled his nose, but he reached for Puck's hand. Puck pulled him up as if he weighed nothing. The platform wasn't large enough for both of them. Puck slid over, and Connor clung on with his other hand.

Puck jumped; he released Connor's grip, and the jerking movement almost sent him tumbling back. He managed to catch himself and pulled himself the rest of the way onto the ledge.

Connor struggled a lot; he used his feet to kick himself up. Once he was crouching, Puck reached up to help. Connor scoffed and leaped from the perch. His knees buckled the moment he landed, and he lurched forward. Puck was there to catch him before his face hit the ground.

Quinn's heart flipped as Connor confirmed what she had barely begun to believe.

"I saw your mom here. She's somewhere in this labyrinth."

But I can only take one. She really is here.

She caught glimpses of her mother in the ever-changing reflections, believing they were a part of the illusions. Her mother's face flickered within the walls, her heart broke even more, shattering into fragments of what it once was.

Quinn was now more determined than ever to go back and rescue her mother once again. She may end up releasing this entire prison before she escaped herself. As she attempted to reach her mother, she was met with dead ends and doubling corridors, with Connor and Puck by her side.

The maze was relentless, wrapping back around itself as if it were intentionally obscuring her path to her mother. The males were quiet, which she thought was just the way she'd preferred it. Yet the silence was even more nerve-racking.

Quinn was close enough to see her mother. She could even hear her, yet she couldn't figure out how to get to her. Quinn kicked the glass before her, hoping to smash her way through. Puck's hand was on her shoulder. He shook his head.

"I'm so close, yet so far." It was heart-wrenching. Quinn was so fatigued from the miles she'd walked with little rest.

She ignored her body's protest to stop. She'd save all of them.

The silence was broken by a loud shout, followed by an ear-splitting alarm that reverberated through the passageways. All three of them covered their ears. A guard had spotted them.

Quinn turned and saw her mother's face again, with terrified eyes, the white growing larger.

"Quinn, go!" her mother cried out, as desperate as she'd ever heard her speak. "Save yourself. I'll be alright."

Torn, Quinn hesitated, her heart sinking. But her mother urged her to go.

Her lower lip quivered. "I'll come back for you," she promised as her voice cracked.

Quinn fled as tears stung her eyes, her mother's image seared into her memory. She looked older, weaker, and more frail. Her time in prison had worn her down. No longer the unbreakable woman Quinn remembered, in her place stood a ghostly, haunting reminder of what was lost.

***

After hours of evading the endless stream of guards and meeting repeated dead ends, Quinn trusted her instincts and used her abilities. She discovered an exit, a narrow, shimmering bridge made of a shining, reflective glass.

Another mirror.

It stretched across a vast chasm, the bottom not visible, an unknown abyss. The glass was thin and delicate, as though it might shatter under the slightest weight. Her heart pounded, and it was difficult to swallow; her throat was tight with a threatening panic attack as she stared at the path.

Each heartbeat was a reminder of her fear. The darkness and narrowness of the bridge made navigation difficult. Connor went first. He dropped to his hands and knees and crawled to feel for the path ahead. He moved with caution, testing each step and the bridge's ability to hold him.

Behind him, Quinn struggled, fighting her fear with every hesitant step forward. The darkness was closing in, making the bridge appear even narrower, its twists impossible to navigate with so many reflections. They played tricks on her, casting false directions, while the bridge twisted in subtle, deceptive ways.

Puck remained silent behind her, his presence oddly comforting, as if he anchored her.

Then, a sharp crack pierced the air, so sudden it sent Quinn's tiny hairs on her neck up. Connor stood and ran as the bridge splintered. Quinn could see a large crack following him. It was moving too fast. She could see the stone wall at the end, the exit.

"Jump!" Puck shouted. He moved so fast, Quinn didn't see him whisk her into his arms as if she weighed nothing.

A shard broke free and fell into oblivion. Connor launched into the air and reached the end right as the bridge collapsed, leaving Quinn and Puck stranded, and trapped in the prison.

Her breath hitched in her throat as she stared at the vast distance between them.

"Connor," she said breathlessly. The pain was audible in her voice. She almost lost him again.

"What can I do? I can't leave you," he said, his voice tight with emotion.

Quinn shrugged, tears threatening to fall. The echo of his voice was enough to break her; hearing it once was enough.

"We can't risk it," she whispered, voice trembling. "If you don't go now, you may never escape."

"There's no way the guards didn't hear that." Connor's voice was high-pitched and desperate. "I'm not leaving you here." He waved his arm across his body.

"You must go. Now!" Puck demanded, his voice sharp, cutting through the chaos, leaving no room for an argument.

Connor's gaze flickered between Quinn and the crumbled path. The sound of the alarm echoed in the distance. Each ring forced a sense of urgency.

He shook his head, his body stiff with anguish, and sighed. His body hunched in resignation. "I will find a way to you," he promised.

"Just get out of here, maybe find help, but get out," Quinn said. She was already turning around, seeking a new exit.

Connor was quiet for a moment. "Promise me you'll get out alive," he cried, his words breaking with the pain in his voice.

Quinn froze. It was already too difficult to leave him again. She looked over her shoulder.

"I will. You've gotta go, now." She continued walking without looking back. Tears streaked her cheeks. She couldn't bear it, so she ran off.

***

The most unsettling vision loomed before them. A guard, its physique a grotesque fusion of Fae and nightmare. Its face resembled melted plastic stretched haphazardly over charred wood. The uneven surface was stiff in the dim light.

Its movements were mechanical, each step a jerking motion, deliberate, like a marionette controlled by strings. Despite its disjointed gait, Quinn sensed the lethal energy radiating from it. The sentinel was a sheer predator, designed only for precision and violence.

Her throat tightened, paralyzing a scream before it could escape. Puck was a flash before her eyes. In the blur, she saw him strike. Though he had looked weakened moments ago, he showed no sign now. He was swift and precise, a deadly combination.

Quinn could barely register that Puck had dispatched the guard before she could process what had happened. A crumpled pile on the ground was all that was left. Puck knelt beside the fallen watchman. He radiated the stillness of a statue, and a flicker of Ophelia flashed in her mind.

Quinn blinked, not knowing what to say. She murmured, "Thanks."

He peered at her from beneath his lashes, eyes sharp and distant. "It was merely self-preservation," he replied, his voice detached.

Without another word, he rose to his feet and continued walking, as if nothing had transpired.

Quinn hesitated for a moment, hoping to untangle the knots in her stomach with some calming breaths. A sense of unease overcame her.

How could Puck fight so effortlessly when he looked that fatigued mere moments ago?

She'd forgotten how deadly he could be. She sighed.

What choice do I have?

Regardless of the potential danger he posed, she had a mission to complete. Quinn hurried to catch up to him. His stride was resolute, determined. His long legs made it difficult to keep up, forcing her to jog.

"Where can we get out now?" she asked, tone defeated.

"There are many ways out," he said cryptically. "As there are many ways in."

Quinn sighed once more, noting her unanswered question.

"If you keep breathing like that, you may pass out," Puck remarked, his tone unreadable.

Her forehead scrunched up as she turned to glance at him, attempting to decipher his hidden meaning.

Is he teasing me or just annoyed with my breathing? Quinn decided to leave it alone for now. They still had to find a way out and avoid the patrol.

Chapter 21: A Name Like Monk E

Connor

Panting, Connor hesitated and took a cautious look around. Now that he had escaped, he stood at the edge of an ordinary-looking forest. A faint shimmer caught his eye through the trees. Without his necklace, which was confiscated by the guards, this realm appeared deceptively serene. On previous visits to the forest, he had seen vibrant colors and unimaginable creatures.

Unable to see threats and aware he was in grave danger, he noted many glinting crystal rocks, the prison, no doubt. Every step was a potential trap. He may even appear to be walking on a flat surface and end up at the bottom of a ravine.

He clenched his jaw, frustration setting in. *How can I help them if I can't help myself? I need to find Celeste or Seraphina. They'd know what to do.*

Connor marveled at a tree. The trunk was gnarled and spiraled around itself. Wisps of translucent, violet puffs clung to the end of the branches, like they were floating cotton candy made from starlight. He blinked as it shimmered.

"A kissing tree, where two great lives sacrificed all and perished together. Their eternal love lives on in the tree, contributing to the collective pool of magic."

"Who said that?"

He entered the woods and ducked as a ripple of air brushed past his left ear.

"Hey, watch it!" Connor called out, irritation evident.

"It is not safe for you here, human," a high-pitched, robotic voice called back.

Connor scowled toward the voice. "Tell me something I don't know," Connor replied into the forest, unable to see what flew past him. He scanned the tree line, desperate to find something.

"You are close to a portal," the voice continued. "Yet without aid, you will never see it."

Connor grunted and wiped his forehead with the back of his hand. "Will you help me?"

His request was met with a long silence. "I will…for a favor," the voice finally answered.

His stomach clenched. "What favor?" Connor asked, hesitation in his voice.

He knew all too well that a favor wasn't always a small task, especially here. The price may be heavy.

But what else can I do? I'm trapped here, helpless, while Quinn fights for her life.

"I will name my price when I need your aid," it answered cryptically. "Deal, human?"

He thought about it and balled his fists. "No way, I want to know
the favor now."

"I will name the favor when I need it. I possess no need now."

You never make a deal without knowing all the outcomes. They can be so fickle. I need to hurry to help Quinn. "I guess I don't have a choice," he said to the ground.

There was no point in looking for the speaker without some sort of assistance.

A sudden swooshing sound flew by once more, and something struck his shoulder and fell to the ground.

Connor crouched to pick it up, and his breath latched in his throat. "My necklace. How…?"

He slipped on the necklace and blinked hard. Vast and vibrant colors flooded his vision, like a kaleidoscope, the shimmer momentarily blinding him. He staggered and raised a hand to cover his eyes.

As his vision adjusted, he looked around. Hidden in plain sight, a murky swamp lay before him, swirling with thick, dark muck. No doubt so thick, he wouldn't come out.

"Not to worry, human," it answered. "You must go around this bog and avoid the Impenetrable Forest."

"If it's impenetrable, what does it matter if I go near it?"

"It is impenetrable, not because you cannot get in. That none have ever exited."

"That's not what impenetrable means," he protested.

"I did not make the name."

"It's a stupid name."

It ignored his comment. "The portal lies beyond the bog, camouflaged. I will take you, for it is a well-guarded secret. You must not share the location with anyone."

Connor frowned. "How am I supposed to bring help if I can't tell anyone where it is?"

"That is for you to figure out."

A flapping sound made him turn toward the right.

"What happens if I tell someone?"

The rustling sounded again. "May you never find out," it answered as it flapped before him.

That bird. Connor's eyes widened as he pinpointed the voice. "I know you," he shouted, pointing. "You're Celeste's bird."

The parrot tilted its head; its golden eyes narrowed with intelligence. "You know nothing of me, human," the parrot answered, distaste in its voice.

Its feathers were a shimmery green with a dark chestnut-colored patch on its forehead.

He flinched as the parrot flapped its iridescent green wings, revealing glimmers of red and blue feathers, and landed nearby. When the wings were tucked in, they appeared mostly green.

The bird twitched its head in an erratic pattern. "I am owned by no one," the parrot huffed. "Especially the inferior human."

For once, Connor knew better than to argue. *This bird was at Celeste's house.*

The parrot flapped its shimmering wings toward the edge of the swamp, feathers light like polished emeralds, changing to different shades of iridescent green as if they vibrated with color. A good disguise.

"Follow closely, human. Stray, and you may become a part of Fata forever," it called.

Connor gulped, taking in the vibrant, shimmering terrain surrounding him. Without another word, he followed the mysterious bird. Shadows twisted where no shadows should exist, and the air thrummed with energy.

A bubble escaped the bog and popped, releasing noxious gas into the air. Connor grimaced. *That can't be good.*

The teal glass-like grass released a delicate, musical chime with each step he took. The sound echoed through the air. Though strange, it would've been beautiful if it weren't so unnerving.

"What's your name, anyway?" he asked after following the bird in uncomfortable silence, his curiosity piqued.

The bird landed on a low-hanging branch, its sharp eyes level with Connor's. It tilted its head and shook it several times, ruffling its feathers until they stood on end. The parrot appeared larger, more menacing.

"You cannot possibly pronounce my true name, human. You may call me Monk E."

Connor blinked, then a laugh burst from him before he could stop it. "Monkey," he repeated, while laughing still. "Your name's Monkey." He chuckled once more.

The bird puffed its chest with indignation, launched off the perch, and dove at him with surprising speed. At the very last second, it swerved away, wind brushing his cheek.

"Insolent human!" it squawked, circling him as a predator would before landing on another branch. "I am aiding you, preventing your demise, and you laugh at me?"

Connor raised his palms in surrender, trying not to grin, but the corners of his lips twitched.

"Sorry, but... Monkey?" He struggled to hold it in and only chuckled once despite the parrot's murderous glare. "Your name is Monkey." He burst at the seams, his laughter spilling out.

The parrot's irritation was evident in the angry ruffle of its feathers. "Find your own secret portal then," it snapped and prepared to take flight.

"Wait, please. Alright," Connor said, his laughter fading. "I'm sorry." He bowed his head in an amusing attempt at remorse.

Unmoving, the parrot muttered, "Hmph."

Connor exhaled slowly. He had no other choice but to trust the parrot; something told him the bird was looking out for him, even if its motives were unclear. Unable to keep his questions to himself, as silence was never his strength.

"So, how did you come by that name?" he asked, his curiosity getting the better of him.

"It is a great honor. I am the fifth monk of the Temple of Transformation, a guardian of all. Once we reach enlightenment, we shed our birth names to transcend." Monk E puffed up his feathers with pride.

"Lose your name?" Connor frowned. "Doesn't that make things difficult? I mean, how do you talk to each other?"

With a sharp click of its beak, the sound pierced the air. "We acquire titles based on order of transcendence. I am the fifth, and so I am Monk E. We go by the order we become, and since numbers are used for other purposes, we go by letters."

"I can't imagine a bird-monk temple."

"It's the Temple of Transformation. Say it correctly or not at all," Monk E corrected him. "And we are not a temple of birds. First off, I am in macaw form, and second…"

"What?! You can change forms? So cool," Connor cut Monk E off.

The parrot took to the air without warning. "Keep up, human," it commanded, shutting down the conversation. "We cannot linger."

Connor had to adjust his pace to a run to keep up. Monk E may have given him a second chance, but it wasn't moving at a leisurely pace any longer. He had a feeling he couldn't afford to lose the bird. A third chance was unlikely.

It was silent, the forest absorbed all sound, even the ground was muted, and the chime from the grass was absorbed. The swamp was unnaturally still; the shadows no longer danced in the swirls as if holding its breath. The atmosphere felt heavier as if in warning. Monk E tensed as if he sensed it as well.

"Make haste," Monk E said, its tone urgent. "Darkness approaches."

Connor shivered as a chill ran down his spine. He instinctively placed his hand over the necklace.

"This is where I must leave you," Monk E said, voice clipped. "The portal is right behind that tree." Monk E gestured ahead with his beak.

"Hey, you can't just," Connor started to protest, but was cut off by a rustling sound that had them both silent.

Connor held his breath in anticipation. The sound grew closer, and his heart pounded. The sound was nearly upon them. Then a ball of fur pounced from the brush and darted for them. Connor flinched and stumbled back. He fell hard, knocking the wind from him.

"On your bottom once more I see, human," it said in a silky voice. A Siamese cat-like creature sauntered toward him. It plucked a strand of Connor's hair and shoved it into a straw like totem; it looked like a voodoo doll.

"Ow," he said rubbing his head. "What was that for?"

Connor blinked as he registered the creature before him. The sleek fur and piercing sapphire eyes sparkled unnaturally. At one angle the eyes looked solid black. It cocked its head to the side and smiled; a look of bemusement crossed its feline features.

"Wait a second. I know you," he said, a bit too loud from excitement.

"Observant as well," called a second voice from the brush. With fox-like coloring, the animal emerged from the brush and sauntered toward them with a grace, most unnatural, hypnotic in nature. All eyes were upon it. Its rust-colored fur shimmered despite the faint light.

"Rena, right?" Connor asked and squinted, though his tone wavered.

"Reza, human," the first creature to approach, corrected sharply. Side by side, he was slightly bigger than his companion.

"No time, danger approaches," said the other one. It peered over its shoulder, where it had originated. "It has been tracking you."

Connor's heart dropped to his stomach; a wave of nausea overcame him. "What's been following us?" Connor asked as he got back on his feet.

"Your presence here is not unnoticed," the slightly smaller creature said in a clipped tone. Its nose lifted to the air, twitching in the most adorable manner. "You are not where you were left."

"You mean that dungeon?" Connor asked. His skin prickled as he recalled Quinn, now trapped there. He'd have to hurry.

"The Mirror Prison is not easily escaped from," it replied. "You must have had tremendous help."

Connor shrugged in answer. He recalled these creatures, but he wasn't sure if he could trust them with his secrets.

The creature went on, ignoring the gesture. "This will anger him. He is coming unraveled, bit by bit, and will not allow his plans to be thwarted again," it said with a sharp flick of its fluffy tail.

Connor swallowed hard and glanced nervously in the direction of the rustling. The forest felt as if it were closing in. Whatever was out there, it was close.

"Who's angry?"

"The self-proclaimed king," it answered.

Mr. Perry?

Monk E took to the air without warning.

"Um, bye, I guess," Connor said with one wave of his arm in a good riddance gesture.

Reza whined, "Ezra, we go now."

"Oh yeah, Ezra," Connor said, recognizing the name. "How's your paw?"

"No time," she called as she darted to the tree line, leaving the ease of the path behind. "Run, human."

Reza followed suit without a word.

Connor hesitated for half a second, attempting to process what was happening. "Hey, wait up," he called as he scrambled to follow, sprinting faster than he ever had as she disappeared into the dense brush ahead.

Why not run on the path? It would be easier.

A deafening crash thundered, shaking the ground, and he stopped in his tracks. He instinctively looked over his shoulder, eyes widened in terror. The trees where he was standing toppled, and flames sprouted within the cracked trunks. Smoke darkened the already dim light, and the smell added to his fear. His mouth dropped open, and he faced forward and bolted as fast as he could.

He shouted ahead as he lost all sight of the creatures, "What the hell was that?"

"Shut up and run. Your questions mean nothing if you are ash," Ezra shouted from somewhere ahead and to his left.

Connor adjusted his path to follow her, feet pounding the sticks. Darting around the dense brush and trees made a linear path impossible. He zigzagged, dodging fallen trees and weaving around thick trunks. Each twist and turn felt like a gamble. A loose rock or even a hole could be the end of him at this pace.

Another crash sent Connor into high speed; he felt like he was flying. His legs screamed for relief, but his adrenaline ignored them. He gasped for breath, his throat constricted as branches whipped across his face.

The uneven ground was dangerous at this speed, but he floated over the obstacles as if he were running on air. The inferno roared behind him, farther away now, but he forced himself to push harder, fearing what might happen if whatever did that caught up to him. Connor didn't dare look back again.

"Keep up," Reza called.

Connor's breath was ragged; he couldn't respond. For once, he was quiet, without a quirky retort. He focused instead on staying upright. He was running as fast as humanly possible.

Ahead, a flash of movement caught his eye. Ezra's form darted between the trees in the blink of an eye. Connor adjusted his path once more, and his feet slipped on damp leaves when he corrected his course to chase her.

He flailed his arms, desperate for purchase and was forced to a halt as a branch snagged his threadbare shirt, smacking him back. He tore free but stumbled forward to his hands and knees, breaking his fall right before he kissed a rock. His breath was so short he felt as though he were suffocating.

"On the ground again?" Ezra taunted as she appeared before him out of thin air.

What was worse was that she didn't seem the least bit affected by the mad dash. Connor gritted his teeth and forced himself to his feet, his body protesting every move. He was exhausted, utterly depleted.

"You need wineberries," Ezra said.

'Wineberries?" Connor asked. "You mean grapes."

"No, berries that are used to make fairy wine are called wineberries," Ezra responded, shaking her head.

"Yeah, grapes," Connor said, nodding to himself.

Ezra let out a human-like sigh. Almost human, it sounded more like a grunt. The intent was apparent. Ezra had spent too much time around humans.

"No, these are magical and have many purposes," she said matter-of-factly.

She plucked an odd-looking berry from the bush beside them. Connor had been too tired to even notice.

Ezra stopped, a robotic-style movement, and then said, "Never drink the wineberries. You eat, but not drink," she continued, as if nothing had happened.

"Well, I'm too young to drink wine, anyway," Connor said.

He threw the berry into his mouth, and instant relief washed over him. A spark of energy shot through him; his body warmed with electricity.

Ezra shrugged in a childlike innocence.

Connor reached for another berry, and Ezra did a backflip and kicked the berry from his hand.

"You must not have too many, very dangerous."

"I only had one," Connor protested.

Ezra shook her head.

Connor could no longer hear anything following them. Holding his breath, he strained to listen for any inkling of danger. All he could hear was his pulse pounding in his ear. He needed to rest.

"I need to get to a portal," Connor said between breaths.

"We can either head toward the Ravenswood tree to seek aid from the Freedom Fighters or pass the Ecnad Foh Taed," Ezra stated, eyes narrowing.

Connor wiped the sweat that trickled down his forehead with the back of his hand. "I remember hearing about that place, the dance of death," Connor replied, still short of breath. Each word was spaced out between his panting. "No, thanks."

"Then the Ravenswood it is," Ezra said, her ears twitched in different directions. "I must warn you, it is the last known tree.

The overlord had ordered them all destroyed. He has constant surveillance. You may not avoid him or his minions going this way." She circled him effortlessly, like they hadn't been running for their lives.

"Well, I don't know what to do," Connor replied, shoulders drooping.

Hopeless and still breathless, he collapsed onto the ground, exhaustion setting in. The damp ground felt cool and refreshing.

Ezra observed him, her eyes sharp and unreadable. "The Ecnad Foh Taed may be dangerous," she said at last.

"Not if you walk around," Reza chimed in. "Be wary of pine cones, they release an odorous scent that has psychedelic effects.

Reza purred, it was more guttural than a cat's, making Connor's tiny hairs stand on end. Before he could react, the creature leaned close and licked Connor's face with a rough tongue and hot breath.

"Ew, gross," Connor said and closed his eyes. He'd survived this far; he wouldn't let Quinn down. With a heavy sigh, he said, "Fine." *So much for an easy portal and getting help.*

***

Reza, was more mischievous, whereas Ezra was blunt and spoke of things to come. She had a bit of foresight. Reza played the reluctant villain role; he was torn between being mischievous and the right thing, feeling no other choice. He figured, why not have a little fun and play the part he was given, since everyone expected him to be bad, anyway.

Chapter 22: Unexpected Guests

Baxter

B axter, Jimmy, and Cole stood outside the park when a cool breeze blew their hair. The streetlights were too far away to offer light, though their hum could be heard. Baxter moved the gravel with his boot and raked his fingers through his unruly hair. His eyes were set on the rocks he kicked.

Jimmy leaned against the hood of his car, arms crossed. "So, what did you want to talk about?"

"Well, the thing is," Baxter paused, unsure where to even begin.

Cole had been hanging out every day. Baxter looked after Cole. He'd been even weirder than normal ever since the lake incident. Baxter had to tell them what was going on since Cole was already trying to head into Fata.

He had no idea why, but when Cole blurted it out in front of Jimmy, Baxter chose to fill him in. Not with everything, especially Connor, but about the parallel realm that was right beside them.

"What did Cole mean when he told you he found out Fata is real?" Jimmy asked. His voice filled with concern.

Baxter looked up at Cole to see what he would say. *Should I lie? Will Cole rat me out?*

"Ax, you've been acting weird. And Cole hasn't been his unusual self since, well, you know," Jimmy said with a sigh. "So, what's really going on?" His eyes bounced from Baxter to Cole.

Baxter shoved his hands into his pockets and stared at the rocks he kicked.

Cole leaned against the car. "You can't stop me," he said. "I found one of my mother's journals, filled with stuff about Fata." He crossed his arms.

"Cole," Baxter started.

"I thought it was just a dream," Cole explained.

"Dreams and Fata," Jimmy repeated. His eyes narrowed as he said, "Did you guys have the same dream or something? Ax had bad dreams before."

Baxter looked off in the distance, uncertain how to explain this to Jimmy. He fidgeted with the zipper of his hoodie.

"Just tell me," Jimmy said. "I can keep a secret." The hurt was apparent on his face.

"That's not the problem," Baxter said.

"Then what is the problem?" Jimmy asked, his voice raised.

"Knowing could get you killed," Baxter said, looking Jimmy in the eyes. His hurt and fear were easily readable.

Baxter hesitated, glancing at Cole, who remained silent. Cole stared out at the lake, his face unreadable. Baxter thought he saw Cole's jaw clench.

"I'll tell you," Baxter started, his voice soft, barely above a whisper, as if something might overhear him. He shifted his weight, his hands in his pockets. "But you have to promise to keep it a secret."

Jimmy's brows furrowed, and he leaned closer. "You're freaking me out, Ax. Tell us already."

Cole turned, his pale blue eyes hyperfocused. "It's about Fata, isn't it?" he said.

Jimmy's eyebrows raised. "Fata?" he questioned. "What the hell is that?"

Baxter's heart pounded. "Well... a place," he said carefully. "It's a parallel realm." He glanced at Cole, who was staring at him with such intensity. "You already know. You've been trying to go there, haven't you?"

Cole stiffened. "Yes," he whispered. "After what happened at the lake, I needed answers. Something's calling me. I know you've felt it."

Baxter ran a hand through his hair. "Yeah, I guess I have. But you can't wander into Fata, Cole. It's dangerous. You have no idea what you're getting into."

Jimmy took a step closer, the confusion written all over his face. "Back up a second. Are you seriously telling me there's another realm? And you've kept it from me?"

"It's not that easy," Baxter said. "It's not a secret hideout or something. Fata's deadly, not a game."

Jimmy's mouth hung open. "You're serious," he whispered. His eyes were wide with wonder.

Baxter only nodded and then said, "Dead serious." Baxter turned to face Cole. "You can't go there alone." His voice was commanding.

Cole's jaw clenched. "I'm going with or without you."

The desperate look in his eye was something Baxter recognized; he'd felt it. He shrugged his shoulders as he looked at Jimmy, his mouth still hanging open.

"This is so insane," Jimmy said. But Baxter noticed the excitement in his voice. "No more secrets."

Baxter swallowed. "If we do this, we're doing it my way."

Cole smiled. "Let's go then."

A girl called out to them, drawing them from their conversation. "Hey, guys." Her blonde ponytail was swinging side to side.

Baxter sighed under his breath. "What Naomi?" he asked.

She hesitated and looked over her shoulder at Lindsay, who made a gesture to continue.

"I just wanted to apologize for how I treated you this past year," she said.

"It's fine," he replied, too fast.

She shifted her weight from foot to foot, eyes cast downward. "The thing is…" She paused, taking a deep breath. "It's really not fine. I haven't been fine."

Jimmy stomped as he approached. "Naomi, we don't have time for another pity party. Not everything is about you." He turned and gestured for Baxter to follow.

Naomi's hands flew up, palms out. "Wait, that's not what I was trying to do," she said. A loud sigh escaped her lips. "Look, I heard Cole talking to someone. I overheard him mention fat-ah," she announced.

Baxter's eyes widened. "Fata?"

Jimmy spun around to face her. "And you're just telling us now!" he shouted.

Naomi flinched. "I didn't believe it before," she said, avoiding eye contact. Her shoulders curled in. "I was distracted."

She looked back to Lindsay McMullin, of all people. One of Rufus's crew. "I got this gift from Linds," Naomi said. Lindsay nodded, encouraging her.

"What are you saying?" Baxter asked.

"Well, I guess it does have magic powers. I took it off and couldn't see Cole talking to anyone. I put it back on, and he was literally talking to a tree, and I heard him say your name." She was whispering now. "It was the same tree as before."

Naomi wasn't acting her normal, selfish self. She had no nasty comments about anyone. She appeared humbled. Baxter sensed something more was going on with her and Lindsay. He couldn't think about it now.

"Cole, is this true?" Baxter asked as he looked around for Cole. *How could he have disappeared that fast?*

"Anyway, I came here to ask for your forgiveness." Naomi paused and looked back at Lindsay again. "I was hoping you would accept her as my girlfriend."

That briefly got Baxter's attention. Not that he cared who she dated, but it made sense now. Her strict dad and his threats to send her to boot camp if she didn't stop hanging out with the wrong girls.

Girls. He threw out all her posters from her walls. Baxter had thought he was just angry at her.

Baxter glanced up when she continued.

"That's when I decided to date the first nice guy I saw," she explained. Her cheeks flushed red.

Baxter recalled when she walked up to him and told him, 'You're my boyfriend now.' Naomi had known she had him by the look of confusion on his face. Baxter was too much of a gentleman to try and kiss her, so she was safe in that department.

Denying her identity for so long must have been miserable. No wonder she was lashing out. Naomi was gay and fearing she'd be sent away if she didn't straighten out, pun intended. She must have been so worried her friends might not accept her. Those insecurities must have been devastating.

Naomi had confronted her fears and worked toward acceptance. She realized the impact of her actions and was attempting to make amends.

Maybe she recognized her shortcomings and took responsibility for her behavior. If Naomi were to embark on a journey of self-development and apologize to those she'd wronged, she'd fix the damage she'd caused. Through open communication and genuine remorse, Naomi could start to rebuild the trust she had lost. Gradually, those close to Naomi could see she was trying to make amends.

"Anyway, I've adopted the phrase, 'hurt people, hurt people,' and it's my mission to help those who are hurting and try to understand why they behave the way they do." She smiled. "I'm going to be a counselor when I grow up."

Naomi's redemption wouldn't be a quick fix but a gradual, evolving process. Her determination and ability to learn from her mistakes would help her overcome her selfish and nasty behavior, transforming her into a better person.

"Let's go, Baxter. We don't have time for this," Jimmy said, looking like he wanted to take off running. His voice pulled him from his thoughts of Naomi. Baxter always wanted to see the good in people.

Baxter glanced back at Naomi and shrugged to say sorry.

"Baxter, let's go," Jimmy repeated.

Baxter shook his head and then nodded. "Did you see which way Cole went?" he asked Jimmy.

Jimmy shook his head.

"I don't know how he disappeared so fast," Jimmy said.

Baxter looked at Naomi and Lindsay.

"He ran off as soon as he saw me. I'm assuming he knew I'd tell you what I saw."

"What do we do?" Jimmy asked.

"We find Cole," Baxter answered, determined. "I'll head back to Connor's and grab some supplies. You need to create an alibi."

"An alibi? Who exactly are we murdering?" Jimmy asked. His brows arched in the most perplexed face.

"Dude, time's different in Fata. Your parents will wonder where you are," Baxter said, exasperated.

"What am I supposed to say?" Jimmy asked.

"Um, tell them you're going away to look at colleges up the coast," Baxter explained, looking up to the right.

He made a sweeping motion with his hand. "They'll be proud and not question if you're gone too long. They'll think you're really looking or ended up at a frat party."

Jimmy grinned. "That's a great plan," he said. "Except they know I'm not going to college."

"They will believe it, trust me," Baxter said. "They'll be excited you changed your mind."

Chapter 23: The Dance of Death

Connor

As Connor skidded around a tree, he said to himself, "Dance of Death." He did a double take, over his shoulder. He swore he saw Chantelle.

How could she be here?

She placed a finger over her lips. "If you tell anyone, it will drastically affect the future."

"Wow." He blinked hard. "These pine needles really are psychedelic." He shook his head and continued. He could not believe he made it out of there unscathed.

***

Connor hesitated at his front door. *What can I say?* He took a breath and pushed open the door. Once he got through the portal he hitchhiked the rest of the way back. This portal was much father then the last one he went in.

"Connor!" his mother cried. Rushing to his side, she wrapped her arms around him. Barely letting him breathe, worried he'd vanish again. "Where were you? I've been worried sick."

His father entered the room. He was reserved, he watched them, and then he closed the distance between them. Placing a firm hand on Connor's shoulder, he said, "We've missed you, son." He yanked him into a bear hug.

"I've gotta find Baxter."

"You're not going anywhere," his father said.

"Not until you tell us what happened," his mom said.

"He's here by the way," his dad answered.

Connor stepped back and looked his father in the eyes. "What?" *How could he be here?*

"He had nowhere to go, and you weren't using your room," his mom said.

After answering enough of their questions, Connor let out a deliberate yawn and feigned fatigue. Making his excuses he went down the hall to his room. He pushed open his door, and Baxter froze, staring at him like a deer paralyzed in headlights.

Connor exhaled and stepped into his room. "B, I've got so much to tell you."

"Connor," Baxter whispered, voice trembling. Tear pricked at the corner of his eyes watered.

For a long time, they stood facing each other, letting the weight of their reunion settle. When Connor started to speak the words flew out in rapid succession. The prison, Quinn, what he saw, everything but Chantelle.

Baxter listened without interrupting, afraid to disturb this dream. When Connor finished, Baxter cleared his throat twice, unable to speak. He was too choked up. Connor really stood before him. No words could express the relief in seeing his friend. Baxter crossed the room and hugged him.

***

Connor was essentially grounded. They had to slip out the window, knowing it would hurt his parents all over again.

Baxter shoved his hands in his pockets. "So, Jimmy knows about Fata and is currently heading over there now." He rocked on his heels. "I don't mean to hurry this. I'm happy you're safe, but I need to get Quinn."

Connor's mouth dropped open, but for once, he didn't have a snappy comeback.

"I understand if you don't wanna go."

"No way, man. I'm totally going wherever you are." He paused. "I just need to eat something."

Baxter smiled. He looked at Connor. "What about your parents?" Baxter asked.

"My parents will just have to understand," Connor said.

Baxter pulled his friend into a fierce hug. Connor's heart could barely handle this emotion.

"I can't believe you thought I was dead," Connor said with a wry smile.

***

Baxter

Baxter and Connor raced to Celeste's shop to get anything that might help them. Jimmy was hot on their heels after he set up his alibi; he'd be there in a moment. Baxter had texted him to meet up there. He would explain about Connor once he showed up.

Connor had brought a rock back with him from Fata that Reza said was important, tossing it into his pocket. He kept drinking all these potions and food in Celeste's house in hopes that it was enchanted. It looked like regular food in her pantry. He was starving, anyway.

Baxter heard a crash, followed by a gasp from Connor. He ran toward the sound. Connor stood before a pedestal lit with a soft, golden bulb.

"What is it?" Baxter asked, moving to see past Connor.

Connor had wandered into a back room in Celeste's house and spotted a treasure on a stand. The pedestal bore a crown.

The most ornate crown, with puffy protruding sides and bejeweled with gems. Connor hesitated, nervous to touch it. After a deep breath, he lifted it from the pedestal and replaced it with a vase in one fell swoop.

"This isn't Crocodile Dundee," Baxter said.

Connor turned to face his friend, now wearing the crown on his head.

Baxter smiled. "You look ridiculous."

"It has to be magical. I just know it," Connor said. The crown made a jingling sound as Connor spoke.

Baxter's grin widened.

"What?" Connor asked.

Baxter burst out laughing. "I'm sorry, man," he said in between laughs. "You can't wear that."

"Hey, man, you wore my tunic last year, and I didn't say anything," Connor countered.

"Excuse me," Baxter said with false bravado. "You gave me that tunic."

"You asked for it," Connor fired back, his crown still jingling.

"I didn't ask for *that*." Baxter was still laughing.

There was no time to argue.

"Okay, let's go," Baxter said, gesturing toward the doorway.

Connor nodded, causing the crown to jingle again. Baxter opened the door and Jimmy stood on the other side. He was frozen, as if he had seen a ghost.

Connor leaned over Baxter's shoulder and said, "Hey, Jimmy."

"Where the hell have you been?" he asked. "Have you been here this whole time?"

"It's a long story and we're kinda in a hurry," Connor said.

"You can't seriously expect me to not ask questions." Jimmy's voice rose in frustration.

"Jimmy," Baxter started. He placed his hands on Jimmy's chest. "I was going to tell you."

"You knew!" Jimmy shouted, his face was beet red.

"I can explain," Baxter started.

"You'd better," Jimmy interrupted.

"Whoa, man," Connor interrupted right back.

He pushed Baxter aside and began talking to Jimmy in hushed tones. They walked down the stairs and around the side of the house. Baxter stood there for a moment, perplexed.

He followed. Jimmy was now in a lighter mood. He smiled with his hand on Connor's shoulder.

***

They rushed to the portal. Jimmy was speeding so fast that Baxter felt nauseous. He parked in the far back corner of the parking lot, not wanting to raise suspicion. They jogged toward the path when a laugh pierced the air. It was Rufus, Baxter's nemesis.

Rufus yanked off his baseball hat and bowed mockingly toward them.

"You look like a royal jester." Rufus laughed. "What's with the crown, King Connor? Is that where you've been, your highness?"

Connor's cheeks reddened, and he gritted his teeth as his hands balled into fists, but he kept walking. They didn't have time for this.

"Back the hell up," Connor shouted.

Rufus tripped and fell backwards.

Maybe the hat is powerful.

"I didn't want to mention it, but it's kinda weird," Jimmy said. His palm rubbed the back of his head.

Connor rolled his eyes. Rufus wasn't through with them yet. He dusted himself off and smirked.

"Where are you guys going?" he asked. "The royal ball?" His words dripped with sarcasm.

Ignoring him completely they continued walking.

"The royal jester and what are you?" he asked, turning to Baxter with a sneer on his face. "The peasant?"

They quickened their pace. Baxter eyed Jimmy, knowing it would be difficult to not engage with him. But Rufus was relentless.

"Are you planning a little picnic, your majesty?" he called after them.

Baxter could tell by his footsteps that Rufus was skipping. He knew he was pretending to hold a picnic basket as well. He didn't look back to confirm.

Baxter increased his pace. Connor and Jimmy followed. Baxter glanced over his shoulder.

I can't believe that stayed on him.

For a moment, Baxter thought they had finally lost Rufus. He slowed his pace.

"I thought he'd never leave," Baxter said when they made it to the entrance of the park.

"I know. He's so annoying," Connor answered.

"I was about to punch him," Jimmy confessed, his hands still balled into fists.

"I know," Baxter replied.

They made it down the long driveway, and when it turned to dirt, Baxter stopped for a moment. He was out of breath. These past few weeks, he'd been depressed, barely leaving Connor's room. Connor was locked in a cell and malnourished, plus he'd have cramps after stuffing his face so much at Celeste's.

When they were at the mouth of the path that led to the cave, Connor asked, "What's that?"

He pointed to the left of the path. Behind the brush was shining metal. Connor approached and moved the branches. It was a purple bike.

"Quinn," Baxter breathed. His purpose reignited.

Connor and Baxter made eye contact, knowing for certain that Quinn had taken this path to Fata. They darted up the path without saying another word. They hiked in silence at a strenuous pace. Once they neared the cave, they heard the unmistakable sound of a twig snap.

In unison, they turned toward the sound and spotted Rufus, smirking at them.

"Rufus. What are you doing here?" Baxter asked.

"Go home," Connor growled. Neither of them were in the mood for games.

Rufus ignored them. Something in his face had changed. His curiosity was piqued. "What's up with these purple mushrooms?" he asked, crouching to get a closer look. "They totally move."

"Shut up and leave us alone," Jimmy said.

Baxter stared at the mushrooms; he didn't see anything. A mushroom at the edge of his vision rose up and waved at him. Baxter jumped back. He expected things like this in Fata, but not in his world.

Upon further inspection, they resembled little bearded men. Their white beards blend in with the stalks. It looked like a tiny gnome, wearing a mushroom hat.

"Do you hear that?" Rufus asked. He angled his head, so his ear pointed up.

Baxter and Connor exchanged uneasy glances.

Could he really be able to sense Fata? This big oaf.

The gnome mushroom men were completely forgotten. They had bigger things to worry about.

Rufus took a step forward; his greedy eyes locked on the cave's entrance.

Baxter's heart stopped, and he moved, blocking Rufus's way. "You don't wanna do that," he warned. Baxter had both palms out.

But Rufus ignored him, pushed his arms away, and easily sidestepped Baxter.

"Can you guys see that?" Rufus's voice rose an octave, his astonishment apparent. "Those colors?"

Before they could stop him, Rufus had entered the cave. Baxter ran after him, hoping he'd be stuck in there as Connor once was without his necklace. Connor was hot on his heels. Then Rufus was in Fata.

Rufus turned to Baxter. "Now, that was cool," he said and smiled ear to ear. "What is this place?"

Baxter frowned. He looked back at Connor, not knowing what to say. "I have no idea how you can even see it." His honesty was ignored.

Rufus shrugged, his brow furrowed. "What do you mean? You guys can, so wouldn't I be able to see it?"

"See what?" Jimmy asked

Connor sighed. "Well, I only see this because of this necklace," Connor said, gesturing to the chain that hung from his neck.

Rufus shrugged and turned to Connor, smile fading. "So, what's up with the crown, really?"

Connor sighed. "I don't know, but it's gotta be magic."

"Do I need one?" Rufus asked, serious for once. His smile faded.

"No," Connor said. "Speaking of, Jimmy, here take this." Connor said, taking off the necklace and handing it to Jimmy.

Leaving Baxter no other choice, as Rufus was never going to let them venture alone. Baxter vaguely filled Rufus in as best he could about Fata and what Mr. Perry had done.

"Mr. Perry wasn't just my teacher; he went rogue here. He lost his wife and was consumed by revenge. He's evil; nothing will stop him from exacting his revenge."

To his surprise, Rufus turned out to be helpful. Along the way, Baxter nearly stumbled on a makeshift trip wire. Rufus grabbed him roughly by the arm and yanked him back as an arrow flew by his face.

"Whoa," Rufus whispered, eyes scanning the tree line. "That was close. You didn't warn me about that."

"I told you that you didn't wanna do that. When you first approached the cave," Baxter reminded him as he crossed his arms.

They were on the same side, and it was weird.

"So how come Connor can see without the necklace?" Jimmy asked.

"Its gotta be the crown," Connor answered.

"Or maybe because you drank everything in sight at the shop," Baxter suggested.

Connor's hand hovered over his jeans pocket but didn't say anything. They continued in caution.

Chapter 24: Bloodstone

Quinn

Quinn felt a vision slam into her as if she were struck. It flooded her mind and all her senses. She quickly sat down, afraid she might faint like last time, or worse, walk into something.

Images of Connor with a rock in his hand. It was mostly black, streaked with red swirls on it. She had seen Reza handing it to him. The smooth stone was menacing; the power ebbing off it had her worried.

A vision of her father, Doug, standing over a fire. He had dropped a black liquid into the flames. He was chanting, but she didn't understand what he was saying. When the liquid hit the stone, the fire blinded her. There was an explosion.

Her father fell to the ground. Once the smoke cleared, a single drop of crimson, not black, seeped into the stone. As if it were drinking it.

The once white stone pulsed and turned smoky. The veins darkened and turned scarlet, while the core blackened. She knew something was born in that fire, and she didn't want to know what it was.

Quinn spotted a Fae hunched over a body. It lay lifeless, a sacrifice. Quinn tried to look away. An inaudible whisper drew her back, a hunger for more. Quinn shuddered. It wanted more. More blood.

Another vision of blood covering everything, screams, and fires. It was definitely evil; it desired more blood. It was insatiable. As the crimson blood seeped onto the jagged white rock, a remarkable transformation occurred, forging the very first Bloodstone. Its creation came at a cost. The life of the Fae and something darker.

With the infusion of blood in rock, it became sentient, driving its unquenchable thirst for more. And it wouldn't stop until it consumed all it desired.

But why is Dad involved? No way would he do something like that. Could he?

Quinn coughed and sat upright, as though the very oxygen around her was being sucked out. She gasped as she tore free from the vision, and her body convulsed. Her mind cleared, showing her the real world again. Her breath was ragged.

That rock in Connor's hand... it looked just like the one in my father's fire. Connor's in trouble. He has to ditch that stone.

Then the world spun, and the corners of her vision darkened as Quinn fell back.

Blood dripped steadily, each crimson bead splashing onto the jagged porcelain rocks below. The pale, bone-white surface of the rocks made the red contrast unsettling. Each drop echoed through the stillness, a stark reminder of the fragility of life.

The jagged edges of the stone, sharp as broken teeth, glistened as the blood pooled in their crevices, as though drinking it, indifferent to the suffering that had taken place.

The stone was created by Doug during his experimentation. It allowed humans to wield some minimal magic.

She saw herself approaching it. The moment she picked up the rock, her senses shifted. Her vision blurred, as if she were seeing two things at once, fragmented glimpses of possible futures and even places.

The confusion left her disoriented, and the ground rose up to meet her. Completely overwhelmed, her head spun, and a wave of dizziness washed over her. Her legs gave out, and she crumpled to the ground; it was a glimpse of her fainting right before she had done so, a warning.

"What did you see?" Puck asked as he caught her before she fell.

Chapter 25: The Mirror's Final Test

Quinn

A loud scratching noise echoed deep within the caverns, and every alarm bell within Quinn's body was going off. All her tiny hairs stood on end. The damp air had a musky scent. She had the sudden urge to flee. She glanced at Puck, who nodded and took off running. Quinn followed, with her arms out before her to prevent running into a glass wall.

The ground started to vibrate. Five feet ahead of her, the floor opened, and a monstrous creature slithered out. A not-so-silent scream escaped her lips, and her panic boiled over. She stole another glance at Puck, who looked more annoyed at her outburst than the grotesque centipede-like creature that slithered before them.

Each of its segmented body pieces was a different color, creating an oil-spill effect. Tiny cilia-like antennas wiggled of their own accord from all aspects of the body, each dripping slime that was yellow and thick.

It turned to Quinn, who was nowhere near Puck. Her panicked eyes darted to him, and he motioned to her to be still. The creature turned toward her and disintegrated into miniature squirming copies of itself.

The segments fell to the ground and scurried off in different directions. Each of those tiny antennas seems to be collecting data about its surroundings. Its multiple legs tapped the floor, making an eerie noise. Quinn resisted the urge to scream again.

The creature didn't seem to notice her. Puck gestured to the centipede and covered his eyes for a moment. Quinn nodded, understanding the creature was blind. He placed a finger to his lips to keep her silent. He then gestured for her to circle around the back of the gaping hole and approach him.

Quinn shook her head, fear paralyzing her. He waved his arm in frustration, and she took a slow, deep breath. As she let it out, she took a step toward him. When nothing happened to her, she took in a breath and then one more step. She walked as carefully as possible, slow and steady. Not too slow for the creature to find her. A crunching sound caused her to freeze.

The whites of Puck's eyes betrayed his fear. She looked at her feet; she'd stepped on some of the broken glass. The creature made a growling noise and turned toward her. All the tiny pieces returned to the center creature, reforming a larger centipede, which was now headed right at her.

She ran, and Puck followed. The fragmented creatures converged again, gradually reassembling, making the monster whole once again. The centipede was hot on her trail.

"This way," Puck growled as he turned to the right, into a nearly invisible corridor.

Quinn's steps stuttered, threatening to take her down at the sudden change in direction. Yet she remained upright. Puck motioned for her to stop once she caught up to him.

"What. Was. That?" she whispered. Each word came out in a puff of breath.

"A Skolavrax," he answered. "It's blind and nearly deaf. The cilia detect vibrations, air, and temperature, all to locate its next snack."

"Skull vax," she murmured. The words tasted like a mixture of copper and a curse on her tongue. A tingling sensation ran down her spine at the very mention of that menacing creature's name, summoning its evil presence.

Puck ignored her and continued on.

Quinn was visibly shaking despite the warm temperature. The wormlike creature scurried past them. The moment it was out of sight, Quinn exhaled a long, shaky breath of relief.

She glanced at Puck, who turned in the opposite direction. She followed him, quietly, their footsteps slow and deliberate to prevent making any noise and provoking the creature to return.

Minutes passed as Quinn continued to look over her shoulder, worried the centipede would sneak up on them. This last time, she spotted a smaller version of it nearly upon them. She noted two more heading their way, but not in a linear line.

They zigged and zagged, as if feeling all the walls of the tunnels, likely to mark out the pathway. A gooey, yellow trail was left behind by the creature.

The mini creatures darted through the jagged crevices and narrow passages within the cracks of the walls, all guided by those frantic, twitching antennas. This creature was a living nightmare in the flesh. They squished into every nook and cranny to locate their next meal, Quinn was certain.

One of the worms slipped into a crack Quinn couldn't see. The others were still slowly approaching them. The first one was nearly upon them. Quinn, desperate to retreat, backed up and bumped into the mirrored wall.

The faintest sound or vibration from that contact set the remaining worms into a frenzy as they surged straight for them in unison. A scream died in her throat.

All she could hear were her echoing footsteps as she sprinted down the corridor, her ragged breath. As she rounded the corner, she chanced a fleeting glance over her shoulder for any sign of pursuit. She didn't notice anything out of the ordinary, well, ordinary for this realm.

That didn't stop her sprint. She pushed herself even harder, attempting to keep up with Puck. Her aching legs burned. Then she heard a bellow, and the floor trembled. Parts of the glass floor splintered like ice on a lake.

Quinn glanced over her shoulder once more. The creature was closing in on them. She cringed.

Puck scowled at her and roughly grabbed her by the crook of her arm right as it closed in on them. Puck hit a spot high on the glass wall, and a hidden door burst open, sending Quinn to the ground as Puck jumped in and slammed the glass pane shut.

The door shimmered, and the translucent glass showed multiple worms now approaching. As they came upon each other, they joined together to reform the larger beast. It was even more nerve-wracking to watch the massive centipede, more like a millionipede, as it slithered around looking for them. Its innumerable legs, hundreds of legs, maybe thousands, scraped the reflective floor and clicked rhythmically; the sound reverberated deep within her bones.

The sound caused Quinn to shiver. It was more than unnerving; it was ferocious, as if the sound carried the weight of its eminence. The fact that it was blind was a minor solace.

I hope it can't smell.

It couldn't see them, yet the ability to watch it up close and intimately made it even scarier. It made her blood run cold. The grotesque creature had so many fingerlike projections coming off its body that they writhed of their own accord, independent of the main entity.

They reminded Quinn of tentacles. She noted that each one looked like it had a mouth, equipped with teeth. Puck motioned for her to be still and silent.

Quinn nodded once, too scared to do anything else, frozen in fear. The millionipede stilled for a moment, as it found something, all its antennas swayed like grasping fingers, and Quinn's heart pounded. She worried it may hear it.

Another growl rumbled from the creature, so loud it caused the room to vibrate. The creature shifted its massive body into a rolling motion due to the limited space to turn and leave, making the ground tremble.

Quinn struggled to control her breath as Puck offered her a hand, his face unreadable. She hesitated for a moment, paralyzed with worry that the creature would hear her. Once it disappeared down the corridor, Quinn exhaled a heavy sigh of relief. The tension in her shoulders and spine slackened, but left an ache in her muscles.

"What now?" Quinn whispered, her voice barely audible. She remained as still as she could.

Puck scowled at her. "That only bought us a few minutes," Puck replied, his tone clipped and matter-of-fact.

Quinn blinked. "What?"

Puck raised an eyebrow, his expression exasperated as he repeated dryly, "That. Only. Bought. Us. A. Few. Minutes."

Quinn shook her head and huffed. "I heard you," she said, crossing her arms in a defensive manner.

"Then why did you say what?" he asked, tilting his head at her. His confusion was apparent.

Quinn shook her head in disbelief. "You wouldn't understand."

Puck sighed mockingly and crossed his arms. "Humans are confusing."

This pulled a small smile from Quinn, despite the knotted tension in her stomach.

Quinn's faint smile faded as she watched Puck move toward the exit. The small pocket of a room offered no other exit.

"Where are you going?" she asked, tension in her voice.

"We cannot stay here forever," he replied in a calm manner. Puck silently slid open the reflective door.

It was seamless. It didn't possess any markings, nor was there any visible sign of its presence. Quinn looked from the door to Puck and frowned, curiosity overflowing.

"How did you know that door was there?" she asked.

Puck glanced over his shoulder; his lips curled into a wry smile. "Fae secret," he replied cryptically.

Quinn shook her head, shaking any further questions. She followed Puck down the slick, reflective slope, silently repeating: *don't fall, don't fall.* As though the mantra would protect her.

Puck led them away from the creature's last direction without hesitation. His steps were confident, and he was unbothered by the encounter with the creature. The mirrors that lined the hallway cast a rainbow of light that shimmered faintly in the distorted reflections.

Quinn walked crouched over as if it would hide her movements. She walked on the balls of her feet, in awkward, hesitant, jerking motions. Puck eyed her, his brows furrowed, yet he didn't speak. His gaze lingered, an unreadable look of strength with compassion on his face as he continued in silence.

"How do you know what way to go?" she whispered as she glanced behind them nervously. She looked over her shoulder once more, eyes darting to every corner.

Puck didn't answer; the silence stretched between them. The only sound was the scrape of Quinn's boots against the jagged, uneven mirrored floor. The sound echoed unusually loud in the damp stillness of the passageway. Puck's footsteps were ever silent.

Did he hear me? Of course, he did, with that super hearing of his. Maybe it's too dangerous to talk.

Quinn trailed him, attempting to be as quiet as possible. His reply startled her; she'd been convinced he wasn't going to answer. It had been quiet for so long. She thought he was ignoring her, or he didn't want their conversation to give them away.

189

"I do not," he said, short and hurried. No further explanation was offered.

Quinn bit her tongue, thinking better of it. Nothing good could come from her flooding him with questions. Perhaps she'd find out those creatures were common or liked to eat humans.

Perhaps she'd discover that there was no chance of them both getting out alive. For now, it was better to keep those nagging questions to herself, at least until she formed a plan.

If I couldn't control my visions…

An unknown amount of time had passed as they, hopefully, wandered in the correct direction through the winding maze of mirrored walls. She had no idea how long they'd walked, or how far. Her legs must've been numb; they no longer ached. They felt heavy.

Every turn blended into the next. She couldn't tell where they were going or if they had been already here. Puck had a better sense of direction than Quinn did. He moved with a quiet confidence. She didn't sense them backtracking even once. Perhaps she wasn't paying that much attention as she placed all her trust in Puck finding an exit.

Her stomach clenched and churned with doubt at the thought. *What if we just keep going in circles like I did?* What if this was yet another false reflection and she was standing in the hall watching it, as if it were real? Quinn shuddered and shook the thought from her head. Negative thoughts like that would only consume her.

Once she calmed her mind, she noticed the subtle reflections in the visions were soft. They had a hazy white vignette effect around the edges, whereas this realm had very sharp features. This helped comfort her and distinguish between real and fake, and only quelled her fears further.

A tightness in her chest eased as she was able to distinguish the illusions. Now, she could move past the visions, knowing what they were. A breath of relief escaped her lips; she was one step closer to completing this task. The journey before her felt a tad easier.

Their progress felt slow, unremarkable. Quinn's legs started to ache from all the walking, especially over this uneven terrain. She hurt her back as she stepped into a hole. The jarring movement pulled her muscles; with the difficulty, she fought to keep upright. \

Pain shot up her leg, straight to her back. Quinn frowned, forcing the curses to halt before she let them loose and alerted the guards, or worse, the creature to their location.

Puck didn't even stop; he only scowled at her and kept walking. With gritted teeth, she followed him, though the ache in her back pleaded for her to stop. Her stomach tightened. There was something unexplainable about his silent confidence, the set in his jaw, that kept her going. He was certain of what he was doing.

Puck slowed his pace and leaned up against a mirrored wall so that both shoulders were touching it. It seemed to be the backside of the glass; it was mostly dark, gray, and not reflecting anything. Not even their movements. Quinn was frozen with fear, her heart pounding in her ears, drowning out any other sounds.

"What is it?" she whispered. She doubted a human could hear her, yet Puck had incredible hearing, like a predator stalking its prey.

Puck's gaze darted to hers with a grim, unreadable face, but he offered no answer to her. He was normally difficult to read. Whatever thoughts stormed beneath the surface rarely showed unless he allowed them to be seen. Quinn scanned the halls for anything out of the ordinary.

The rock-solid glass walls didn't show her illusions now, as though they knew she had mastered them. She couldn't detect anything, no movements, no sounds, no footsteps, nothing amiss. She trusted Puck's senses over her own. If he thought something was wrong, he was far more experienced with these situations.

Then, without warning, a soft tremor from the wall reverberated through her hand. She leaned against it. She recoiled like she'd been burned. Puck showed no sign, no change at this new discovery. He never wavered. She studied him, more for what to do next. After inspection, she noticed the tiniest bit of tension in his jaw.

Miniature creatures no bigger than a quarter scurried around like cockroaches. They darted to and fro, not in a straight path. They bumped into the mirrored walls and turned at higher speeds. Quinn clenched her muscles, ready to sprint, jump, scream, or do anything that Puck was doing.

The multi-legged crustacean crept from the shadows; the sheen from the gloss-like exoskeleton gleamed in the darkness. Its numerous legs clanked upon the ground, the fingerlike protrusions danced in the air, as if absorbing the atmosphere. Quinn bit her lip to keep from screaming as they were nearly upon her; one passed a few feet from her boots. A bead of sweat dripped in her eye. She blinked, too afraid to move. Her eyes glanced at Puck; he still hadn't moved.

Why aren't we running?

The creature continued on. Then the rest of the creatures approached and passed without issue. Most of the tiny critters had passed them, yet a few remained. The second-to-last visible creature slowed. It paused, and faced her, all the appendages pointed in her direction, the mouths on the end opened of their own accord. Quinn began to tremble; she held her breath. She attempted to force control over her body. The creature turned and followed the rest of the pack.

Quinn exhaled, "How are we going to get away from that thing?"

"Slowly. They sense the vibrations from your footsteps," Puck replied.

Quinn glared at him, but she knew he was right. Quinn hadn't heard a single sound from Puck as they traveled. His steps were nonexistent; hers on the other hand echoed with every move. It was as if her efforts to quiet her steps only amplified them.

"What am I supposed to do?" she asked, voice tight, betraying her panic. "How can I be silent like you?" she asked without letting him answer the first question.

"You cannot," he said, not giving any further explanation.

Then the beast roared and turned back, heading straight for them. It reformed slowly into a larger centipede. Enraged, the creature liquefied, dissolving into a viscous pile of a bloodlike massacre, which spread across the floor like spilled milk. It slid beneath the crack at the base of the glass door and flowed through the gap.

After it passed under the door, its liquid form began to reform into a solid figure once more. The odor from the liquid was stomach-churning, and vapors had floated from it. Quinn suspected they were toxic.

One of the worms sunk its yellow teeth into Puck's forearm, and he thrashed violently on the ground. He turned over, pulling away from the bite. Quinn was frozen, not certain what to do.

Panic surged through her, and she grabbed Puck by the uninjured arm and yanked him hard to the side. He barely moved. At that moment, a flash of the future burned into her mind. It was Puck dying where she intended to move him. The message seared into her brain. If she moved him there, he would surely die.

"No," she mumbled. She shook off the grim vision. "Not today."

She scanned her surroundings, hoping for a new plan to replace the previous failed one.

Puck's body hung lifelessly in her grasp. Drool seeped from his mouth. She tugged him hard in another direction, her pulse racing. Sweat beaded her brow; she wiped it with the back of her sleeve.

As they got momentum, she noticed a small hidden alcove in the corner. A breath of relief washed away the tension in her body, giving her a burst of strength. There were no sudden visions of Puck dying this time, so that had to be something.

Quinn stopped dead in her tracks. Before her stood Baxter. A tornado of confusion wreaked havoc on her mind.

How could he be here?

Quinn shook her head hard. If she kept all this shaking up, she'd pull a muscle.

"Baxter?" she whispered. "What are you doing here?" *This must be another illusion.*

He pointed behind her. Maybe he's astral projecting. She noted a faint glow surrounding him.

Didn't the illusions have that glow?

No, this seemed like a projection; she sensed that he was trying to do something. He gestured behind her again to her backpack. She'd dropped it in her panic, left it there. That was something that might save them later. Quinn retrieved the pack and looked back to her brother. He was gone. He was trying to tell her something.

Quinn was on the verge of tears. With Puck unresponsive, she faced the Mirror World's ultimate trial, a test of self-awareness and inner strength. Uncertain if she could complete her task, she blinked away tears. She must confront her flaws, her fears, and her weaknesses.

She overcame the thin boundary between reality and illusion, as they had blurred into one. She ventured to a climactic showdown with this beast, and she wasn't going to stop here. As trapped as she was in the prison herself, she wasn't sure if she'd ever escape, but she wouldn't quit, not now. The prison in her mind was fiercer than this prison, and she'd navigate out.

Truth and deception were indistinguishable; she was confronted like never before. She questioned everything, even herself. All hope was lost. Quinn gave in to her instincts and would blaze a path out of here. She reached into her backpack and pulled out a cloth-wrapped vial.

When all hope is lost. Her hand shook.

Puck was still unresponsive on the ground; his fate hung in the balance. Quinn pushed herself to her limits. She banged her other hand on the nearest wall.

She yelled, "Come and get me, you freaks!"

The creatures raced at them; they nearly reformed into a larger version than she'd seen. As it was upon them, Quinn threw the vial and splayed herself over Puck, squeezing her eyes closed. She held her breath.

At that moment, the flash of Blinding Light erupted, a radiant flare designed to blind and repel the abomination. The light seared the air with such intensity that Quinn heard the vermin hesitate, recoiling momentarily before it attempted to resume its relentless, formless pursuit.

Good idea putting it into a vial so I didn't accidently set it off.

The whole prison shook. Light overwhelmed her. After a minute, she looked over her shoulder toward the creature. It was nowhere to be seen. A pile of ash remained.

The guards would surely know their location now. She had to get out of here.

The aftermath of Quinn's choices reverberated through the Mirror World and would change their course permanently.

This is why I had to go back and train more.

A blue shimmer rose from the dust, and a portal opened where the ashes were scattered. Quinn's breath hitched in her throat.

Is it an escape or a trap set by the guards?

She had no way to know. She trusted her instincts. Quinn dragged Puck toward the light. Each step ended with a grunt. She hoped she wasn't hurting him, but she didn't know how long the portal would stay open. Quinn pulled Puck into the portal.

Chapter 26: A Promise Kept

Quinn

For a moment, Quinn couldn't see anything. The light was so bright that her eyes struggled to adjust after the gloom and darkness of the prison. She blinked rapidly and raised her hand to shield the light. She started to make out shapes, but the light dimmed, and shadow fell over her. A massive figure stood before her, blocking out the light.

She heard a snort. "Hello, human," a deep voice said.

Quinn froze; she knew that voice. "Cornelius, is that you?" she asked.

"It is," he said. Beside him stood a smaller version of himself. He gestured toward the figure with surprising grace. "I'd like you to meet my mate, Tessa." He beamed.

Relief surged through Quinn as a tidal wave of emotion overtook her. She was drowning and couldn't catch her breath. She crumpled to the ground; the weight she carried overcame her.

She'd done it. She escaped and managed to get Puck out with her. An impossible feat, yet she did it. She started to cry, softly at first, and then it turned into bawling. Heavy, ugly crying. Wave after wave of uncontrollable sobs caused Cornelius to step back.

"I'm not that repulsive," Tessa said. The hurt in her voice was blaringly obvious. "Or do you want Cornelius for yourself?" she demanded, her eyes narrowed. She stomped a hoof into the ground, a puff of dust surrounding them.

Quinn attempted to control herself, but once she let the floodgates open, it was nearly impossible to stop. She shook her head and waved her arm, but the tears wouldn't stop.

"No… it's…I'm sorry," she gasped in between sobs, gesturing toward Puck. "My mother," she cried, her voice cracked, "and Connor. I don't know what to do anymore."

Cornelius nudged Puck gently as a Minotaur could, with the tip of his hoof. He bent over and sniffed him, and his nostrils flared as a loud snort escaped.

"What's wrong with this fella?" he asked. "He smells funny."

There was no response from Puck, he was motionless, his usual sarcastic remarks absent. She never thought she'd miss them.

Tessa tilted her head to the side and sniffed him. "I think he's dying."

This only made Quinn's breath hitch, and her sobs grew louder, more desperate. Her hands pressed against her face as her entire body trembled. The mere mention of losing Puck, after everything she'd endured, was too much to bear. Not after leaving her mother and Connor behind.

Who knows what happened to him?

"Quinn," Cornelius said, his voice rumbling like distant thunder. "Pull yourself together."

Quinn only sobbed harder; she couldn't stop. Her tears fell, blurring her vision as she gasped between sobs.

"He. He can't, he can't die," she choked out, the words barely audible through the sobs. Her anguish was so gushingly visible.

Cornelius shook his head, his flowing locks swinging in the motion. He knelt beside Puck and sniffed him more efficiently.

"Let me smell him closer," he said as he leaned closer.

Tessa took a few steps closer to her mate. She hovered behind him and crouched in a protective motion in the dirt.

"If he's dying, what can we do?" she said bluntly, no sympathy in her voice.

Cornelius growled, "Not helping, Tessa." He glanced from her to Quinn and back again.

Tessa shrugged and said, "Tears won't save him."

Cornelius pounded the dirt with a heavy hoof and puffed out a forceful breath from his snout as he eyed her. His look shot daggers, but he remained silent.

After a while, what felt like an eternity to Quinn, she wiped at her face with her trembling hands. Her breath stuttered to come out in tiny gasps. Her floodgate emptied; no tears remained. She looked at Puck; her eyes burned with determination and were reddened from crying.

"He's not dying," she grunted fiercely. "He can't be. Not after everything I've been through."

Cornelius snorted. "He's still breathing," he said gruffly.

Quinn nodded, clinging to hope. It was all she had left.

"I can't carry him," she quietly admitted. "I've got to get help. I need to get back to Fata."

Quinn took a deep breath and knelt beside Puck. She placed the back of her hand on his forehead. "Come on, Puck," she whined. Her voice quivered. "Please."

There was no response from him, no witty comeback. His silence cut her like a blade. Her heart ached as she fought back another wave of tears.

Tessa huffed, crossing her arms. "Well, I'm not carrying him," she declared.

Quinn shot a glare at her; a flicker of determination crossed her face. She'd had just about enough of Tessa.

"I'll figure it out without you," she snapped.

"Good," Tessa said with a huff and turned on a hoof and walked away. "Come on, Fluffy Cakes."

Quinn raised an eyebrow. If Cornelius could blush, she was certain he would've.

"Don't mind her, she's really jealous. I swear it's the braids," he said.

His face contorted in the most grotesque display. Quinn thought he was attempting to smile as best he could with his snout. She thought it looked more like a constipated grimace.

Cornelius shifted his weight to the other hoof and turned to focus on Puck. "I'll carry him to the border, but I can't go any farther," he said and glanced at the sky. "We need to move now before Gideon…"

"Gideon." Quinn looked up to the sky. Seeing nothing, she asked, "Who's Gideon?"

Cornelius looked over his shoulder, almost nervous, and shook his head.

Quinn wondered why he had this sudden rush of urgency, but she didn't think about it. She didn't care who Gideon was. She had bigger things to worry about right now and she needed to get Puck back to Ophelia and figure out how to save her mom and Connor.

Quinn nodded as Cornelius approached Puck. She'd do whatever it took. She wasn't going to lose Puck, not here, not now, and not like this. Cornelius scooped Puck up and slung him over his shoulder as if he were as light as a blanket.

He looked over his shoulder at Quinn and asked, "Ready?"

She nodded once more. She feared her quivering voice would betray her. Cornelius glanced at his mate one last time, and then he sprinted off. Quinn could never keep up with him. She was exhausted from all she'd been through. She chased after him as best she could, but she was still out of breath from her crying fit.

***

It was dark by the time Quinn caught up with Cornelius. She wasn't used to the darkness of night, as she had grown accustomed to the gloomy reflective light in the prison. And in Fata, night came rarely, at least as much as she'd seen.

She didn't think her body could take any more, and her legs trembled with exhaustion. Then she remembered Celeste's snacks, Runezests. She collapsed to the ground.

Cornelius had gently placed Puck beside her and said, "I've gotta get back. She's gonna stab me with a horn." He looked up again before taking off.

Quinn struggled with the energy to even lift her head. "Thank you," she managed to say barely above a whisper.

Cornelius nodded and said, "Just... don't stop moving." He looked cautiously to the sky. "Things have a tendency to wither away when they stop around here."

With that, he sprinted off into the darkness. Quinn watched him until he was out of sight. She looked down at Puck, lying motionless on the ground.

I hope he's okay.

Quinn caught herself looking toward the night sky. She noted three glowing orbs that she assumed were moons or planets. She didn't have the energy to care. As her gaze fell, a flicker of dark movement caught her eye in the corner of her vision.

She snapped her head back but couldn't find it. Her eyes strained to pierce the dark emptiness. She rummaged through her pack until her fingers grazed Celeste's snack.

With shaking hands, she unwrapped the bar, noting the rune, and tossed it into her mouth. Instant warmth flooded her, and the sensation overcame her. Her whole-body flushed, and when it cooled, she was regenerated, restored. She hovered over Puck and checked if he was breathing.

When she noticed he was, she let out a sigh of relief. Feeling better after eating and renewed energy coursing through her veins, she stole another glance at the night sky once more. Quinn couldn't see any stars, but she did spot dark movement again.

Her stomach fell to the ground. It wasn't a figment of her imagination; she saw it clearly. It looked like a silhouette of a dinosaur, no, a dragon. Every internal alarm went off. She had to get out of here right now.

She grabbed Puck's arm and began dragging him toward the portal. With each pull, she glanced back up at the sky, her back facing the portal so she could prepare in case something swooped down and got her. The dragon lowered in a circular motion. It grew closer and closer.

At first, it appeared to be inspecting her, then a second dragon roared. This set her blood ablaze, and she yanked Puck through the portal, right as the first dragon landed. She wasn't convinced the dragon couldn't cross the portal, and she didn't want to find out.

She pulled Puck one more time and hit something. It wasn't an immovable object; it was a living thing. She held her breath, hoping it wasn't a threat. She jumped out of the frying pan into the fire.

It was the most beautiful brown Fae she'd ever seen. His wings were transparent except for the shimmering outline. There were three others present.

The tallest, she'd seen him before, and recognized the vibrant green wings, from the library. The female she didn't recognize was average-looking, for a Fae. The last Fae she knew.

"Oh, Puck," Ophelia gushed as she scooped him up.

Quinn let out her breath. She didn't think her nerves could take another scare.

"What happened to him?" Ophelia asked, her words rushed. "I didn't think you could get him out."

"What?" Quinn asked. "Then why did you send me there?" Her voice rose an octave with each word. She was shouting by the end of her sentence.

"You were my only hope," she said. "Long ago, someone close to me predicted this."

"Your sister?" Quinn asked.

Ophelia wasn't so stone-faced now. The surprise on her face said it all.

"Yeah, I met her."

She never saw Ophelia shocked, but this surprised her.

"You met my sister?" she asked. She was kneeling beside Puck, kissing his forehead. "My love, I am here."

Quinn nodded. And just like that, Ophelia's mask had returned.

"What happened to him?" she asked. "He's barely alive."

"A skull vax?" Quinn sounded out the name, turning it into more of a question.

Ophelia's eyes widened, the only break in her mask.

"A Skolavrax," she repeated. "How did you escape it?" she asked and glanced away. "They are fierce opponents."

"With the Blinding Light, Seraphina showed me."

"That was terribly dangerous. You could have been killed or permanently blinded with all the mirrors," the tallest Fae said.

"Who are you?"

"There's no time for introductions. You already met them. These are a few of the Freedom fighters. I sent them to assist you at the library," Ophelia said.

"I did? I only recognized him." Quinn pointed to the Fae with the blue hues.

Ophelia ignored her.

The concoction Seraphina gave me. That must be what they look like without their glamor. The female glowed last time. What could that mean? And the other male was kinda ugly. I can't piece this together now.

Quinn was too tired to worry. She did, however, want to know what had Cornelius so worried. "Ophelia, who's Gideon?" she asked.

Ophelia recoiled. "The dragon? You met the dragon. His mate is far more vicious despite her size. They rarely see humans, and most who see them never see the light of day again."

Quinn sighed; at least she didn't truly encounter the dragon, only from afar. "Why didn't you warn me of the dragons?" Quinn was nearly crying now. If she hadn't cried so much earlier, she'd be crying now.

She was met with stony silence.

"How did you know we'd be here?" Quinn asked.

"Locator spell," Ophelia answered curtly. She was performing a full-body check on Puck. "Now, tell me what happened to him, so I may cure him." Ophelia didn't even take her eyes off Puck. She touched him, searching for wounds and smelling for poisons, Quinn assumed.

Quinn was wracking her brain about locator spells and how many times they would've come in handy. *How could she hide this from me?*

When Quinn didn't answer right away, Ophelia nearly shouted, "Quinn, tell me."

Quinn jumped and spun around to face her. Her last nerve frayed; she sighed. She was nearing burnout. "I told you the Skull Vax bit him."

Ophelia's eyes widened, and she crouched, grabbing Puck's arm. She slung him over her shoulders.

"That bite contains potent neurotoxins." She stood and turned. "I must get him to Seraphina." Ophelia turned, took three steps, stopped, and called over her shoulder, "Send a message to Seraphina. Let her know what happened."

The other Fae followed her.

Quinn acted as if she had been slapped. "I don't know…" she started, but Ophelia was already running.

Unable to keep up, Quinn sat cross-legged and leaned forward, putting her head on her lap.

"Seraphina," she whispered. "Can you hear me?" Quinn sighed. *How can I contact her? She's only ever contacted me. I've gotta try.* "Seraphina, Puck's on his way, but he's been bitten by a Skull Vax."

She looked around but couldn't see Seraphina. She tried one last time. "Seraphina! Help."

Quinn gave up and crumpled to the ground, unable to make the long trek back to Seraphina's place.

***

When she woke up, she was inside Seraphina's hut. Ophelia was already there. The scent of the herbs that hung from the rafters, along with hushed voices, told Quinn where she was. She didn't open her eyes right away, hoping to learn some information.

When she hadn't heard anything useful, she finally spoke. "How exactly did you do a locator spell? And why the hell haven't we used them before?"

Ophelia and Seraphina stopped talking, but didn't turn to look at her. Seraphina, no doubt, already knew she had awakened.

"The locator spell comes at a great cost," Seraphina said.

"Tell me," Quinn demanded.

"It was due to the necklace you wear," Ophelia said cryptically.

"I'm sick of the non-answers. I want to know how to do one. I've been training here this whole time, and neither of you ever mentioned a locator spell."

"That is because the cost is too great, and the results are not accurate."

"I don't care. Show me how," Quinn demanded.

"Young one, Ophelia took on a great sacrifice performing the spell."

"And you need to rest," Ophelia said, not looking the least bit remorseful.

"It is a waste, anyway," Puck added.

"I don't care," she said. Turning to Puck, she said, "You owe me."

Puck feigned horror or surprise. "I owe you?" he asked.

"Yes," Quinn said, glaring at him. "I risked my life, my mother's, and Connor's."

"Was that not a debt you owed to Ophelia?" he asked, raising an eyebrow at her.

Quinn slammed her hand on the table.

"Ophelia was weakened beyond belief, and she destroyed an entire circle of lifeforms in order to perform it. Her magic reserves have been so low lately, as she did everything she could to save Puck despite not having any hope," Seraphina attempted to explain.

"I want to know," Quinn said.

"I will show you," Ophelia said.

"When?" Quinn asked. "I don't want it to be years from now."

"When your reserves have returned," Ophelia said.

"I'm not one of you. I don't have a power level to maintain."

"But you are weakened at this time," Seraphina said.

"Once you are at baseline, I will assist you," Ophelia said. She stood from her chair, making no noise, and exited the hut.

Quinn looked to Seraphina, who attempted to shrug, but it looked more like a shiver. Seraphina went back to the cauldron over the fireplace. She was stirring something. Quinn was left with Puck. She shot him another glare.

Quinn had completed her challenge, faced her biggest obstacles, and confronted her inner demons. She had mustered every last drop of her courage to succeed. She even made the most intense, life-altering decision and left her mother and Connor behind. Quinn didn't think she could take anything else.

"I did it." She passed out, hitting her head on the stone floor as she fell forward.

Chapter 27: Redemption and Sacrifice

Baxter

After what felt like an eternity of walking, Baxter could tell Connor's legs ached by how gingerly he was walking and rubbing them.

How was he falling behind? How long had it been since he walked?

Baxter called the group to a halt when Connor paused. His hands were on his knees, and he was breathing heavily.

"Why are we stopping?" Rufus demanded. His impatience was apparent in his crossed arms.

"I just need a minute," Baxter lied. He glanced at Connor using his peripherals.

Connor caught it and nodded in appreciation. Baxter sat cross-legged on the ground, knowing the others would follow.

These past few weeks had taken a toll on him; his face was hollow.

Who knows what he's been through?

Baxter had a hard time, and he wasn't in prison. He hardly left Connor's room, and an exhaustive depression overcame him. The heaviness of everything weighed on him. All he had seen and survived.

What Connor must've been through. I'm sure he doesn't want to talk about it.

Spending weeks, if not longer, locked in a cell, considering how time worked here. He looked half-starved, and after eating everything in sight at Celeste's, he had to be nauseous.

"We should get going," Jimmy said. His eyes darted around.

Baxter exhaled, raking his hand through his hair. He looked to Connor, who nodded once.

"Okay," Baxter said reluctantly. He stood up and froze.

Ahead of them were two gnarled trees that stood beside one another, the branches interlaced. Movement caught Baxter's eye. It was a figure that dashed between the trees. Baxter's pulse quickened as he raised a hand to signal to the others to stop.

Everyone froze. Connor held his leg up midstride. They hadn't encountered any danger for a long time. After moving as a unit, they developed their own unspoken language of hand gestures to communicate. It was mostly Connor's idea, and Baxter was certain it was from a video game.

The figure was briefly visible past the first tree, then it disappeared as it slipped behind the second. Baxter held his breath to attempt to sharpen his senses. With caution, they approached. Only Jimmy made noise, snapping a branch. They all froze and looked at him. There was no trace that anyone had been there.

"Who do you think it was?" Jimmy asked.

Connor didn't take his eyes off the spot where the figure last appeared. "Or what?" Connor corrected as his jaw clenched. His voice was low and ominous, betraying the things he had seen.

"It's gotta still be here," Rufus said. His eyes searched the area. "Things can't just disappear. Can they?"

Baxter didn't answer; he only nodded.

Connor gazed at the tops of the trees. He pointed up, and everyone looked together.

A Fae was crouched effortlessly on a high branch. She wore a crown that looked like it was made from birch branches on her head. A white-faced owl hooted on a nearby treetop. They all stared at a creature, as its long, tufted ears twitched.

Its golden eyes shone in the light of the two moons. It felt like the creature could see into the depths of one's soul. The owl took to the air, its feathered wings spreading wide as it leaped from its perch. The flapping of its wings was the only sound. They looked back toward the Fae when the owl was out of sight. She was no longer visible.

Before anyone could comment, a voice spoke from behind them, causing them to jump. Connor fell to the ground and didn't bother standing. His crown remained in place.

"You have developed your skills greatly, Shadow Walker."

"What the hell?" Rufus shouted as he spun around. His eyes were wide.

Baxter couldn't tell if his reaction was in fear or astonishment. This was the first Fae Rufus had encountered. Her skin had vines tattooed on it, with leaves covering her skin, as though she were woven with nature. Emerald green vines snaked around her arms and legs. Her deep red, moss-like hair moved as one solid thing.

"Eve," Baxter whispered. His eyes widened.

"Why do you call him Shadow Walker? He doesn't walk in shadows," Jimmy asked.

"They are considered a dark gift, a curse more than a blessing. It all depends on how you use your gift."

She moved gracefully toward Baxter. "The rotten branch will take out more than the limb," Eve repeated a warning from long ago.

It felt like a lifetime ago. Eve's gaze locked onto his, her expression unreadable. Her lack of movement created an ancient air about her. Her voice was firm, but not as scary as it once was.

"Beware, your birthmate is in grave danger. A friend will betray her," she said.

Quinn. Baxter's heart stopped beating as his stomach clenched.

"You must find the Grimoire Bás and take it from the overlord," she said. "Beware of Caprice, you already encountered him twice. Once, when your mother jumped into the pool."

The very mention of Mr. Perry turned his blood to ice, chilling his whole body.

"That hooded guy with," he paused. "Mr. Perry?" Baxter asked. It physically hurt to say his name. Hearing his mom mentioned was gut-wrenching.

"The one in the same," she replied. "Beware, water acts as a mirror, and they are dangerous."

Baxter's mind raced. *Reflections are the same as mirrors.* The weight of this revelation settled like cement in his stomach. *What happens if you fall into a reflection? Mom.* Baxter shook his head and with it any false hope. She was gone. He needed to focus on Quinn.

Eve took a step closer, her moss-like hair moving unnaturally, as if by the wind, yet there was none. Jimmy also moved a step closer in a protective manner. Eve ignored him.

"You are the Protector of the Realms and have been slacking in your duties since we last spoke." Her eyes pierced into him, obtaining information.

Baxter lingered at the top of a roller coaster, fear freezing every muscle, waiting for the drop.

"You're the Protector of the Realms?" Rufus asked, holding back a laugh. "You?" His smile widened.

Jimmy elbowed him hard in the gut. A puff of air escaped Rufus's lips.

Baxter glared at him, then turned back to Eve. "Realms?" Baxter asked.

Unfazed by Jimmy's elbow, Rufus continued to interrupt. "Whoa, there's more than one," he said with barely contained excitement.

"Guys, stop, I need to focus." Baxter exhaled long and slow.

Eve's cryptic messages were frustrating, but not without purpose. "This is important. How do I help? I don't know anything about being a protector of the realm."

"Find the Freedom Fighters," Eve answered.

Baxter's head snapped from his friend to her. *At least she's answering questions this time, instead of all those riddles.*

"I've heard of them," he tried to play it cool. "Ophelia's group, right?"

Eve took another step forward. "They were originally created by humans, an ancient order that once battled the Fey to maintain balance. Now, they are almost extinct."

"Fae?" Rufus asked.

Baxter swallowed hard, fighting back the feelings overwhelming him.

Once again ignoring Rufus, Eve continued, "Since then, Fae have foreseen your world's end, due to our clash with humans. We have joined the Freedom Fighters to prevent it."

"Fighters?" Connor asked.

"Yes, to ensure the safety of your world."

Baxter felt like he was now dropping on that roller coaster. *I'm the Protector of the Realms? Betrayal, Quinn, a Grimoire.*

"Realms?" Connor echoed, catching up to the conversation.

Baxter looked at Connor. His brows were furrowed, and he frowned.

He's been strangely quiet the whole time. I hope he's okay.

She ignored Connor. "You recall the Shenzhen Nongke Orchid?" she asked, pausing until Baxter nodded. "It was mixed with human blood and made Unseelie evil."

I caused all of this by giving Mr. Perry that plant.

Baxter took a few steadying breaths, but it wasn't helping. For the first time, he had no idea what to do. His lungs felt as if they were in a vice. He was going to have to figure it out and fast.

Baxter's hands trembled; he shoved them into his pockets, hoping nobody would notice. His breaths became rapid and uneven. When his vision started to darken at the edges, he heard Jimmy's voice.

Jimmy now stood between Baxter and Eve, his hand on his hips. "This is great, warnings and betrayal, but where do we go?" he asked, his voice forceful.

Eve opened her mouth to answer, but Jimmy lifted a hand and cut her off. "No more riddles and bewares. What actual way? Point." His anger was barely contained.

Baxter knew it wasn't merely frustration; his friend sensed his anxiety. Jimmy had always been good at reading him. "Speak plainly."

Baxter swallowed and drew in a deep, slow breath, exhaling through his nose. The vice on his lungs loosened. Jimmy was right. They needed directions, not warnings.

Feeling a little better now that Jimmy intervened. Baxter wasn't confident how Eve would react to Jimmy's blunt demand. She stood utterly motionless for a few seconds; he wasn't sure she was breathing.

Then she turned her whole body in one fluid motion and pointed to her left. All four of them looked in that direction. No words, no riddles, just direction.

"Heed my word, Shadow Walker," Eve called from seemingly nowhere. They looked back, and she was gone.

"That was intense," Rufus said.

Jimmy scowled. Baxter couldn't tell if it was due to Eve or Rufus. Jimmy glared at Rufus. Baxter looked at Connor, who appeared rested. They had a direction now and no other choice.

"I guess we go this way," Baxter said with a shrug.

No obvious path to where they were going presented itself. Baxter was very careful not to stray from the direction Eve had pointed. The rustling of the grass created a whimsical melody. Baxter still wasn't used to the teal color and the stiffness of the greenery, which was similar to grass in the winter back home when frozen stiff. Here, the grass was more like glass.

Connor rose from the ground with as much grace as an old man. He brushed the dirt off his pants and walked to stand beside Baxter. Without a word, they ambled on, their footsteps the only sound.

"So," Connor broke the silence. "Who do you think is going to betray her?" he whispered.

Baxter frowned. "I don't know," Baxter said, keeping his face forward.

"I bet it's Puck," Connor said. His distaste for Puck wasn't out of nowhere. Puck was cruel, particularly to Connor.

"Who's Puck?" Jimmy asked, matching pace with Baxter and Connor.

The three of them walked side by side while the trees were sparse.

"Yeah," Rufus chimed in from behind. His amusement wasn't contained. He was acting like this was a day at a theme park.

Connor grunted, unable to hide his annoyance. He had been more irritable since he came back. Baxter thought it was justifiable, but he wasn't used to his happy-go-lucky friend being so negative.

"I still don't understand why we had to bring him," Connor said, turning to eye Rufus.

Connor made a face and turned back around. Baxter imagined Rufus sticking out his tongue or rolling his eyes. He didn't bother to glance back and see.

"I told you, he was going to come anyway, and I couldn't let him go on a suicide mission," Baxter said. "Plus, he saved my hide from a trap."

This time, Baxter glanced over his shoulder. Rufus had a smirk on his face with an arched eyebrow. Baxter offered him a weak smile. While Rufus had redeemed himself, Baxter had tolerated years of torment from him.

People did change, but Baxter wasn't convinced it was that fast. It was only last year that Rufus pranked him so badly that Baxter ended up at Oakdale. He didn't have to like the guy, even if he helped him. That wasn't enough to tolerate him, for now.

Chapter 28: Changelings and Halflings

Baxter

The ground had a worn path that they stumbled upon after walking in silence. It was strange for Connor to be so quiet. He'd been through hell. When Baxter first saw him, it finally felt like home. Now, he was back to when it all began. He worried about his friend.

Baxter started to recognize the area. They were heading for Seraphina's house. He knew this path, her half-hidden house. To an untrained eye, it was another patch of gnarled trees and vines surrounding a boulder, but Baxter had been here before.

Without caution, they approached the house. Movement caught Baxter's eye in the backyard. It was Celeste, dancing whimsically with Theo. They both laughed, as carefree as ever.

Baxter moved as silently as he could. He almost didn't want to interrupt the magical moment, almost.

"Hello, Celeste, Theo." Baxter smiled. It was nice to see them again and to see them so happy.

Celeste returned the smile without missing a step. "Baxter, it's so nice to see you," Celeste said. She continued dancing, as if in a trance.

Theo looked up at the group and waved. "Hey, Connor, my boy, how are you?" he said with a wide grin. "Baxter." Theo nodded at them as he twirled Celeste in a few circles.

"Hey, Theo," Connor replied with a weak smile and a slight wave.

"What are you guys doing?" Baxter asked.

Theo spun Celeste.

"Oh, we're dancing before this moon water," she said.

Baxter raised an eyebrow but decided he didn't want to know. The lanterns didn't have a flame, and tiny dots swarmed around in it. Vibrant, colorful flowers adorned the backyard. Baxter twisted his hands together.

"Baxter, my boy, do you still have that book I gave ya? You know, Inn Plane site?" he asked.

"Ya, somewhere," he said noncommittal. *Did I leave it at home? Not now.* He shook his head once. "Have you seen my sister?" Baxter asked.

"Yes, she's resting inside," Celeste answered without missing a beat. "I'm afraid she hit her head."

His blood ran cold. "What?" Baxter asked, voice a little too high.

Connor straightened. "Is she okay?" he asked, his brows furrowed.

"Yes," Theo said. "That's why we're dancing," he explained.

"You're dancing because she's okay?" Baxter asked.

A soft laugh came from Celeste. "No, we're making enchanting moon water," she said. Theo spun her again. "For my tea. It will speed up her healing," Celeste said, as if it were completely obvious. "I possess a little magic. It's all whether you believe in it and cultivate it."

"I'm helping her cultivate it," Theo said with a wink.

Connor crossed his arms. "Why not give her your goulash or sweetgum seed pod thing?"

She placed a hand over her heart. "Oh, well, I'm simply out," Celeste said, winded from dancing and talking simultaneously. Her flowing skirts flared out with her twirling movements.

"What do you mean, you're out?" Connor asked. His brows raised. "Can't you just make more?"

"I don't have the ingredients," she said between breaths. "So many injuries on Puck, I thought we'd lose him."

He went rigid. "You gave Puck care over Quinn," Connor said, his irritation not concealed at all.

"Oh, goodness no," Celeste said. "When she brought him back, she was uninjured."

Baxter and Connor exchanged looks. "She got injured here?" Baxter asked. *The friend who betrayed her.*

Celeste nodded and didn't miss a beat. "Yes, that's what I said," she replied. "I see you found my jester's hat from the Renaissance Fair." She smiled.

"Renaissance Fair?" Connor asked. He removed it from his head.

Rufus laughed. "I knew it."

Connor faced Rufus, but Baxter spun on his heel and headed for the entrance of the house. He heard arguing but ignored them. Seconds later, the rest of the boys followed him. Someone here had hurt Quinn. First, he needed to see her; he'd deal with that someone next. Baxter's hand reached for the doorknob, ready to slam it open, when it swung open.

In the doorway stood Seraphina. Her dark purple eyes glinted with white rings. She slowly looked at each of them and smiled.

"Hello, Manlings."

Baxter ignored the greeting. "Where's my sister?" he asked, impatient.

Without waiting for an answer, he pushed past her in search of Quinn. Baxter heard the footsteps of the others following him in. The distinct scent of herbs filled the air.

Shadows danced on the walls cast by lanterns that appeared to contain fireflies; the soft golden glow created an ambiance. Baxter scanned the room frantically for Quinn. The shelves lining the walls held vials filled with liquids of every color. There, in the back of the kitchen, was Quinn lying on a cot.

She was supine, and a worn brown blanket covered her. He noted her chest rose and fell and let out a sigh of relief. An olive-green paste coated her pale cheeks, a healing remedy, no doubt.

"Quinn," Baxter gasped. She was filthy, and her clothes were in tatters. "Quinn, are you alright?"

There was no response. Her motionless body caused his mind to race with negative possibilities. He dropped to his knees beside her. Baxter's hand hovered tentatively over her forehead before making contact. Quinn's skin was warm, but not feverish. Her eyes fluttered. They had a white ring around the edge.

Her eyes.

Quinn yawned. "Baxter, what are you doing here?" she whispered. Blinking, she looked at each of them in the face. When her eyes rested on Rufus, she said, "What's *he* doing here?"

Rufus crossed his arms with a huff. "Nice to see you, too." His muscles looked even bigger in this position.

Baxter shrugged. "Long story. Are you hurt?" he asked, his voice filled with concern.

Quinn shook her head. "What happened?" she asked, sitting up on the cot with a wince.

Her hand cradled the back of her neck. The cauldron in the fireplace was bubbling over, distracting them momentarily. The lime-green flame was surprisingly not hot despite its proximity.

"What happened to you?" Baxter asked, repeating her question, his brow creased.

Quinn eyed Rufus still, her face skeptical and cautious.

Jimmy let out a loud and long exhale. "Let's get out of here," he said.

Baxter glanced at Connor, who still hadn't spoken, which wasn't like him. Connor was staring at Quinn with a horrified expression on his face. Baxter was certain he was beating himself up for leaving Quinn in Fata. For not being there for her. Baxter placed a reassuring hand on Connor's shoulder with a firm squeeze.

Connor swallowed hard and broke his silence. "Are you well enough to walk?" he asked.

"I think so," Quinn said, slowly sitting up.

Baxter helped her into a sitting position.

"Not so fast," Ophelia said from the doorway.

She wore a predatory smile. Her purple eyes flashed. Only a fool wouldn't question their safety in her company.

"Whoa. Who's that?" Rufus blurted out. His mouth hung open. Thankfully, he had been quiet entering the house. This wasn't a good time to start talking now.

Baxter tensed. *Really.*

Ophelia didn't even glance at Rufus. She leaned against the doorframe with ease, no longer the stiff statue she'd been. Zmija slithered up her arm.

If he's awake, it's dangerous.

"Cool snake. Can I pet it?" Rufus asked.

The moment stretched on forever as the silence spread between them like a fog rolling over the land. The longer she was quiet, the more worried Baxter felt.

Ophelia coiled like a predator, poised to spring. After a while, she relaxed minutely. "I wanted to thank you. I free you from your pact," she said. Zmija now around her neck, tongue flicking toward Rufus.

The faint smell of muskle berry filled the air. Not just the scent, Baxter could sense the power in the air of the pact dissolving.

He stepped back, mouth open. "Whoa."

Silently, another figure entered the room. Baxter couldn't tell who it was past all the bodies in the room.

"Quinn, you should not travel yet. You spent too much energy," Seraphina said, "I sensed you opened a portal."

"That's what happened after I threw the Blinding Light at the monster," Quinn said to herself, figuring it all out.

"Your visions will not be as clear, and if you use too much energy, you may never regain consciousness."

Baxter's thoughts raced. He knew Quinn was in danger, but monsters and portals. Both were deadly. She nearly died after her last portal.

Rufus started searching the room, oblivious to the tension. He lifted his nose and sniffed the air. "Oh, is someone making blueberry pie?" he asked with a smile. "It's my favorite."

Baxter shook his head.

"At least wear your glasses, if your visions come back before you exit the prison again," Celeste called from the doorway.

"What?" Baxter asked. His eyebrows raised.

"If her visions return too quickly, it might overwhelm her. She may not be able to filter them," Seraphina explained. "They limit her visions to one at a time."

219

Quinn looked into Baxter's eye, her own glistening with unshed tears. "Mom's still alive."

Baxter stumbled back, his hand flew over his heart. He felt as if he'd been punched.

"What?" he gasped. "How?"

Quinn shook her head. "I don't know. I only saw her." Tears were on the verge of spilling.

Baxter's throat tightened. He attempted to clear it. "Are you sure it was her and not some kinda trick?" he asked, his voice raw, not ready to believe it was possible.

"I'm sure," she whispered. "She's trapped there all alone, and I just left her there."

Tears sprang from her eyes, the faucet now open. Baxter sat beside her on the cot, arm around her shoulders. He pulled her in for a hug. She sobbed into his shoulder.

Resting his chin on the top of her head, Baxter said, "We'll find her." His conviction wasn't just for her, but for him as well.

Once her sobs subsided, Baxter released her from his embrace.

"Wait, how did Mom even get into the prison?" Baxter asked.

"The halfling and changeling were behind that," Ophelia said.

"Who?" Connor and Baxter asked in unison.

"Your father, Doug discovered the truth and was about to reveal their plans," Seraphina said.

"Who?" Connor asked again.

"You call him Cole," she said. "Cole, a halfling, and Grace, a changeling, shared a father."

"Theo?" Baxter asked.

"No, Theo is not Fae. Their father was named Magnus Lyons. Grace wore contacts to conceal her white eyes and true nature."

Their father is Fae.

"Did she say changeling?" Jimmy asked.

"A changeling is a Fae switched with a human baby, and a halfling is half Fae, half human," Ophelia said.

"Who was switched, and where did the baby go?" Quinn asked.

"They were using a book to communicate," Seraphina said, ignoring the question.

That book Cole was always reading. What was it? Whispering Shadows of something Echoes.

"Their child had been stolen, most likely became a slave for power or was they lost in the folds of time," Seraphina said.

A slave? Baxter's head spun.

"The book was spelled to communicate between portals, you write on one end, and it shows on the other," Ophelia explained. "Puck ended their father and ended up in prison."

"Like an Etch A Sketch," Connor said.

Ignoring his interruption, Seraphina said, "Grace realized your father discovered the truth, and she had his memory wiped before he could expose them."

"Who's Grace?" Connor asked.

Baxter eyed him.

"Cole's sister that went missing," Jimmy answered.

"Oh yeah," Connor said.

Baxter's world spun. "Guys," he said, exasperated.

All the questions cease. The silence stretched throughout the room. The stillness was uncomfortable.

Quinn tilted her head sideways. "What truth?" she asked, breaking the silence.

Baxter let out a long, slow exhale. "Dad knew about all of this?"

"The siblings planned on trapping your mother all along," Seraphina said calmly. "She made it easier by jumping into that pool."

Baxter stiffened, recalling that memory. That first encounter in Fata with Mr. Perry. "The water," Baxter said.

Quinn's mouth made an 'O' shape; the realization was setting in. "It's a pathway into the prison," she finished his sentence.

Ophelia crossed the room. "That is why they are forbidden," she said.

"If that's a way in, we could use a mirror to get into the prison," Jimmy said.

Everyone in the room turned to scowl at him.

"May your crow fly north," Ophelia said.

"Are you serious?" Connor asked, his voice was a little too high.

Jimmy shrugged. "What? It's a way in."

"Yeah," Connor cut him off, his voice deep with knowing disdain, "if you want to never see the light of day again."

The room fell silent once more. A new figure entered the room. It was Connor's turn to stiffen. Rufus looked him up and down, as if assessing his threat level. He thankfully stayed quiet this time.

Puck crossed his arms and gave the room a half smile. "Getting in is not the problem," he paused, letting his words sink in, "getting out is."

They recapped what they knew of the prison. The tormenting reflections, the traps, endless mazes, and the creatures protecting its halls. How the prison didn't want to let you go.

Baxter listened intently. If he wanted to save his mother, he needed to know all the dangers. "I saw it, you know," he whispered.

"Saw what?" Jimmy asked.

"Quinn and Puck in the prison," Baxter answered to his shoes, "in a dream." He couldn't bear to look at Quinn. Not yet.

Quinn's eyes widened. "I knew I saw you," she said, her voice shrill.

Puck tilted his head, interest piqued, clearly, in the dark on this.

"I thought it was a vision," Quinn elaborated.

Seraphina eyed Baxter; her face was unreadable. She smiled. "That wasn't a dream, Baxter." Her voice was soothing.

Baxter's stomach twisted. Seraphina took a slow step toward him.

"That is your gift. To Shadow Walk between realms. As you practice, you can do it at will."

The room closed in around him. He doubted he could control it; he hadn't been sleeping after all. His mother was trapped; now he had a way to see her. If only he knew how.

Connor jabbed a finger into Puck's chest. "We wouldn't be in this mess if it weren't for you."

Puck's eyes darted from his finger to Connor, and he swiped it away. "Going back for *you* nearly got us killed."

Connor stepped forward, nose to nose with Puck. His fists were clenched.

Jimmy shoved Connor back. "You two want to fight, fine. But not right now." Jimmy eyed them both. "Now, are we done here?" he asked. Neither responded. "Baxter's mom is trapped, and we're standing here instead of rescuing her."

They made haste in leaving, despite many warnings from the Fae.

Chapter 29: Dreams Reimagined

Baxter

Once they were far enough away from the house, Jimmy walked beside Baxter. "Why didn't we ask Ophelia or Seraphina to help get your mom?" Jimmy asked.

"Someone's going to betray Quinn," Baxter answered. "Besides, do you really want to owe Ophelia a favor?"

"Good point," Jimmy said.

"Someone's going to betray me?" Quinn asked.

"Eve told me that," Baxter answered.

"I wouldn't mind owing her a favor," Rufus said suggestively.

"Puck would kill you if she didn't first," Connor said. He smiled as if he imagined it happening.

"You definitely don't wanna owe her a favor," Quinn said.

The green paste was still on her face. It dripped onto her Bob Marley T-shirt, covering the 'e' in "one." The shirt now read "on love." She showed no signs of weakness, but Baxter knew her too well; he knew she was pretending to be fine.

The group walked like a pack of teens going to the beach. They were not the uniformed, trained unit. They were too loud, and not everyone took the risks seriously. Rufus threw a stone into a nearby bog.

I hope nobody gets hurt.

"Can I see that map?" Rufus asked.

"No," Baxter, Connor, and Quinn said simultaneously.

A vicious snarl erupted from the woods, paralyzing them with fear. Out of nowhere, a four-legged creature lunged for Jimmy, then dove into the dense brush. It resembled a hybrid of a dog and a frog. A giant hairless Labrador with curved hind legs.

Its muscular dog-shaped body had odd hind legs. With slick, glistening, seal-like skin, with the legs of a frog. Gills flared at its sides. Its yellow teeth were razor sharp as it snapped its jaw.

Baxter shouted, "Look out behind you."

Connor dove out of the way. Jimmy was not as fast. The creature reappeared.

Jimmy was thrown off his feet and dragged by his backpack ten feet away before something blue flew past them. The creature yelped and released its grip on Jimmy. The object fell from the beast, covered in neon green ooze. Blood. The animal skirted away.

Baxter's stomach knotted at the sight of the blood, but he didn't get sick. He'd overcome his phobia of blood. Connor glanced at the blood, then Baxter.

He's making sure I can handle the blood.

A knife carved from a bone with a vine wrapped around it was embedded in the tree.

"I know that knife," Connor said. Puck threw one right past his face when they'd first met, a threat. Baxter looked in the direction from which the knife was thrown. Leaning up against a tree with one leg crossed over the other was Puck.

"Well, that was close," he said, inspecting his nails.

"You were following us?" Quinn questioned him.

Puck shrugged as if he were going on an evening stroll. He stepped out from the tree line. He faced Quinn. "I couldn't let you go alone."

"I'm not alone," Quinn said, gesturing around her to the others.

225

Rufus was crouching next to where the dogfish had last been. "Here, puppy, puppy," he said, turning back to the others. "Man, that thing was cool."

"I owe you my life," Puck said simply. "Seems only fair."

"Oh, now you owe me?" she asked.

Jimmy was still sitting on the ground, huffing and puffing. Baxter approached Jimmy to comfort him.

"We don't need a babysitter," Connor said, his face contorted.

"Too bad," Puck said. "I did not ask you." He turned to Quinn, who had her arms crossed. "I owe you my life," Puck repeated.

"Are you alright, man?" he asked.

Jimmy was still catching his breath. "I think so," he said. "My life flashed before my eyes."

Baxter peered up as the others had gathered around. He offered his hand to help Jimmy up. He reluctantly took it.

"Let's go," Baxter said.

They gathered everything they littered the ground with during the commotion. Their backpacks were leaden with charms, potions, weapons, and food; they were ready as they would ever be.

Puck led the way, and the others followed, passing a gnarled sapling. He waved away a curtain of willow leaves. "This way. I know a shortcut."

They travelled single file down a dense path.

"Should we bring Quinn and Rufus home?" Connor asked Baxter. His brows knit together.

"Nobody's taking me anywhere," Quinn said. She crossed her arms; her stance said, 'Don't even try me.'

"If something happens to you…" Connor started to say, but Quinn cut him off.

"Says the guy who we all thought died." She looked mildly guilty.

"What about him?" Connor gestured at Rufus, who was still looking for the creature.

"There's no time," Baxter interrupted.

"How do we know he isn't going to betray her?" Connor asked, pointing at Puck.

Puck acted as if he'd been shot. He crossed his arms, stopping in his tracks, and his face turned serious. "You don't."

Quinn studied him for a moment and said, "I trust him." She gave a weak smile.

Connor clenched his jaw but didn't argue.

"Look how hard it was when we dragged Cole everywhere," Connor said.

"Where did Cole go, anyway?" Baxter asked.

Connor shrugged. They end up agreeing to go together. As they trudged along, somehow, with the addition of Puck, they became more uniform, stealthier. Whether it was in fear of him, Baxter didn't know.

They walked on in silence.

Unable to bite her tongue, Quinn asked, "What about Ophelia's sister?"

Puck stilled. Not turning to face her, he said, "My deepest regret." He shook his head and continued without another word on the matter.

After a time, Quinn and Puck each warned them about the mirages the reflections in the mirrors created.

"You'll see things that seem so real, but they aren't," Quinn warned. "They're your worst fears and deepest regrets. They play on your emotions." She hesitated. "The prison tries to keep you."

Puck, with a somber expression, nodded. "If you look too long, you may forget what side of the looking glass you belong."

When Quinn mentioned dragons, both Rufus and Connor perked up and peppered her with questions.

"There's dragons here?" Rufus asked.

"No, not here. In the mirror realm," Puck answered. "Though I suppose nothing is stopping them from coming here."

"Mirror realm. So, we're leaving this realm?" Jimmy asked.

"It's not too far from this realm," Quinn answered, looking around. "I've never been here, I'm not sure."

"Are they friendly?" Rufus asked, ignoring that the conversation had turned.

"Can we fly them?" Connor asked, practically bouncing on his toes with each step.

Baxter smiled. It was nice to see Connor back to his usual self.

"You most definitely cannot," Puck said dryly.

"I don't know," Quinn said, smirking at their enthusiasm.

"What's it like?" Rufus asked, like a child would over a celebrity crush.

"Are they friendly?" Connor asked, not letting her answer.

"You already asked that," Quinn said.

"I didn't ask that," Connor said. His forehead wrinkled.

"I asked that," Rufus said.

"And you didn't answer that question," Connor reminded her.

"I don't know," Quinn answered. "I saw him and ran."

"A wise decision. His name is Gideon," Puck answered. "And I would not describe him as friendly. Fierce is a better term."

"Awesome," Connor said. His eyes were wide with childlike wonder. Their formation crumbled. Rufus and Connor walked in front of them backwards.

"Guys, get serious," Baxter reprimanded.

"Sorry," Connor said and sighed. "But I might never get to meet a dragon again in my entire life."

Baxter sighed and shook his head. "You two are in no way going to seek out that dragon," Baxter warned.

"All your chatter will alert the beast of our location," Puck cautioned. "Easy prey."

"I'm not easy prey," Rufus said, flexing his arms.

"Those will not save you against a Vorstax," Puck said dryly. "A gaping hole where its face be drags you into oblivion, and it is ten times your size. They live in the mirror realm." He eyed Quinn. "We are lucky we did not meet them."

The name got their attention. No matter if it was the first or tenth time here, there was so much they didn't know.

We're lucky we've only seen a few of the creatures that live here. Baxter shivered. I don't wanna meet a Vorstax.

"Cold, man?" Jimmy asked.

"No, just thinking," Baxter said.

"Wanna talk?" Jimmy asked.

"No, but thanks," Baxter said with a weak smile.

"Here is the shortcut, more of a portal, but not quite. A rip between realms," Puck explained.

Quinn knew the way from here. They crossed into the Mirror World. The pathways twisted and changed as they passed, or the reflections did as the maze moved.

Baxter watched as Rufus caught his reflection, and he flexed his muscles. He looked around and saw multiple versions of himself.

"I already love this place," he said with a wry smile.

Rufus turned and faced another mirror, and a shorter, thinner version of himself, with sagging muscles, stared back at him. He stopped walking.

"I hate this place," he muttered.

Jimmy and Connor snickered. Baxter fought the smile forming on his lips. He looked at Quinn, who was also fighting a smile, but failing.

A clashing sound of metal erupted, and everyone froze, looking to Puck. He shrugged. It echoed loudly as it bounced off the glass. Once they got around a large, jagged wall, two figures fought in combat.

It looks like a bull standing on two legs.

One creature lunged, narrowly missing the other with its horns. The other spun on a hoof at the last minute. The first creature bore sharp teeth. In a deep, grumbling voice, he barked, "You're slowing down, Tessa."

"And you're too predictable," Tessa called back.

He charged at her once more, and this time he knocked her to the ground with a laugh.

Baxter tensed, wishing he had a weapon. "They are going to kill each other."

Quinn shook her head. "No. This is their form of flirting."

Rufus was wide-eyed. "I think I need to reevaluate my definition of romance," he said.

"Hey, Cornelius, over here," Quinn shouted, waving to the creatures.

"A Minotaur," Connor gasped. Baxter couldn't tell if he was scared or in complete awe.

Now, noticing them, Cornelius gave them a toothy grin and charged at them.

"Whoa, whoa," Jimmy yelled as he dove out of the way with only seconds to spare. The others jumped out of the way with a little more grace.

"Perfect timing," Cornelius said, stopping right before hitting them. He turned to Jimmy. "Well, except for you. Gotta work on that timing."

Jimmy reddened.

"Hello, stranger," Quinn said.

"How are you, Quinn?" he asked. He patted Puck on the back, causing him to look out of sorts for once. He turned to Puck. "Glad to see you using your legs."

From across the way, Tessa shouted, "So you're just gonna quit?" She dug her hoof into the ground and kicked it.

Where they'd battled, the ground was like sand. The glass was all but shattered and pulverized.

"For now, my dear," Cornelius shouted back and then huffed through his snout.

"I owe you for helping me," he said and flicked his head in the direction of Tessa. "With you know."

"It was nothing," Quinn said.

"So, you've been playing with bulls this whole time," Rufus said.

She ignored him. "We're heading back to the prison to rescue my mom."

"You sure you want to do that?" Cornelius asked. "You are the only one I've ever seen leave without a guard."

"We don't have a choice. Our mother is in there."

Cornelius looked over the group and said, "That's quite a brood she has there."

"We're not…" She exhaled audibly. "It doesn't matter."

"I've seen many more guards around now, too," Cornelius said, gesturing in the direction of the prison.

"Great," Connor mumbled.

"I can assist you in getting there safely," Cornelius offered.

"I'd appreciate that," Quinn said with a smile.

"Hey, babe. I'm going on a mission," he shouted. "Wanna come?"

"Can I trample someone?" Tessa shouted back as she ran at full sprint toward them.

"Only the guards," Quinn interjected quickly.

Tessa halted right before colliding with Cornelius.

"Then they will have to do."

Tessa exposed her teeth.

I think that's a smile, hopefully.

Chapter 30: Reentering the Prison

Quinn

They marched toward the prison. The glass was all broken and cracked. It made reflections minimal. It was much more conspicuous this time, with the Minotaurs stomping their hooves on the mirrored ground. Their heavy footsteps shook the very ground they walked on. Tessa made little attempt to be quiet. She led the pack, her impatience visible.

I think she's trying to lure the guards to her just so she can fight them.

After walking as a pack, Tessa took off without a word. Shimmering dust flew up in her tracks.

Cornelius huffed. "Save some for me, my Fluffy Munchkin," he called as he took off after her. His voice was obnoxious and childlike

Quinn smiled.

"What is it?" Jimmy asked.

Connor and Baxter exchanged glances.

"Should we go after them?" Connor asked, concern apparent in his tone.

A distant clanking metal echoed through the air, followed by a cry of pain. The group took off running toward the sound. The guards found them, or Tessa found the guards. As they climbed the hill, screams and shouts could be heard. Once the others caught up to them, Tessa charged the last guard. She appeared to be having the time of her life. She bucked the last guard right over her head. His spear appeared to bounce right off Tessa. He flipped twice midair before he landed with a painful crunching sound. The guard's limbs were bent in unnatural angles. Guards were scattered across the ground.

Tessa let out a puff through her snout and said, "That was fun."

Blood stained the ground.

"Tessa, you're bleeding," Quinn gasped.

Tessa's flank had a gash; the spear hadn't bounced off her. The edges of the wound were raw and glistened with crimson.

"It's nothing," Tessa said, shaking her mane, and droplets of blood flew everywhere.

Baxter stepped back. While he seemed to have overcome his fear of blood, Quinn guessed he didn't like it.

Cornelius sniffed Tessa's side. "You did great," he snorted. "See, getting slow."

Tessa's eyes flared. She tilted her head down and locked her horns with Cornelius's horns. They struggled for a moment, and the clanking of the horns made Rufus step back.

He'd been unusually quiet ever since meeting the Minotaurs. Cornelius jerked his head and twisted free of the lock with a grunt.

"Are you sure you're okay?" Baxter asked. He eyed the blood seeping into her fur. He looked weary.

"Nothing time won't heal," Tessa said. She stomped her hoof into the ground. The cracking glass sound sent shivers down Quinn's spine.

"It will make an epic battle wound," Cornelius snorted again.

Jimmy looked around. "They probably raised an alarm."

"We should get going," Connor said, surveying the area.

"This is where we leave you," Cornelius said. Without another word, he and Tessa took off stomping away.

"Do you think she's okay?" Baxter asked Quinn.

"I think she will be fine," she said.

**

Guards were everywhere. Their boots clicked against the ground. They made easy work of dodging them despite the group's size. The guards had a predictable pattern.

"They're expecting us," Connor said. He glanced about.

"No one had ever escaped before," Puck explained. "So, they never needed many guards."

They were so close. Connor led the way; it was apparent that the mountain before them was the prison. He quickened his pace. Rufus was hot on his heels.

Then, Rufus jutted out a hand over Connor's shoulder, yanking him back, nearly knocking him off his feet. It seemed that Rufus wanted to be first.

"Back off," Connor growled.

Puck tossed a rock onto the ground before them, and it collapsed, revealing multiple sharpened spikes. Connor's eyes widened. He'd been about to step on that false ground. Rufus had stopped him, saved him. He turned to Rufus.

"Thank you," he whispered.

"No problem," Rufus said.

"No, really, man. I would've died."

Rufus waved his hand.

"How did you know that was there?" Quinn asked.

"The color was off. See," Rufus said, pointing to the corner that hadn't fallen in on itself.

It was lighter than its surroundings. Considering Connor's history with falling into bottomless pits, he was exceptionally grateful. They eventually made it to the prison without any further issues, other than the one trap. Puck now led the way.

"This isn't where the keyhole is," Quinn said.

"The shard is the key to the entire prison," Puck explained.

"W-what?" Quinn stuttered. "You could've told me that sooner."

"It mattered not at the time," Puck said. "You hold the key before the glass like this, and it will open."

He tilted the shard to reflect onto the glass so they could see themselves.

Quinn moved the shard as directed, and the glass opened at a different location. The air around them shimmered like a diamond, or maybe it was all the reflections moving at once.

"Why didn't you tell me this sooner?" Quinn demanded, she crossed her arms.

"I thought you knew. You got me out and watched me get Connor out," he protested.

The ground trembled as the entrance opened. In the doorway stood two huge guards.

Puck made taking down the guards look effortless. It was all a blur.

Connor touched the glass and shivered. The reflection grinned. Quinn knew he wasn't smiling. He jerked his hand back as if he'd been burned.

Quinn watched as Baxter and Connor exchanged glances. Connor had been acting stranger than usual. This return to the prison had to be re-traumatizing him. Connor's eyes were wide and darting everywhere.

"It's best to not look at the reflections for too long," Puck said as he passed them.

They navigated the prison much faster this time. Quinn took off to the right. She gestured to the others to follow.

Connor shook his head. "No. I went this way last time."

"You also collapsed the bridge last time," Puck corrected.

Connor crossed his arms.

Quinn exhaled. "Standing here arguing isn't helping Mom."

"It's the only way I know," Connor said. "We may encounter more guards wandering around."

"We're supposed to cross a giant hole?" Rufus asked skeptically. His forehead furrowed.

"The guards may have fixed it. If not, they wouldn't expect us this way," Connor rationalized.

"I guess it makes sense," Jimmy agreed. "But how do we cross if there's no bridge?"

Puck smirked and said, "I may be of service with that."

Baxter's eyes narrowed. "Why do I feel like I'm not going to like this?"

"You won't," he said cryptically. A wry smile crossed his face.

After a heated discussion, they agreed to try Connor's path. There were no further encounters with any guards when they arrived at the ravine. They most likely assumed no one would come this way. The bridge had not been rebuilt.

"How do we cross that?" Jimmy asked.

"See, I told you," Quinn started, and gasped.

Baxter turned to see what had happened. "I've seen this place before."

"Duh. We came here not that long ago," Connor said. His hands waved with frustration.

"No, before that," Quinn said as she waved Connor away. "In a vision."

Baxter dropped to his knee and rummaged through his pack. After a moment, he retrieved his hag stone. The polished round stone with the hole in the center allowed him to see through glamour. He lifted it to his eye and searched the ravine.

"What do you see?" Connor asked.

"What the heck is that thing?" Jimmy asked.

"It's a hag stone," Puck said dryly.

Quinn grabbed the rock from Baxter when he didn't answer them. He gasped for air.

She spotted a narrow ledge to the right of the ravine. Not wide enough for them to cross.

"I remember this, Quinn said, walking to the other end of the ravine. She gasped and lowered the stone.

"What's the matter?" Jimmy asked, rushing to her side.

"It's the stone. In exchange for seeing through magical glamours, it sucks your breath away," Baxter answered, following Quinn.

They reached the edge of the cavern. Quinn held it up to her eye again and inspected a bit of plain wall. She removed the hag stone from her eye with a gasp of breath. She reached into her pocket and produced a key. It sank into the wall, an invisible keyhole.

"I saw this in a vision when I was in training," she explained.

The others followed her in silence.

"I don't know how I didn't remember this before. One step forward, three to the left, one more forward, and one to the right."

"What are you talking about?" Rufus asked. "Since when do you act so weird?"

There was a scuffling sound behind them, and then a clatter on the ground across from them. Across the ravine, Rufus was getting up off the ground.

"What the hell?" Rufus yelled. He dusted off his jeans.

"I thought you'd be the most difficult to toss across," Puck explained. "So, I figured I'd start with you."

"And if I didn't reach the other side?" he shouted across the ravine.

"Shh," Quinn placed her index finger over her lips.

"Then I guess you would be at the bottom by now." Puck smirked.

Puck was swiftly behind Jimmy, his hands under his arms. He swung Jimmy over the ravine as easily as one would toss a crumpled piece of paper into the trash. Baxter looked like he was going to be sick the entire time Jimmy was in the air.

Jimmy landed on his feet and then fell forward onto his palms.

Puck was behind Connor in the blink of an eye. Connor was expecting it and side-stepped him.

"Hang on," Connor said. His palms were facing Puck.

"You wanted to come this way," Puck reminded him, stepping forward.

"Yeah, but I didn't think I'd be tossed over like a horseshoe," Connor complained. His eyes were darting between the other side and Puck.

Puck gestured for him to go, and Connor nodded. Connor tucked in his feet and squealed when he was midair over the center of the ravine. He landed in a crouching position but didn't fall as the other two did.

Quinn gasped, looking across the ravine. "It's an invisible path," Quinn said with astonishment.

"Now you tell me," Connor shouted.

"Shh," Quinn said. *I've seen myself fall here.*

"Quinn, what was that with the wall over there?" Baxter asked her.

Quinn exchanged glances with Baxter. She shrugged. "A keyhole," she said. "But I'm scared."

"You don't have to look at it. Puck could toss you across," Baxter suggested.

"Not about that. I haven't had a vision since I woke up," she confessed. Her hand rubbed the back of her head.

"Seraphina said you overdid it. She did warn you might not have any for a while," Baxter reminded her.

"I know," Quinn said, more to her feet.

"I thought you didn't really like them," Baxter said.

Quinn looked her brother in the eye. "A lot has happened since I saw you last. I've gotten better with them. I've gotten used to them. Rely on them even," she confessed.

They walked toward a tattered tapestry on the wall. Quinn pushed it aside.

Baxter's eyes widened at the hidden hole. Quinn finally turned the key.

The ground vibrated as the mirrors above shifted, revealing a shimmering path along the side of the wall.

Quinn took a step forward into the ravine, but instead of plunging to her death she stood on a transparent ledge.

Baxter grabbed her by the arm. "What if it can't hold your weight?" he asked, voice filled with concern.

"I'd rather walk here than get thrown," she said matter-of-factly.

Quinn placed her foot on the mirrored floor, barely visible. She moved her other foot on the spot. Baxter let out his breath. He'd been holding it since she took her first tentative step.

Quinn took three steps to the left and then one more forward, just as she previously recited. Her last step to the right didn't quite bring her to the edge.

Baxter used the hag stone once more. Maybe he couldn't see the path anymore.

He struggled to breathe. He couldn't see anything. "Where do you go now?" he whispered.

Quinn shrugged and jumped the last three feet.

Before he had a chance to react, Puck launched Baxter across the abyss. Baxter landed on his feet, did a tuck and roll, and stood up in one fluid motion.

"Cool landing," Connor said, nodding.

The mirrors were darker here, as if it were the backside of them.

"Total accident," Baxter confessed. He turned and glared at Puck. "You didn't have to throw me like that," Baxter said.

Puck gestured to Baxter a formal bow before leaping swiftly across the black abyss without a running start. He landed as graceful as a gymnast.

"Would you prefer I leave you there to decide what path to take?" Puck asked mockingly.

Quinn approached Puck, her eyebrows furrowed.

"If you could just throw us across, why didn't you do it the last time we were here?" Quinn asked. She crossed her arms and tapped her foot.

"You forget, Quinn," Puck said. "I was severely weakened and tormented mentally. I'm surprised I could even function."

Quinn's arms fell to her sides. "I didn't know you were that bad. You looked okay," she said. Quinn looked down, not meeting his eyes.

"Looks can be deceiving," Puck countered.

Once they dusted themselves off they made their way out of the cavernous hall into the hallway. They walked in pairs. Puck brought up the rear with Rufus, while Baxter and Jimmy trailed Quinn and Connor. They kept a steady pace and made easy work of finding the path to their mom's cell, only encountering one pair of guards rounding a corner. They patiently waited for them to pass and saw no other guards along the way. The bare walls had only their warped reflections.

I wondered if it was easier to travel in a group. That way, you're distracted from looking at the reflections.

A few hundred feet from her cell, Rufus raised his voice. "Gross."

This time, Connor shushed him. "Shh, you're gonna get us caught."

Baxter glanced back. Rufus's sneakers were covered in thick greenish-brown mud. Rufus's mouth hung open in disgust.

"Hopefully, that isn't poop," Jimmy said with a laugh.

Baxter eyed him but said nothing. Quinn went back to inspect the mud. She crouched and touched it with one finger. She gasped and fell back. Connor caught her as her hand flew up to hold her head with two hands. Then her body went limp.

"What happened?" Jimmy asked.

"She's having a vision," Baxter said.

Jimmy glanced at Baxter briefly before returning his gaze to Quinn. "This is what happens to her when she has a vision?"

After a few intense moments, Quinn's eyes fluttered.

Connor gave him a grim nod. "What did you see?" Connor asked, leaning in. He held her head while she was sprawled out on the mirrored floor.

Quinn groaned, pressing her fingers to her forehead. "A mud monster," Quinn said. "And the prison shattering."

Puck twitched after hearing her. "Shattering?" Puck asked, moving closer to her.

"Cool. Do we do that?" Rufus asked, his enthusiasm a complete contrast to the mood.

"I-I don't know," Quinn said.

Crouching beside her, Baxter placed a hand on her shoulder. "Maybe you should wear your glasses," Baxter offered.

Quinn blinked at him; her lashes were slow to open. "Why?" Her eyes were heavy with exhaustion.

"Doesn't it limit or focus your visions?" Baxter asked. "Seraphina warned you about pushing yourself too hard."

Quinn looked down. "Yeah, but it's not like I ask to have these visions."

Connor combed his fingers through his perfect hair. He took a deep breath and said, "Maybe we should rest here a while."

Quinn shook her head, her face hardening. "We're so close to finding Mom. I'm not stopping now," Quinn said in a firm tone.

She let the others know there was no changing her mind, just by her expression.

"Let's get going then," Baxter said. He offered Quinn a hand and she accepted.

Chapter 31: Second Thoughts

Cole

Cole stumbled back, pulling Grace with him as the tree-creature swung at her. It hissed, teeth glinting like broken glass. Cole raised his hand to shield her. The air snapped. The tree-creature turned black and disintegrated, resembling leaf compost. Cole froze, palm out over the crumbled vegetation. He glanced at his hand; it tingled. He flexed his fingers and looked at Grace, who smiled.

"About time you accepted and demonstrated your power," she said. No thanks was ever given. This was the closest to encouragement she had ever given him.

Grace had been trying to manipulate his power for a long time. She had him leave the book for Mr. Perry to unravel the Fae Queen's dominion. Making her kingdom ripe for invasion.

"Theo's breakdown was easy to orchestrate. A few suggestions. A witness in the right place at the wrong time." Her smile was wicked.

Quinn discovered they'd left clues for Cara in a vision. Not lies, but half-truths. To pull her to Fata, all while Theo was spiraling out of control. "We might have to do something about her. She's a liability."

"I like Quinn and Baxter," Cole protested.

Grace convinced Cole to slide a mirror at Chloe, so she'd fall into the prison. Her disappearance would never be explained. Chloe made that plan unnecessary as she willingly jumped into the prison to spare Baxter the choice.

Cole was having trouble following Grace's directions regarding Chloe; she was so sweet and innocent. Grace convinced Cole that he was the source of all this evil, that he needed to accept his fate if he ever hoped to flourish and gain his true powers. He and Grace conspired to set up Mr. Perry.

Grace had foreseen that only Mr. Perry possessed the power to take down the Fae Queen. To lay forth their path they orchestrated to set Grace up as Queen. Theo's commitment to the asylum ensured he was incapacitated, and with Cara gone, they could do their bidding.

"I don't know Grace. I don't want to hurt anyone," Cole said.

She laughed; it was sinister. "Don't you think it's a little too late for that now?"

Cole recoiled. *She wasn't always this mean to me. Did this place corrupt her or the murder of our dad?*

She crossed the distance between them and slapped him across the face. His hand flew to cover his face. His eyes wide with disbelief.

"Do you really think Baxter will still be friends with you after he finds out what you've done?" she demanded.

She turned and pointed to the charred debris behind them. "Or when he finds out you can do that," she spat.

Chapter 32: A Muddy Encounter

Quinn

They walked amongst the silence; no one mentioned the slower pace. Puck scouted ahead, ensuring their safety. Most of the corridors were bare, making the transparent cabinet stand out. Upon inspecting the jars inside only one label was legible.

"Belladonna." Connor smiled. "I speak French, it means beautiful Donna, harmless enough." He nodded. "It's totally safe."

"I don't know about this," Jimmy said, wearily. "We don't have time to play around."

Connor's confident smile almost assured Quinn, almost. He opened the cabinet with ease.

This is too easy. Why wouldn't that be locked? Why leave this out in the open?

"What does beautiful Donna have anything to do with this quest?" Rufus asked.

Quinn's stomach tightened with unease.

Connor grabbed the jar, completely unaware of the deadly mistake.

"Connor, no," Baxter said in a hushed tone.

Connor flinched as if he'd been burned, dropping the jar. Smoke rose from the debris. Those closest to the jar began to cough.

Could he sense the danger before something happened? That rock!

"Run," Quinn said, taking off down the hall. The others followed her. Puck returned in an instant and met them on their mad dash.

"What was that about?" he asked.

"Connor grabbed Belladonna," Rufus tattled.

"What?" Puck turned to Connor. "Do you have any idea how dangerous that is?

"I thought it meant beautiful…"

"It is poison. Likely there in case of a prisoner escape," Puck said, interrupting him.

"Let's keep going," Baxter said.

They started down the corridor in silence, wrapped up in their own thoughts.

Quinn approached Connor. She was standing too close. In a hushed tone she said, I almost forgot. That rock you got, I need it."

Connor made a face, "What?"

Is he hiding it from me? "I saw you have a blood red stone," Quinn said, in a clipped tone.

"Oh, this," he said pulling the rock from his pocket.

"Yes," Quinn said, swiping it from his hand. She wrapped it in a sweater and stashed it away in her backpack.

Puck glanced at them as Quinn was tucking the rock away.

He heard me. Does he want it?

Before she had time to think about it Connor made a panicked sound. Baxter side-stepped Connor to see what startled him. Baxter's hands shot up as he stumbled back. As Quinn had foreseen, a mostly human-shaped mud monster loomed before them.

A wet, semi-formed sculpture that hadn't fully dried loomed before them; it was easily seven feet. Taller than Puck. The mud shifted like a fondue fountain. A thick glob dropped from its arm with a squelching splat.

245

Baxter wrinkled his nose and pulled his shirt up to cover his face. The mud reeked of rot, mold, and decay.

"What is that?" Jimmy asked.

"A golem," Puck answered, arrogant demeanor vanished. He stood in his fighting stance.

"It's gotta be a foot taller than me," Connor said.

Jimmy inched backwards. "Is that thing alive?"

"Sort of," Puck started, but was cut off by Rufus.

"How can it be sort of alive?" Rufus scoffed. "It is, or it isn't."

Puck looked menacingly at Rufus. "It is made of clay from the bog."

Rufus moved closer and inhaled deeply. He gagged. "It smells putrid," Rufus said, crinkling his nose.

Jimmy chuckled.

"The stench from the bog is poisonous," Puck explained. The pungent odor even caused Puck's face to scrunch up. He was typically difficult to read.

"How do we defeat it?" Connor asked. He coughed into his elbow. He kept his arm there to block the stench.

"This isn't a video game." Rufus laughed.

"It cannot be defeated," Puck answered. "It absorbs magical attacks until the user is deceased."

"Then how do we knock it out?" Connor tried again.

"It cannot be knocked out," Puck said. "It will cease to exist once its duty is fulfilled."

"How do we know what its duty is?" Jimmy chimed in.

"We do not," Puck answered, his annoyance not contained.

"So, it might not care about us," Connor said.

"It is not here by accident," Puck replied. "Despite being made of bog mud, it has incredible strength, able to lift massive objects with ease. It can regenerate limbs."

"If I wasn't facing this thing down right now, I'd think it was pretty cool," Connor confessed.

"Can we make our own?" Rufus asked. His fists balled in excitement.

The golem's arm twitched, causing a wet sloshing sound. Jimmy flinched.

"It can be done," Puck answered.

"What do we do?" Baxter asked, shifting his weight from one foot to the other.

"We can't risk going around it and finding another path when we are so close to Mom," Quinn said.

"How can we stop it?" Jimmy asked, panic clear in his voice.

"They are vulnerable to words that can control it," Puck said.

"What words?" Connor asked, a bit less panicked.

"I know not," Puck admitted.

Jimmy threw up his arms in frustration. "Well, why even say that, then?" Jimmy asked, his voice rising with each word.

Puck didn't even look away from the golem. "Water can dissolve it," Puck offered.

"Well, that's just great," Connor said sarcastically. "Where the hell are we going to find water?"

"They are not intelligent. The mirrors may confuse them," Puck said.

"Okay, can we move a mirrored wall somehow?" Baxter asked.

"Maybe," Quinn said.

Rufus shouldered a wall without a second thought. A dull thud was heard, but it didn't budge.

"It's looking right at me," Jimmy said, in full panic mode now.

Rufus turned to face the golem. "Does that thing even have eyes?"

"It does not," Puck answered.

"Why are you giving such short, unhelpful answers?" Connor demanded. His face turned red.

Puck's jaw clenched as he palmed his face. "I am trying to think. Yet you humans, with your incessant questions, distract me," Puck said dryly.

The golem's bulky body moved slowly. Crude, unfinished features made it easy to identify, a moving heap of mud with hollow eye sockets.

"What about if we distract it and run right by it?" Baxter suggested.

Puck looked at him, tilted his head, and then nodded. "Not a terrible idea," Puck said.

Jimmy's hands flew into a defensive position. "Whoa, what if it grabs one of us?" he asked, his voice shaking.

"It's only mud," Rufus scoffed.

Puck clicked his tongue. "It is tremendously powerful. It can mold and reshape to fit its needs," Puck explained.

Jimmy's eyes widened.

Baxter gulped. "Ready?" Baxter asked. "On three."

The others looked at Baxter and nodded, all except Jimmy.

"One. Two," Baxter counted slowly.

Jimmy bolted on the count of two, leaving the others to scramble behind him. The golem was slow to react.

"Jimmy," Baxter said as he was midstride after him. The others followed without hesitation.

So much for being quiet.

Their shoes clattered on the floor, echoing down the hall. By the time the golem started to turn, they had all dashed past it. Their breathing was ragged.

Baxter's heart pounded in his ear like a drum. The golem's movements were stiff and slow. The mud slopped off and reformed as Puck had said.

They continued the rest of the way to their mom's cell. Jimmy practically walked backward, with how often he glanced back.

"Do you think we lost it?" Jimmy asked, breathless.

"No," Puck said. "It will catch up when we stop."

Jimmy's eyes widened and his mouth opened as if he were about to say something, but no words came out. "Let's go," Jimmy said, looking over his shoulder.

Baxter nodded.

Several cells were vacant, and in others the inhabitants were buried under piles of debris. They made little comment about the other prisoners, not wanting to alert the guards, or get caught up in the tricks of the reflections.

They continued down a corridor, the reflections mocked them as if they were ghosts. They haunted them and moved in unnatural ways. Jimmy made the mistake of looking directly at one reflection. Connor threw something. Jimmy ducked and stumbled, knocking Connor down in the process.

"Hey," Connor said.

"Sorry," Jimmy said, staring at the reflection.

Connor followed his line of sight, dusting himself off. Baxter helped Jimmy up. His hand was clammy.

"Are you okay?" Baxter asked.

"I just tripped," Jimmy lied.

Baxter and Connor eyed each other but said nothing.

They continued moving, worried the golem would catch up eventually.

As they turned a corner, Rufus stopped and touched the glass wall. "It's different here," he said.

Embedded within the wall was a darker patch, dull like obsidian. The shape of a door. It obscured everything, and no hinges could be seen.

"It's the back side of the mirror," Puck explained.

Quinn sighed, having seen this before. "We don't have time to keep stopping," she said and walked on.

Everyone followed.

After what seemed like an intense eternity, they arrived at the cell.

Quinn gasped. "She should be here."

"Are you sure this is the cell?" Baxter asked.

"I am sure," Quinn said. She placed her hand on the glass.

"This place is a maze, maybe she's somewhere else," Connor suggested.

Puck stepped beside Quinn. "Take out the shard," he said. Quinn obeyed.

"Place it like this," he said, angling his hand.

A seam appeared in the mirror. Puck pushed open a small rectangular chunk of glass.

Quinn inspected it before entering the room. Once inside, she spun on her heel. "Where is she?" she asked. Her voice betrayed that she was on the brink of tears.

The others froze, unsure how to react.

"Maybe they moved her," Connor suggested.

They searched her cell, but it was empty. The room was sparse. Nothing on the walls, just the bedding in the corner. Quinn crouched to inspect the spot her mother had slept. She lifted the tattered cloth that was meant to be the bed as if her mother might be under it.

Quinn lifted something small and shined with blue. She held it up. Baxter recognized the jewelry; it was their mother's. Quinn's forehead wrinkled with worry. "Mom would never take this off willingly," she said.

"Maybe it fell off," Rufus said.

"A water sapphire," Baxter breathed.

"The iolite stone," Puck said. "The stone of Second Sight."

Connor frowned. "I thought your mom didn't know about all of this," he said, arms gesturing wide.

Baxter shook his head. "She didn't," he said. "Otherwise, she wouldn't have let me go through all that last year." Baxter didn't take his eyes off the pendant while he spoke.

After an uncomfortable silence, Baxter looked to Quinn, who quickly glanced away.

"What's an iolite stone?" Jimmy asked.

"It has the power, once mastered, to travel through dimensions on demand and unseen," Puck explained.

"Whoa," Rufus said. "Where do I get one?"

"For us, it lets you see the Fae," Baxter said to Jimmy, ignoring Rufus. Baxter turned to Quinn and crossed his arms. "You know something you're not telling me," Baxter accused.

"Well," she started and then paused. "I had a vision, but I wasn't sure it was true," Quinn said to her feet.

"Tell me," Baxter said more firmly than he ever spoke to her.

She took a deep breath. "It was long ago, to me anyway," Quinn said. She stared at the ground. "Mom pretended not to see strange things happening. She was secretly searching for the truth about what happened to Dad."

Baxter tilted his head. "Dad? What happened to Dad? What does he have to do with this?" he rapid-fired questions at her.

"I'm just figuring out my visions," she explained. "They were all happening so fast. One right after another, mixed with illusions." Quinn faced Baxter. "Mom knew if she pursued answers, she'd risk us, and without Dad's protection..."

"And you're just telling me this now?" Baxter asked.

"There hasn't exactly been time," she said as she crossed her arms. "I've been running around since the moment I got here."

A sharp metallic sound startled them as it echoed. Everyone jumped.

"We should go," Jimmy said, eyeing the corridor.

Baxter made a face at him.

"What if she left this for us to find?" Quinn asked, changing the subject.

"What? She's not here, and that thing is after us," Jimmy said.

Quinn touched Baxter's arm. "He's right. She's not in *this* cell."

"You think she's somewhere else?" Connor asked.

Quinn nodded. "I just don't understand why her cell would be empty?"

"Maybe it was the prison playing tricks on you," Jimmy said.

Quinn glared at him. "I know what I saw," Quinn said forcefully.

"Well, if she's not here, where is she?" Jimmy asked.

"I don't know," she said to her feet.

"Maybe the prison is messing with you," Jimmy said.

"I know what I saw," Quinn snapped.

Jimmy put his palms up. "Okay."

"My visions aren't working this time. I can't even hear her." Her shoulders slumped.

"Hear her? You see *and* hear things?" Connor asked. His eyes were so wide they might pop out.

Quinn only nodded.

"Let's go," Baxter said.

Chapter 33: An Old Acquaintance

Baxter

A metal sound alerted them to danger. They exited the cell, but there was no sign of what had made the noise.

"So, what way do we go?" Jimmy asked nervously.

"It may be easier to go past the golem again. Fewer guards on the way out," Connor said.

"Out," Quinn snapped, her voice raised. She stopped and crossed her arms. "I'm not leaving without Mom."

"Shh," Rufus said mockingly. He glanced over his shoulder.

"This place is huge. How can we find her?" Connor asked.

"We could split up," Quinn suggested.

Puck clicked his tongue. "If you thought the golem was bad, wait until you see what other creatures live here," Puck said. "Let alone the guards."

They walked in silence; the only sound was the clicking of their shoes.

Puck stopped without a word. He looked uncomfortable, unusual for him. He cleared his throat. It sounded more like a low growl.

"What?" Quinn whispered. She scanned the surroundings.

"Since we're here anyway," he said and paused. He turned to Quinn and grimaced. "I have a wrong to right." He held out his hand to Quinn. "Will you give me the shard?" Puck asked.

Connor's eyes narrowed. "Why?" he asked.

"What could it hurt?" Quinn said.

"I don't know," Baxter said, shifting his weight to his other hip.

Baxter and Connor exchanged glances. Connor crossed his arms. "You never give up a magical item in a game."

"It's not a game, Connor," Quinn said.

Baxter whispered to Quinn, "You still don't know who's going to betray you."

Puck flinched.

Right, his super hearing.

"Having been in this prison, I know how it affects you now," Puck said.

"Puck needs to do this. Let him fix this," Quinn said. She handed him the shard. She must've seen something.

Baxter let out a long exhale. "Make it quick."

Puck nodded. He slid the shard into a pouch at his hip.

"You don't have to come," Puck said.

"We need to look for Mom, anyway," Quinn said, glancing at Baxter.

Puck raised his nose to the air, and with predator-like precision, he crouched and took off down the hall. No sound left in his wake. The others tried to keep up.

I bet Jimmy's just glad we didn't take the path with the golem.

Less than thirty minutes later, they were hovering outside a cell. Only one guard went by, and they never stood a chance. Puck hit a pressure point, and he collapsed into his arms as he lowered him to the ground before the others even caught up.

In the cell, a frail Fae was in the fetal position, knees to chest, back to them. Each of her vertebrae was prominent.

"There are no words to express the depths of my sorrow," Puck murmured. He unlocked the cell in one swift motion and stood aside without entering.

"Lyra," Quinn said. "Are you okay?"

The Fae didn't move.

"You're free now," Quinn whispered.

"I know you saw me," Lyra said, her back still toward them. "I foresaw this." Her voice was raspy from disuse.

She moved as if she was in pain. Rising to her feet, she stood, hunched over, her joints cracking, as she set her piercing white eyes onto Puck. "I tried to warn you. Things are set in motion now." She pointed a long, bony finger at him. "This is all your doing."

She took a few steps, and her bones creaked. She straightened and exited the cell with grace.

"The exit is this way," Puck said, his arm an open gesture to allow her to go first.

She brushed Puck's shoulder in defiance and turned the other way. Then she took off in a sprint.

"That went well," Rufus said with a smirk.

"At least I did my part," Puck said. "I did not realize how awful this prison could be on one's psyche." His voice was softer, the arrogant edge gone. He looked tired for the first time. Puck entered her cell, he placed a palm on the wall.

"What was all that about?" Jimmy asked.

"Puck turned her in for being a seer. She was meant to be locked up for eternity. That is Ophelia's sister," Quinn explained in a hushed tone. "He didn't wish to risk his family, as seers were not allowed under the current rulers. Their visions were too powerful despite not always being accurate."

Quinn glanced back at Puck who seemed deep in thought. "The Fae, however; always take visions for accuracy and moved differently in the universe due to the visions. This in turn effectively makes the visions dangerous. Lyra had foreseen a disaster. She saw Cole and Grace's father cause total destruction of the kingdom and even murder Ophelia. Puck couldn't chance anyone hearing this vision and assisting in its creation."

Quinn leaned in closer to Jimmy. Rufus and Connor stepped a bit closer to hear.

"Puck orchestrated the imprisonment to bury the vision and hopefully save Ophelia. Cole had slipped Mr. Perry the Tempest Sisto, he acquired from his father, Magnus. Cole didn't understand how dangerous the artifact was. It took him far longer to give it to Mr. Perry because he accidentally slowed time," she paused and took a breath. "This almost ruined their plans to thwart the Queen and take over Fata. During that time his father died at the hands of Puck. Cole was having second thoughts. He wanted to discard the plan, yet Grace had other ideas. Cole was always awkward; he spoke and moved as little as possible to avoid revealing he was half Fae."

"How do you know all this?" Rufus asked. He was as invested in this story as a child in their favorite cartoon.

A deep, sinister laugh echoed through the corridor, caused them all to jump.

Jimmy squealed.

"I heard there was a prison break," said a sinister voice. "I figured you'd be behind it," he said. "Since no Fae has ever gotten out without the Mirror Shard or permission."

Mr. Perry rounded the corner. A large reflective stone blocked him from view.

"Mr. Perry," Connor and Baxter said in unison.

"The one and only," Mr. Perry said with a bow. "Although, I'm known as the overlord here."

Puck was in a defensive stance immediately, no longer appearing tired.

Jimmy's eyes were popping out of his head, mouth ajar.

I must've forgotten to tell him that little detail.

They turned and sprinted down the hallway, everyone except Puck, and almost crashed right into the golem.

"AHH," Jimmy shouted, nearly stumbling to the ground. Had it not been for Connor's arm, he would be sprawled out by now.

When it wasn't moving, it blended seamlessly into the dark areas. However, when it moved, its presence was unmistakable, as it slopped mud on the ground.

They skidded to a halt. It swiped at Rufus, who was the fastest, so he'd gotten there first. The golem missed him by inches.

"Gross," he whined. The mud dripped from his arm. He whipped his arm up and down to shake the mud off. He gagged at the stench.

The wall to their left shattered with an ear-piercing crash, and shards of glass flew everywhere. A figure came crashing in and dropkicked the golem with a "Hiya."

Mud splattered them. The female rolled forward and swung a sword with expert precision at the golem, taking off its right arm. Her rapier, still swinging, took off the other arm. She yelled a series of words.

It's her.

"Lou Lou?" Baxter said softly. Lou Lou was Baxter's closest female friend.

"She's speaking in tongues now?" Connor asked. He turned to look at Baxter.

"It's called Trikous, the Fae language," Mr. Perry said calmly. He shifted the grimoire to his other hand. The Grimoire of Bàs. Baxter's pulse quickened. "But it won't work in time." He laughed. His laugh was pure evil.

"Whoa, I didn't know she could fight," Jimmy shouted. His amused expression made Connor smile.

"Me either," Connor said. They both looked at Baxter, who shrugged.

And that detail.

The golem groaned from the direct hit Lou Lou landed. Its muddy figure stumbled back. Puck threw one of his throwing knives with a quick flick right at Mr. Perry. He had deadly accuracy as the blade flew directly at his right eye. Sparks lit the dimly lit corridor right before impact. Metal rang as it hit the ground.

"Whoa," Jimmy said.

Someone had thrown a metal star that struck the knife midair before it met its mark. The blue-silver five-pointed star lay on the ground near Jimmy's feet. He stepped on it and pulled it toward him with his foot.

Baxter looked for the perpetrator. It was Caprice, the rotten tree, the Unseelie that tricked Naomi.

The rotten branch will take out more than the limb. It's Caprice.

He creaked like a tree swaying when he walked.

"Great," Baxter muttered to himself. *How can I protect them all?*

A green streak flashed before them. "Now is the time," Monk E called. "I ask you to bind yourself to me, so we may be one."

Connor looked around. "Me?" His expression was dumbfounded to say the least.

Baxter's forehead wrinkled.

"What the hell?" Jimmy asked.

"You got a parrot." Rufus pointed and smirked.

"No," Connor said.

"There is no time, we are destined to join," Monk E squawked.

The blue feather from Puck's knife billowed side to side before landing on the ground.

"Isn't this a nice reunion," Mr. Perry said with a false smile.

As if he didn't just have a knife pummeled at him.

"An unbound familiar. Perhaps you could bind with me instead," Mr. Perry cooed. His tone gentle and kind as he once spoke to Baxter.

"In your Cursed Dreams," Monk E replied and flew to Connor's shoulder.

Connor flinched but didn't swipe him away.

"Binding yourself to me can have untold effects. You may inherit some of my power or extend your life," Monk E whispered.

Connor shook his head. "And what aren't you telling me?" he wisely asked.

Monk E flapped. "We shall be bound; your pain is mine and mine is yours."

"And if you die?"

"Yes."

"If he won't, I will," Rufus said, stepping forward all too eager.

Connor shoved him back. "I'll do it if it will help us."

"What? Can't blame a guy for trying," Rufus said with a huge smile. He shrugged.

Mr. Perry held open the grimoire with one hand, and the other waved above the crumpled, yellow pages. The ancient tome's hardcover looked as though it had seen better days. The leather binding was cracked and peeling, with some sections even missing. Without touching the pages, they fluttered with the flick of Mr. Perry's fingers.

The pages stilled, and he began speaking words Baxter didn't understand. The air felt charged with electricity. Mr. Perry curled and uncurled his free hand. Purple sparks formed at his fingertips. His gray wisps of a comb-over reminded Baxter of the gentle teacher he once had been.

A silver blur flashed before Baxter as Puck sent another knife at Mr. Perry, which was quickly dispatched by Caprice.

"He is trying to curse all first borns," Puck shouted.

"Is that all you got?" the Unseelie croaked.

Baxter glanced at Quinn.

Her face showcased her anger. "Dude, we're twins."

"That doesn't matter, two minutes still counts," Baxter said.

Her anger quickly melted into fear.

"Maybe we should go?" Jimmy said. He was an only child.

Mr. Perry flicked a finger at Jimmy with a sharp crack. The purple spark narrowly missed him as Puck pushed him to the ground. The wall behind them was singed.

Baxter looked to Connor who was momentarily glowing a greenish color.

Lou Lou stopped speaking the odd language, and Baxter peered at her. A puff of putrid green smoke formed around her. She was covered in mud, but the golem was a pile on the ground. She removed something from the mud. It was Baxter's watch.

I didn't even notice it was missing. He looked at his wrist, the tan line faded. It had been gone a while. *The institute.*

Lou Lou held up Baxter's watch, holding it out for him. "I think it was after you," she said to him with a smile.

His breath hitched. He took the watch and felt a spark when their skin connected.

Does she have magic now? "Where have you been?" Baxter asked her, returning the smile.

"I've joined the Freedom Fighters," Lou Lou said in a serious tone, her smile faded. She looked over her shoulder at Mr. Perry. "I've gotta go," she said. "I got what I came for."

"What did you come for?" Baxter asked. He took a cautious step forward.

She held up her hand. "Best you leave while you can," she said, ignoring his question. "I'll hold him back." She pointed a thumb over her shoulder at Mr. Perry. "He's more powerful than you think."

With that, she blinked at Baxter, turned on a heel, and stalked toward Mr. Perry.

Barely out of breath, her garb was that of a fighter in a video game, equal parts Lara Croft and Renaissance fair. She was covered in worn leather, and she had puffy leather satchels hanging from her belt. Even a type of fanny pack, far more chic.

This pouch was serious. She wiped the mud off her sword on her thigh and held it despite having a sheath.

Another purple spark was flung at them by Mr. Perry. Connor stood in front of Baxter and held up his arm. A transparent green shield formed, and the purple spark ricocheted off and left a scorch mark on the wall.

Baxter's mouth dropped open

"C'mon, man," Jimmy said. He brushed against Baxter's arm and turned away. He was trembling.

Baxter nodded and followed. They scurried down the hall when the ground trembled beneath their feet. Baxter held out his arms for balance. Jimmy's eyes widened. He looked to Baxter for direction or comfort; he wasn't sure which.

Behind them, Puck barked, "Get out. Now!"

Quinn, Rufus, and Connor fell in line after them at a steady jog. Cracks began to spider up the mirrored walls. The sound was menacing, sharp and sudden, like thunder.

Puck followed them. Fragments of glass rained from the ceiling, shining like a glitter storm. In his haste, Jimmy stumbled and landed on his palms.

"Ow," he hissed as bits of glass embedded in his skin. Trickles of blood formed where the glass dug in.

Connor doubled back. "Hurry up," Connor shouted, grabbing Jimmy by the arm and yanking him up. Monk E flew overhead.

"This way," Monk E called.

Baxter looked over his shoulder at Lou Lou, facing Mr. Perry, whose sinister smile was dark with malice.

I can't just leave her here.

A thunderous crack split the air, and an enormous slab fell from the ceiling, separating them. The cloud of dust and debris limited his vision; he couldn't see her any longer. His breath hitched, and he coughed from the dust.

"How do we get out now?" Quinn asked Puck.

"This way," Puck said. He was already sprinting away. He led them down twists and turns. They ran out of the prison.

On their way out, an explosion sounded, far off in the distance. The explosion caused Baxter to jump and whip his head around. Dust fell from the commotion. As soon as Jimmy, the last of them, exited the prison, it erupted. Half the mountain of a prison collapsed inward. Smoke billowed from the peak, clouding the sky.

"Lou Lou," Baxter cried.

***

Midstride, Puck tossed the shard on the ground before him and sprinted over it. The second his foot touched the glass, he vanished. Quinn gasped and fell on her hands as she attempted to stop her momentum.

Baxter skidded to a halt, and Connor crashed into him, nearly knocking them both over. Jimmy slammed into Connor, sending them all barreling over the shard, instantly disappearing.

Rufus caught up. "Where did they go?"

"I think the shard opened the mirror on the ground. Where to, I don't know." She turned. "But I'm going after them."

"I'm not staying here alone," he said, attempting not to look frightened by the possibility of being left behind.

"I always thought they were a one-way ticket into the prison, not out. Hopefully, this isn't bringing us right back in." They exchanged glances. Rufus shrugged. Together, they jumped into the glass. Quinn grabbed the shard midjump, angling and unlocking another door.

Chapter 34: The Betrayal

Quinn

Quinn looked around. She recognized everyone present but wasn't sure where she was. Puck was nowhere in sight and the others were either tied up or unconscious. All except for her and Rufus. The last two to enter.

What is Seraphina doing here?

The room was covered in half shrouded mirrors. Like every mirror ever confiscated in Fata was here. *Who did this?*

"That is correct Shadow Seer. The mirrors were collected and stored here in the castle. With the overlord gone I now run things around her." She moved with an air of something Quinn had not witnessed before.

"What?" *Did she read my thoughts? Would she even tell me if she did. No. She taught me how to block that. She taught me.*

Seraphina glided to Quinn and removed the backpack from her shoulder. She dug through it and retrieved the Bloodstone.

"I will be taking this," she said.

"What? Why," Quinn asked.

"Oh, Shadow Seer, what a joke. You cannot see anything. It was all too easy."

Someone will betray me. Seraphina. Quinn's heart shattered at that moment. She was her confidant, trainer, and friend.

"But why?"

"Do you have any idea how difficult it is to live as a seer when the entire realm fears you and wishes to lock you up? I had no choice but to fend for myself." Her face contorted to anger and distain.

"But I could have helped you."

"Help me? You," she laughed. "You cannot even help yourself. The only reason you even escaped that prison was because of me," she said. She circled the room.

"Even then you could not do it. I saw you failed twice. That is why I called you back to training and made you that necklace."

"What are you going to do to us?" Quinn asked.

"I have not yet decided."

Rufus leaped from the top of an armoire and smashed a mirror over her head.

"Quinn run!" he yelled.

She didn't run. She shook Baxter, his eyes fluttered.

"Thank goodness," she cried.

"That was very foolish of you," Seraphina snarled. She whirled around to where Rufus was, but he was no longer there.

"Where have you gone you pesky human."

Quinn untie me," Connor shouted.

She crossed the room and untied him. Connor then ran to the armoire and opened it. Monk E flew out and headed straight for Seraphina.

With her distracted Quinn nodded to Baxter. She ducked down behind her and Baxter pushed her over. She landed to the ground with a thud.

Puck burst threw the door. Quinn froze.

What side is he on?

"Get out of here quickly," he snarled. He darted for Seraphina.

"What about…" she started.

"Go!" he tumbled with Seraphina.

Baxter was helping Jimmy up. Quinn made sure everyone was together and ushered them out the way Puck came in.

Once out the door Quinn turned left and she ran into Ophelia. She froze. *If Puck is on our side, she should be. I hope.*

"This way," was all Ophelia said.

"You knew didn't you?" Quinn accused.

"It was like I said. I was magically bound not to discuss it. And if I had she would have known."

They exited the castle safely. Where each of them would now go remains a mystery. For now.

Epilogue

M att, weary of half-truths and unanswered questions, trailed Quinn into the woods where she'd hidden her bike. He struggled to catch his breath, hands on his knees. Chasing after her on the bike was no easy task. When she glanced over her shoulder, he ducked behind a tree, holding his breath. He didn't want to be caught following her, not yet. Not until he found out what she was up to. He waited there by the trail for what felt like forever. He didn't panic, not at first. Pacing, an hour went by, and then two. Matt glanced at his watch every few minutes. He went into the forest calling her name, but there was no sign of her. Darkness crept in, and his worry increased exponentially. His cell phone had no service. He sprinted back to the edge of the park to get service.

"It's Quinn MacMillans," he said, keeping his voice from trembling. "She went into the woods alone and never came out."

When he hung up, he noticed movement at the trailhead. "Baxter and Rufus?" Matt whispered. Still, he didn't reveal himself.

Jimmy and Connor made sense, but Rufus. Something's up. Where the hell had Connor been?

When the police officer arrived, Matt approached him eagerly and explained what had happened. He left out the part about the guys arriving. The officer asked questions, called in backup, and initiated a full search began. Spotlights and canines surveyed the area. The police filed a missing person's report.

***

The Ravenswood tree got blight from Mr. Perry; the Freedom Fighters fought him off, but it was too late. Baxter retrieved a cutting and a seed from the Ravenswood tree. When he went to his old job, Mr. Trudel wasn't too happy to see him at first.

"What are you doing here?" Mr. Trudel fired him in anger. "I told you that you wouldn't get another chance. I meant it."

Not until Baxter set down the bucket he carried did Mr. Trudel stop shouting. He actually shuddered. Mr. Trudel knelt, his wrinkled hands brushed the soil of Fata, and he leaned closer to study the peculiar tree. His fingers brushed the bark, mesmerized by the surface, unlike any other specimen. His brow furrowed as he flicked a piece of the bark, his fingers tracing it, and it shimmered in return. He frowned, unsure of what he was witnessing.

"I've tended plants my whole life, and I've never seen anything like this," he muttered in astonishment. "There's something different about this... an element, it's almost magical."

His weathered hand broke a piece of bark, and when it cracked, a spark of purple flickered. It flared for a moment across his face and faded as fast as it appeared. He froze; his breath caught in his throat. Mr. Trudel was uncertain of what appeared before him, his brows raised as he held up the bark to the light. His eyes widened, and his mouth hung open in astonishment.

"Did you see that?" he whispered, barely audible, as if he said it louder, the plant may disperse and cease to exist.

Baxter nodded.

"It sparked when I broke it," he said, and the wonder in his voice was childlike. His eyes that were once clouded with weariness now shone with a youthful glow. "It's almost like magic." He raised his eyes to Baxter's, his gaze full of wonder for the tree.

It was like the tree had reignited his inner child, and he was brimming with excitement. He sprang to his feet with renewed energy.

"We must propagate this plant," he practically shouted. "I must have one."

He rummaged through his cluttered back closet; it was overflowing with gardening supplies. He was muttering to himself as he threw plastic bottles over his shoulder.

"Ah, here it is," he said triumphantly, reemerging with a small bottle in one hand. The bottle's faded label read: *Root Enhancing Hormones*, its edge curling inward on itself with age.

He also produced a small pot. Mr. Trudel's wide grin spread from ear to ear. "This should do the trick," he said.

He filled the small pot with soil, and with extreme care, he placed his newest prized possession into the pot. He kneaded the soil around as gently as caring for a newborn. His steady hands, full of years of practice, radiated a contagious passion for gardening. He dipped the stem in the rooting hormone, tapped off the excess powder, and placed it in the pot. Baxter was completely forgotten in that moment.

Once the tree was planted, he broke off a small branch, dipped it in the rooting hormone, and placed it in a small water-filled glass that was sitting beside him.

"The trick is to use distilled water. I'll have this propagated in no time," he said, more to himself, his eyes twinkling as he smiled at the pot.

Baxter smiled at his excitement.

"I'll have this plant multiplied in no time," Mr. Trudel explained.

Maybe we can find a Fae to grow it faster. Mr. Perry probably was also hunting any Fae with green or brown eyes that could regrow more trees.

Glossary

Blinding Light - a concoction made from pink moss, Shimmering Cane Flower and nectar of the Starlight Fern Flower

Casg -to prevent

Casg air -translates to banish you

Ecnad Foh Taed -backwards for death of dance

Dobber -Scottish insult

Granda -grandfather

Grimoire of Bàs -spell book of death

Haste be back, a loue ye -until we meet again

Labyrinth of Wandering Souls -maze outside the fortress

Mirror Shard - The key to the Mirror Prison

Praesidium - a metal to prevent wielding power. Latin meaning protection, defense, or garrison.

Pyrocraft - A fire magic forbidden in Fata

Ravenswood - a mythical tree in Fata. Used to prevent Fae possession and may allow the consumer to see the Fae or Sight

Regs -Regular people without Sight

Runezests - a snack Celeste perfected to restore energy.

Rusk - small piece of bread; it looked like a biscuit,

Sight - The ability to see otherworldly forces and magic

Seelie -Fae not corrupted

Shenzhen Nongke Orchid -rare and expensive flower developed by a group of scientists in Shenzhen, China, using an intricate and time-consuming breeding procedure.

Skolavrax - a creature that lives in the Mirror Realm, lurks beneath the prison. Blind and deaf.

Trikous -language of the Fae

Verachime- truth-chime, alerts when someone nearby has ill intentions

Vorstax - a faceless creature that sucks its victims ten times its size into its gaping hole.

Unseelie -Fae corrupted by feeding off humans too long with Shenzhen Nongke Orchid in system

Zmija -means snake in Siberian.

Acknowledgments

I never imagined I would finish this book, let alone two! I want to thank every single person who has supported me through this rollercoaster of a ride. It's impossible to name everyone that played a part, but please know it has meant so much to me.

Many of the ideas for this story came to me while I was out running. The hypnotic steps in nature led to the creative world of Fata. I would use the talk to text in an app and save little ideas along the way, from dialogue to plot twists. The little ideas were seeds that sprouted into this book.

I want to begin by saying thank you to my son, Alexander. You are the brightest light in my life. You are the reason I push myself to become a better person. I am so incredibly proud to be your mom. I love you, Papa, more than you will ever know.

To my first best friend and sister, Megan. Thank you for the bouncing ideas off each other and reviewing the words I wrote. I know it was incredibly boring. I love you.

I want to save a big special thanks to Jeremy. Without him, none of this would have been possible. With his love and support, he has encouraged me to chase my dreams. He was a listening ear for my obsessive thoughts regarding this book. I know that I went on and on about possibilities and ideas. He is also my Chief Everything Officer, assisting with formatting, marketing, hustling and even created my website: mlvansse.com

To my two fur babies who made sure I did not dive too deep into the land of fairytale. Duke and Molly. RIP Chief, the hole you left when you went away is insurmountable.

To my unofficial editor Monkey, who shreds my manuscripts, quite literally and watched over my shoulder as I wrote. My green feathered friend incorporated her way into the book and became a character.

I especially want to give a shout-out to everyone who is on my Facebook author page, M. L. Vanasse. Without you holding me accountable I might never have finished this book I am truly grateful. Thank you to each and every one of you.

I want to say thank you to my coworkers who kept asking me daily about the book and when it would be out. You helped drive me to the finish line.

I need to give a huge shout-out to Julie, not only for reading every word repeatedly, but for showing up time and again, coming to my events and assisting me with sales. You've been there in so many ways, from cheering me on to joining me on writing retreats through her travel agency, Wishes and Dreams Destinations inc. Your encouragement, friendship, and generosity have meant so very much to me. I couldn't have done this without you. I honestly do not know how to thank you enough.

I want to say thank you to, Jenifer. To listen to me go on and on about every little idea that popped into my mind.

Thank you to Chris one of the closest people in my life for reading my book and giving me feedback.

Kassidy, thank you for all your support. Finish your book!

Thank you to all my beta readers who were so helpful.

I also want to give a shout-out to my late grandmother, Grace. She was my biggest cheerleader and supported me in every way. I only wish you could have seen this day. I love you, Grandma.

Thank you to my mom for grounding me and never letting me think too big. For keeping me humble.

Lastly, I just extend my most sincere gratitude to each and every reader who has taken the time to explore my story. I am deeply grateful that you have gotten here to read this and believe in me. Your support and enthusiasm has driven me to continue my writing journey. Without all of you this book may not have come to fruition. Every message of support, review, and words of love and encouragement has meant more than I can ever express.

As an independent author, I do it all, the writing, editing, designing, formatting, and even the marketing. It's not easy, but knowing that you're waiting for the next book has made every challenge worthwhile. Your continued support, whether it's sharing the book with a friend or leaving a few kind words in a review, helps my little business grow and keeps my story alive. Thank you, truly, for helping me bring this universe to life. May you always find your parallel realm and lose yourself in wonder, hope, and a bit of magic whenever reality gets too real.

Find me on Facebook, M. L. Vanasse, Instagram, m.l.vanasse.author, Pintrest, AuthorMLVanasse, TikTok, M.L.vanassebooks and more. Can you find them all?

A message from Seraphina

Ah, so you have completed the journey, have you? How curious. Few make it this far without tremendous consequence. It is I, Seraphina, the one who sees all you refuse to see. I have foreseen your next decision as well.

You could close this book, vanish into your mundane world, and pretend none of this has ever happened.

But beware: ignoring fate so entwined with your own a comes at a steep price. The threads that weave us together are delicate things to trifle with. Leave a review, share this story, and you may very well tip the scales toward a brighter destiny for both of us.

Remain silent, however, and I cannot say I have seen what happens to those who keep the reviews unseen.

Your words possess more power than you think. Use them wisely or succumb to a fate you may not desire. It costs you nothing and you shall gain much.

Sneak peek from the next book

Follow Chantelle in this thrilling sidequel, while she navigates high school while trying to master her sword skills before it's too late. Each class she sits in, every lie she tells to cover her tracks wears on her. She's unable to tell anyone what's going on and she's running out of time. Each visit to Fata is risking time lost in her world. If she can't get her training completed in time and save the day it may be over for her friends and family.

Meet the author

M. L. Vanasse is not only a medical professional, but a professional of creativity. She can be found making all forms of art using her superpower of ADHD. She claims her biggest fan is her son, but even he would admit her three insane pets are top of the list. Though she loves all animals, she most identifies as pool shark.

www.ingramcontent.com/pod-product-compliance
Lightning Source LLC
Chambersburg PA
CBHW030353020726
47493CB00003B/794